The White Star of Twilight

Russell Sebring

This is a work of fiction. Names, characters, places, and incidents are products of the author's imagination or are used fictitiously and are not to be construed as real. Any resemblance to actual events, locations, organizations, or persons, living or dead, is entirely coincidental.

World Castle Publishing, LLC
Pensacola, Florida

Hardback ISBN: 9798882661662
Paperback ISBN: 9798891261587
eBook ISBN: 9798891261594
First Edition World Castle Publishing, LLC, March 11, 2024
http://www.worldcastlepublishing.com

Cover: Cover Designs by Karen
Cover-designs-by-karen.com
Editor: Karen Fuller

For those who choose the lens of a camera
over the crosshairs of a gunsight
when shooting wildlife.

CHAPTER 1

The last thing Valeria Cortez's mother ever said to her was, "Everything will be okay. They just want to keep me overnight in the hospital and run a few tests. Stay here with Abuela and be good. Don't give her any trouble. I'll be back to pick you up in the morning."

It was nightfall in East Los Angeles.

Valeria got out of the car and quietly walked off without acknowledging anything her mother said. She went up and knocked on the door to her grandmother's apartment, heard it being unlocked from the other side, and let herself in.

Abuela, preparing for bed, was dressed in a bathrobe. "How's your mom?" she asked.

"I have no idea." Valeria made her way to the sofa in the living room, lay down, and resumed texting one of her friends. "You know I don't talk to her." She grabbed the remote control from the coffee table.

"You're still not upset with her about those rings, are you?"

"Yes," said Valeria. "And I'm not going to get over it or forget. What she did wasn't right."

"You're as stubborn as an old mule." Abuela went into her bedroom and returned with a blanket and pillow, which she handed to Valeria. "Those rings weren't yours. They belonged to your mom, and what's done is done. It's in the past now."

Valeria pretended not to hear her. "Can I watch TV?"

"Sure," answered Abuela. "Go ahead, but keep it down. I'm tired." She went into the bathroom, turned on the faucet, and started brushing her teeth. "If you're hungry, there's some leftover pasta in the fridge," she mumbled through a mouthful of toothpaste. "Heat it up if you want."

Valeria's mother, Rosa, had complained of a stiff neck and throbbing headache earlier in the day. By late afternoon, she felt sick to her stomach and went to a nearby walk-in clinic. There, they found she had a low-grade fever and advised her to take some ibuprofen when she got back home to help ease the discomfort.

"More than likely, you've caught the flu," said the doctor who saw her. "A bad strain of influenza is going around. Just about everyone's coming down with it."

That night at the hospital, Rosa Cortez slipped into a coma, was put on a ventilator, and died the next day. The bacterial meningitis that had infected the tissues around her brain and took her life was discovered too late. She was thirty-five years old.

Valeria sat next to her grandmother in the first pew, dabbing her eyes now and then with tissues, while a clean-shaven young priest, who'd never met or knew Rosa, oversaw her funeral Mass.

The priest stood at the church podium before a modest gathering of mostly coworkers and longtime neighbors and spoke glowingly about Rosa but in a forced and colorless monotone voice, void of emotion, which irritated Valeria greatly. She especially disliked how he had chosen to add his own little embellishments about her mother's life and personality that she knew weren't true. Toward the end, the priest snuck a peek at his watch and made sure Rosa's Mass finished on time. Everyone was out the door in less than an hour.

Later, at the gravesite, a parade of well-wishers took turns putting their arms around Valeria, holding her hands, and offering their condolences. Although she knew they meant well and were only trying to ease her suffering, she began to despise the same easy-to-remember sentiments, which were repeated too many times again and again. "I'm sorry for your loss" was polite enough and sounded nice, but "God must have wanted your mother for a reason" made her head explode. A few also added the one cliché, which Valeria came to dislike the most: "Your mother is in a better place."

Dolores, owner of Sparkle Visions hair salon, where Rosa worked as a nail technician, reached for a lock of Valeria's hair. "Who did your hair, dear?" she asked.

"My mom," Valeria answered, "…before she…"

"Oh, my. How sad. I can do better," said Dolores. "I know what all the young girls like these days. You're how old…? Fourteen? Yes? Do come by this next week, and I'll make you beautiful. No charge." She paused, then added, "There's no reason to cry. I know it's hard, but you should be happy. Your mother is in a better place."

Valeria smiled weakly and thanked her.

A small wake, lasting no more than an hour, was held in the community center at her grandmother's retirement complex. Except for a few of Rosa's closest friends, not many people bothered to make the twenty-minute drive from the cemetery to the center. Some of Abuela's elderly neighbors came by to pay their respects. Valeria had seen several of them in passing before but otherwise had no idea who they were.

"Is this your granddaughter?" asked one of the neighbors, a heavy-set elderly man with a gruff voice.

"Yes." Abuela stepped to one side and introduced her. "This is Val."

The man stared at Valeria for a moment with a wooden expression. "Oh, okay," he said. "I thought I'd seen her being dropped off by someone occasionally in front of your building, but I wasn't sure who she was." He then turned abruptly and made his way to the buffet table.

On the ride back to Rosa and Valeria's apartment, Abuela broke down and became inconsolable. "No parent should ever have to bury their child," she moaned bitterly. "It's not right! And that old dress your mother's going to be buried in…is that really the best she owned? I should've had the funeral home put her in something more elegant; a long white satin gown would've been perfect, but I couldn't afford it. I live on a fixed income and don't have much money."

"It's okay, Grandma," said Valeria. "Mom looked nice."

"Rags." Abuela sighed. "How can my sweet girl, and only child, enter the kingdom of heaven if all she's wearing before God is everyday rags?"

Back at Rosa and Valeria's small two-bedroom apartment, Abuela's outbursts continued. "Who in this country can afford to bury a loved one?" she groaned. "I had to sign up for a loan at the funeral home to pay for Rosa's casket and grave. Later, when you feel up to it, Val, you can help me choose a nice headstone for your mom. It can't be anything too extravagant, just something simple that doesn't cost a lot."

Abuela went into Rosa's bedroom and went through her dresser and closet, straightening and organizing things as she went.

"Come in here, Val," she said. "Look at all this. Tell me, how in the world can one person accumulate so much junk?"

"She liked to shop," said Valeria.

"I can see that."

Valeria stood in the doorway and watched Abuela pull some of Rosa's belongings out of a dresser drawer and lay them on her mother's bed, including her old beat-up jewelry box, which played Johann Pachelbel's Canon in D when it was opened. Rosa had found the discarded box at a thrift store shortly after she had divorced Valeria's father, Ray.

When she was very young, Valeria would sneak the box into her bedroom so she could try on her mother's jewelry, open the wooden lid over and over, and listen. The song was the most beautiful she'd ever heard, and at various times, it had the power to soothe her, make her smile, or move her to tears. She also adored her mother's miscellaneous pieces of jewelry, and especially two rings, which she came to secretly love and cherish for what they represented.

While Abuela rooted through the closet, muttering to herself, Valeria walked over to the bed and opened the box. Canon in D began to play. Everything was there just as she remembered, except for the two rings, which were missing. She closed the lid.

"We'll need to sort through your mother's clothes and see which things, if any, you want to keep," said Abuela. "The rest, if it's in decent shape, we'll donate to a homeless shelter or some other charity."

With a nod, Valeria left the room to find somewhere else to cry.

For three days and nights, she stayed in her bedroom, shutting out the rest of the world. Gradually, the initial shock of losing her mother was replaced by intense feelings of guilt. She couldn't stop sobbing and regretted not telling her mother she loved her one last time. Why did she let her mom drive off without at least giving her a hug? She'd never even said goodbye.

A few of Valeria's classmates and friends texted to say they'd heard the news and were sorry for her loss, but not one called or came to the funeral. So, she stopped texting them back.

In the afternoon of the fourth day, Abuela knocked on her

door. "It's time to come out," she said. "I have something for you."

Reluctantly, Valeria emerged and sat across from her grandmother at the small dining room table near the kitchen. Abuela was sifting through a stack of mail.

"What are you doing?" asked Valeria.

Abuela looked up. "There are bills here that need to be paid; they keep coming, and some of these are sympathy cards from relatives and other friends of your mom, offering their condolences." She paused before continuing. "But there's also an envelope here addressed to you. It's from your dad." She handed it to Valeria.

"Why is he writing to me?" asked Valeria, her voice tense and angry. "He hasn't come to visit or see me for five years! What does he want?"

"I contacted him."

Valeria opened the envelope, and a printed ticket of some kind dropped out onto her lap. There was also a folded note inside, handwritten on yellow lined paper.

She pulled out the note and read it aloud:

Dear Val,

I know how much your mother meant to you. No one will ever replace her in your heart. She was a good person, kind and caring. I want you to know I'm here for you. It's you and me now.

Love, Dad.

p.s. I've enclosed an airline ticket for you. I'll be waiting at the airport to pick you up.

Abuela took the ticket from Valeria and inspected it. "This is for a one-way flight to Jackson Hole Airport in Wyoming. It leaves from LAX on Monday, less than a week from today."

"What does this mean?" asked Valeria.

Abuela stood up and paced the floor. She took a few moments before answering. "You have to understand… I live in a retirement center for seniors where they don't allow children or young adults to stay as residents, and even if they did make an exception, it would only be temporary. They'd never let you live with me for more than a few months." She set the ticket on the table. "Most of my life savings went into buying the place, and I don't want to move."

She sat back down and sighed. "When you were little, Val, your mother was granted custody of you as part of the divorce settlement, but now that your mom is gone, those legal rights over who you live with will be given back to your father." Abuela paused to wipe her eyes with a tissue. "There's nothing you or I can do about it. But maybe it's for the best."

Valeria groaned and darted back into her bedroom, slamming the door behind her. "I'm not going!" she shouted. "I want to stay with you and be near my friends." She lay down on her bed and stared up at the ceiling. "I don't even know where Wyoming is."

CHAPTER 2

Two hours or so into the flight, the earth outside Valeria's window turned white. As she looked westward beyond the plane's extended wing, all the way to the horizon, the midmorning sky was a deep, rich blue. A fast-moving snowstorm had swept through western Wyoming the day before, and it had been a harsh, cold winter. And though it was now the middle of March and the start of spring, according to the calendar, the ground below was blanketed with snow.

"Wow," said Valeria.

The middle-aged lady in the aisle seat next to her had her tray table down and was busy sipping a mixed drink and nibbling on crackers. She leaned over. "Have you ever seen snow before?" asked the lady.

"No," answered Valeria. "This is my first time."

"It's beautiful, isn't it?"

"Yes. The snow looks amazing. I've only seen it on TV and in pictures."

A stewardess came down the aisle with a tall plastic bag, asking to take people's empty cups and trash. The lady next to Valeria took a last sip, gathered up everything in front of her, and handed it all to the stewardess. She folded up her tray and leaned her head over a bit to peer out again. "There's something magical about snow," she told Valeria. "Everyone loves it, but if you live or work where it snows a lot, you can grow tired of having to shovel it constantly."

Valeria didn't respond as she continued to take in the breathtaking landscape unfolding in the distance. The ground had begun to undulate; soon thereafter, a few small mountains came into view.

"You look like you're from Southern California," said the lady. She leaned back in her seat. "Am I right?"

"I was born near Los Angeles. I've never been anywhere else," answered Valeria. "Why do you ask?" She really didn't want to get into a conversation with the woman. Until now, they hadn't spoken more than two words to each other during the entire flight.

"You're not dressed warm enough, my dear. When you walk off this plane at the Jackson Hole airport, you're going to freeze to death. That light jacket you put in the overhead bin won't protect you from the cold. I hope whoever's picking you up has a heavy coat for you to wear. Who's coming to get you?"

"My dad." Valeria looked away. More mountains were beginning to appear outside.

"Men! They can be such dummies. Before you got on the plane, your dad should have prepared you better for what you're in for," said the lady. She reached into an oversized leather satchel by her feet, pulled out a chocolate brown cardigan sweater, and handed it to Valeria. "Here. Take this. I don't want you to catch pneumonia."

"Thank you, but I can't. It's too nice."

"Keep it. I have a ton of wool sweaters at home. It might be a little big on you, but it should keep you much warmer until you get where you're going. You can wear your light jacket over it."

Valeria leaned forward and put the cardigan on. "Thank you," she said.

A few minutes later, the seat belt light came on, and the

captain made a brief announcement saying they would soon be arriving at their destination and for everyone to return to their seats. He told the flight attendants to prepare for the landing.

The plane began its descent. Valeria felt her ears pop from the change in pressure. Then suddenly, on the left, a huge, magnificent mountain range came into view. It rose skyward from the edge of a wide valley. For the second time, Valeria said, "Wow!" Everything–the valley, mountains, trees, all she could see–was all covered in snow.

The lady next to her again leaned over. "Those are the Teton Mountains. The highest peak you see there in the middle is called Grand Teton. The entire mountain range extends for about forty miles. No matter how many times I see these mountains, they still take my breath away. They're unbelievable, aren't they?"

"Yes." Just like with snow, Valeria had never seen such rugged mountains as these. Except for the beaches, her mother had seldom taken her anywhere beyond the neighborhood where she had grown up.

They touched down. The majestic mountains Valeria had seen from the sky continued to loom nearby. The snowbound world outside her window was varying shades of white and gray. With just one runway, the airport at Jackson Hole looked tiny compared to the one in Los Angeles. The passengers stirred as the plane made its way to a small terminal. After they came to a stop, a metal ramp on wheels was rolled up next to the plane to let everyone off. Valeria again thanked the lady for the sweater, grabbed her carry-on, and made her way off the plane. The lady was right–it was much colder than she'd expected. She could see her breath, and her hands and face felt frozen.

Valeria wasn't sure she'd be able to recognize her father. It had been more than five years since she'd last seen him. He and her mother had divorced shortly after she was born, and his numerous jobs tended to take him far away. Eventually, he moved out of state. For a while, he worked as a long-distance truck driver. That job led him to Alaska, where he quit to work on an offshore crab fishing boat in the North Pacific. He later took a job as a roughneck on an oil rig in the Gulf of Mexico. From there, her father, Ray, disappeared for long stretches of time. Seemingly oblivious to cell phones and the Internet, he'd send her a postcard or short letter now and then, hastily written, from little-known places throughout the country. Valeria never understood why, but he rarely spoke to her directly, and months would often go by where she didn't hear from him at all. The one exception was her birthday. He never forgot it. Every year, he'd send Valeria a nice card along with a little money. She had no idea what he was doing in Wyoming.

Inside the terminal, Valeria glanced around for her father as she made her way to the baggage carousel, but she didn't see him. A moment or so later, she heard someone behind her call out her name, "Val! Are you Val?"

Valeria turned to see who it was. Before she could answer, a slim, attractive woman wearing a parka was throwing her arms around her and giving her a tight, enthusiastic hug. "It's good to finally meet you, Val. I've heard so much about you!" The woman paused and took a step back. "So, tell me. Did you have a good flight? How are you feeling? You poor dear. You must be mentally drained from what happened. I know you loved your mom. I lost my mother years ago, and it killed me for a long time. I still think about her. You never really get over it."

Finally, the smiling woman took a breath and stopped talking.

"Who are you?" asked Valeria.

"I'm Lauren, a friend of your dad's. He had to help out with an elk feeding. So, he asked me to come fetch you. How are you, dear? You're growing taller, I see. Are you hungry? I'm going to take you out to see your dad. But first, why don't we get something to eat?"

An elk feeding? thought Valeria. Before she could ask any questions, her suitcases were gathered off the carousel, and she was being whisked away in Lauren's four-wheel-drive Jeep. A small magnetic sign attached to the passenger side door read TETON PASS VETERINARY CENTER. Inside, on the armrest between them, was also a small stack of papers attached to a clipboard. Typed at the bottom of the top sheet was the name "Lauren Ross, DVM."

"What does 'DVM' stand for?" asked Valeria.

"Doctor of veterinary medicine. I own an animal clinic and hospital here in Jackson," answered Lauren with an amused expression. "You need to buckle up, Val. In case some moose or bison wanders out onto the highway in front of us, I don't want to lose you. I might have to brake fast. You just never know. The snowplows cleared the road to the airport, but the drifts are piled so high on either side, it's sometimes impossible to see what's coming around the bend."

Valeria sat back and looked out. Beneath the vivid blue sky was an incredible world. As they made their way, the vast snow and its whiteness extended as far as she could see. The snow drifts were indeed high, but no wild animals jumped in front of them. Soon, the buildings of a small town appeared. This was Jackson. Lauren drove past an attractive archway made of elk antlers, down several side streets, and parked the Jeep in front of a rustic-looking building. A wooden sign in the window of the Silver Beaver Eatery said, HOWDY STRANGER.

They went inside and sat at a table. Several people who were eating nearby looked up and greeted Lauren warmly when they saw her. "Hi, Doc," said one. "How's it going, Doc?" asked another. An older man wearing boots and a rust-colored cowboy hat rose to leave. On his way out the door, he tipped his hat to Lauren and said, "Later, Doc." To each, she responded with a pleasant hello.

Across the dining room, mounted high on a wall, were the large head and shoulders of a real buffalo. The animal's resolute but gentle expression seemed to say, *All is well. I feel fine.* Its watchful eyes looked very much alive. Valeria couldn't stop staring at its face.

"His name is George the buffalo," said Lauren. "He's been in this place for as long as I can remember. Everyone around here knows him."

A stout middle-aged woman wearing an apron approached the table with menus, a pot of coffee, and a cup. Without asking, she set the cup in front of Lauren and poured. "I see you have a friend with you today," she said politely. "What can I get you to drink, dear?"

"I'd like a large orange juice if you have any," answered Valeria. She hadn't thought about food the entire morning, but the delightful smell of freshly baked muffins, bacon, pancakes, and whatever else was permeating the room was suddenly making her feel hungry.

"This is Val," interjected Lauren. "You remember, don't you? I told you about her. She's Ray's daughter. She's come all the way from California. Val, I'd like you to meet Hazel. She owns the Silver Beaver and a few other businesses around town."

"Nice to meet you," said Valeria.

"Oh, yes. You too, dear," said Hazel. "You know, I've always wanted to visit California. I've heard it's nice." She left for a moment and returned with two glasses of ice water and an orange juice. "I'm dying to ask you. Did you ever see or get to meet any famous movie or TV actors around where you lived? How close did you live to Hollywood?"

"Not anyone too famous," answered Valeria. "I lived

maybe thirty minutes from Hollywood Boulevard and all that stuff, but my mom never took me there. Where I'm from, almost nothing exciting ever happens, but I liked it. I miss my friends already." She took a sip of water then added, "Sometimes you might spot a real fancy car or stretch limo driving by, and you'll maybe think there's someone famous inside, but the windows are always tinted black to protect their privacy, so you can't see who it is."

"Did you hear about the mountain lions?" Hazel asked Lauren.

"No," answered Lauren. "What happened?"

"A mama mountain lion with her four cubs were seen strolling through the Taylors' backyard outside of town. It happened the day before yesterday. They were able to catch them on video with their home security cameras."

"That's good news. Hopefully, they'll find enough to eat to survive till spring," said Lauren. She then turned to Valeria. "There are a lot of local hunters and other people around here who refuse to understand just how important the large predators are. The mountain lions and wolves are at the top of nature's food chain. They help keep the entire ecosystem in balance."

For some reason, talk of the mountain lion sighting suddenly made Valeria think about her mom. Her eyes welled up, and she began to cry. She plucked a tissue from her pocket and blew her nose. "Excuse me," she said.

A few people in the room looked up. Others paid no attention. "There, there," said Lauren. "It's okay. Let it out if you need to."

"Was it something I said?" asked Hazel, confused. "Can I bring you something, dear?"

"No," said Lauren under her breath. "The poor girl lost her mother recently. She's still in mourning. We just need to let her work through the grief on her own. It'll take time."

After a minute, Valeria composed herself. "Can we go see my dad?" she asked, sniffling. "I'm not sure I want anything to eat right now."

Lauren leaned forward and took Valeria's hands. "You've been through a lot. I can tell you haven't been eating. You look thin. Let's get some food in you and build up your strength a little before we journey out. It's kind of a long drive." She turned to Hazel. "We'll go ahead and order. Maybe she'd like some of your special homemade pie to start off with. And when we're done, we'll order some carry-out and bring it to Ray. How does that sound?"

Valeria nodded.

Hazel took their order, smiled, and disappeared into the kitchen.

The buffalo on the wall was still staring at everyone, seemingly at peace with his fate. "George doesn't have much to say, does he?" said Valeria.

"No, he doesn't," answered Lauren. "But sometimes I think he has a secret he keeps to himself."

CHAPTER 3

The snow-lined road to the elk feed ground ran north, then eastward. It began on paved, level ground and eventually ran beside a long, winding river. There were countless rolling hills and rocky mountain peaks, smaller than the Tetons, as well as sweeping valley vistas that gave way to more hills and summits through a remote backcountry seemingly void of humans. An hour or so later, the paved road ended, turning into what appeared to be no more than a narrow dirt lane. The Jeep bounced and shuddered abruptly as Lauren, at times, slowed to dodge loose rocks and downed tree limbs that had somehow made their way onto the path. Between the evergreens, Valeria spotted a lone moose, the first she'd ever seen, but they continued without stopping.

Finally, they reached an expansive snow-covered valley and followed a line of tire tracks to the south until they came to an end. Before them were more than a thousand elk. They were clustered along a quarter mile arc behind a horse-drawn sleigh loaded with hay bales. Many had their heads down as they ate the rationed hay, while others walked beside the sleigh, waiting for more fresh hay to be laid out. Two large black horses were pulling the sleigh, driven by one man, while three other men were busy cutting the bales and distributing the hay behind them in a long, continuous line.

Lauren parked the Jeep but left its engine on so the heater

would continue to run. "Let's stay in here a little bit where it's warm," she said. "Do you see your dad?"

Valeria wasn't sure which of the men was her dad. All four were dressed in winter caps and heavy jackets and were too far away. "No," she answered. "I can't tell them apart."

"He's right there in the middle, the one on the back of the sleigh helping with the bales."

From where they were, it was hard to make out his face, but Valeria nodded. After a moment or two, she said, "It's been so long… He's like someone I don't even know. I stopped wondering and thinking about my dad a long time ago."

"I understand," said Lauren. "But you should know your father talks about you all the time. He's very proud of you."

Not wanting to interrupt the men just yet, the two remained in the Jeep and watched the elk following the sleigh and eating the hay being laid out for them. "Why are they feeding these animals?" asked Valeria.

"The state has been feeding the elk in Western Wyoming every winter for well over a hundred years. They do it to keep the elk from wandering onto local cattle ranches and eating the haystacks meant for private livestock."

"That sounds kind of smart," said Valeria. She'd never seen an elk before. "There are so many of them!"

"Actually, the elk numbers are way down from previous years. It has some people concerned," said Lauren. She paused, then added, "I'll tell you the truth. Feeding them is mostly about hunting. During bad winters, the elk die by the thousands because the grass they eat gets buried under too much snow. The locals are afraid that if they stopped feeding the elk, too many of the animals would die. Fewer elk would mean having to put restrictions on hunters during hunting season. And more hunters means more money for the local economy. So, they help keep the elk alive during the winter with these feedings so they can hunt and kill more of them the rest of the year."

Valeria couldn't imagine anyone wanting to shoot an elk. The herd looked like something you'd see on a Christmas card, and they certainly weren't hurting anyone.

"It's time," said Lauren. "Let's go reintroduce you to your dad." She turned off the engine, and the two stepped out.

The bitter subfreezing wind passing down the surrounding mountains and hillsides and through the valley, hit Valeria hard. She crossed her arms and shivered. "Oh, wow! It's really, really cold."

"Your body will get used to it soon," said Lauren. She reached back into the truck and honked the horn. She also pulled out a heavy jacket and wool scarf from behind her seat. "Here. Put this warmer jacket on, and take this and wrap it around your neck."

Halfway across the valley, the men looked up. Valeria saw her father say something to the others and leap off the back of the sleigh. He waved and jogged toward them.

Valeria went to run to meet him, but Lauren grabbed her shoulder and stopped her. "Don't go out there," said Lauren. "Elk might not look dangerous, but they can be aggressive, especially the males. They can attack you without warning."

"Val!" yelled her father as he ran. "Hey, Val!"

When he was closer to them and a good distance from the herd, Valeria broke free from Lauren and ran to him. Soon, they embraced. Her father lifted her off the ground and spun her around and around. There were no tears, just smiles and laughter. Eventually, he put her back down. "Oh my God, Val!" he said excitedly. "Look at you! You're so much more grown up now."

Lauren stood nearby and quietly watched. Ray let go of Valeria. He turned serious. "I'm so sorry," he told his daughter. "Your mother was a good person. She didn't deserve what happened to her. I feel terrible. I know I haven't been around, but I want to make it up to you."

Valeria thought about crying but didn't. She was genuinely glad to see him. "What are you doing here, Dad?" were the first words she could think of to say.

Ray pointed to a shiny metal badge pinned to his jacket. Around an engraving of a leaping pronghorn antelope, it read, "Wyoming Game & Fish Department." "I'm a game warden," he answered. "There's no cell service in these remote areas, and I needed to make sure these men were okay. They got trapped out here by a blizzard yesterday and last night. When the weather cleared this morning, I came to check on things."

"No, Dad," said Valeria. "I mean, why are you in Wyoming? Why would you want to live here?"

He wore a slightly puzzled look, as if he were thinking, and didn't answer her immediately. Then he said, "I used to occasionally travel through this part of the country doing other work, and I never wanted to leave. Whenever I was somewhere else, I found myself wanting to return. The great people and this amazing Wyoming land lured me back again and again. Eventually, I came and stayed."

Ray turned to Lauren. "Thank you for bringing her. She can tag along with me for the rest of the day. Do you have all her clothes and stuff?"

"You're very welcome. It was my pleasure," said Lauren. "I do need to go and check on several of my sick four-legged patients at the center. I'll take Val's things back to my place for now. You can come over and pick them up this evening."

All three turned and walked back to the Jeep. Ray's game warden pickup and two other trucks were parked nearby. Ray had his arm around his daughter's waist. "It's been a long time, hasn't it?" he said. "I've missed you so much."

"I've missed you too, Dad."

Lauren got in and rolled down her window. "I'll see you

both later," she said. She quickly rolled it back up, waved, and drove away.

Ray led Valeria to his dark green double-cab pickup. The same department logo that appeared on his badge was on the front doors. "I'm sure you're a little tired from the flight and the change in altitude. It'll take a few days for you to adjust," he said. "I'll drive you home in a bit so you can get some rest, but first, while we're out this far, I need to go by Goshawk Pass Ranch and talk to the owner. He says a good-size wolf pack has been killing his cows."

"This place has wolves? Seriously?" said Valeria. "I'd like to see one. Are they dangerous?"

"Yes. Wolves can be very dangerous. Thankfully, they tend to avoid humans. If you ever cross paths with a wolf or spot signs of one, be sure to steer clear of the area and keep your distance. They're skilled predators and not like dogs. You can't domestic them. These are wild wolves, and they kill to eat and survive."

Ray turned right at the unpaved road and drove east, farther into the wilderness. Not much was said during the ride except for a few quick observations about the scenery and cold weather. More snow-covered valleys and hills came and went. Much higher rock cliffs soon emerged to the south. In places, the road narrowed greatly along steep ascents. It followed a nearby river and the natural landscape, rising and falling as it went. They crossed a creek, and eventually, the road ended, but they didn't stop. They turned onto a tight path, barely the width of the truck, and drove through a stand of aspens until they reached yet another beautiful open valley, enclosed on all sides by old wooden buck rail fences.

They stopped in front of a wrought iron entry gate with stone pillars on either side and a huge decorative wooden arch above it. A welded metal sign hanging just below the archway read, GOSHAWK PASS RANCH. Ray got out and moved aside the gate, drove through, and then closed it behind them.

A large herd of cattle could be seen on the property, mostly clustered together in two pen areas located near a few buildings and a barn. Several men wearing dark cowboy hats were moving about inside and outside the pens. Ray pulled up close to a ranch house and parked the truck. "You can come with me," he said. Valeria got out and followed him to the house.

Before they could knock, a tall, burly man with bushy gray hair and a wide mustache stepped out to greet them. Like the other men nearby, he wore a weathered cowboy hat, a winter jacket, blue jeans, and boots. From somewhere inside, Valeria heard an older woman call out, "Who is it?"

"It's Ray, the game warden," the man answered. He had a deep, booming voice that matched his size.

"How's your mom?" asked Ray.

The man rubbed his chin and sighed. "Mom's eighty-two now. Can't hardly see and walks with a cane, but she's tough as old boots. She hasn't slowed a bit." He paused, then added, "Good to see you, Ray. Who's this with you?"

"This is my daughter," Ray answered. "She's come all the way from California. Val, I'd like you to meet Mr. Hardin. His family owns this ranch."

Mr. Hardin bowed slightly and tipped his hat. "It's a pleasure to meet you," he said.

Valeria smiled. It was the first time anyone had ever tipped their hat to her, and she liked it. "You too, Mr. Hardin."

"There's no need for formalities, dear. You can call me Butch." He stepped past her and walked toward the pens. Ray and Valeria followed him. On the way there, he momentarily stopped and looked around. "We've been cattle ranching here for more than a hundred and twenty years," he said. "My son, Jesse, will be the next generation to work it. He's like his grandma.

There's no slowing that boy down."

When they reached the pens, Butch spoke to one of the cowboys, "Sam, where's Jesse? Have you seen him?"

"He's around here somewhere," said Sam.

"Well, go fetch him," barked Butch. "And tell one of the guys to saddle up three horses and a pony." Sam nodded, then disappeared into one of the buildings adjacent to the pen.

"Where's the carcass?" asked Ray.

"Jesse's the one who found the kill. He has a natural gift for tracking. He said the cow's remains are a half-hour ride from here, somewhere east of Crystal Peak in the direction of Grizzly Basin. If the weather stays clear, we shouldn't have too much trouble locating it," Butch answered. "Damn wolves! I hate them. This is the fourth head we've lost this winter."

"How did the cow get loose? There's no way a wolf pack could have dragged it that far."

"We found several rails missing from a section of fence on the far side of the property. I assume that's where it got out." Suddenly agitated, Butch raised his voice. "Listen, Ray. If I find the pack responsible, I'll shoot every last one of them."

Ray walked up to Butch and looked him in the eyes. "You know, it's one thing if a gray wolf wanders onto your property to hunt," he said calmly. "You certainly have the right to defend your livestock, but if one of your cows gets loose due to your own negligence and strays onto federal land…well, that's on you. And you know full well it's against the law to kill wolves in the parks and national forests. And it's not yet hunting season.

"But wherever this cow was killed, the law says you have the right to put in a wolf kill claim with the state to be reimbursed for damages as long as I can validate what you say happened is true."

Butch frowned but said nothing. He turned his back to Ray and walked off in a huff toward one of the buildings.

Standing beside her father, Valeria studied the cattle in the pens and the ranch hands busy working with them. She watched their icy breaths escape their mouths like little clouds. The cows looked content and serenely oblivious to what was in store for them in the coming months. She also thought about Butch Hardin. She'd just met him for the first time, but she could tell he was accustomed to doing whatever he wanted and didn't much like the law or being told what he could and couldn't do.

Not long after, Sam, the hired hand, came out of one of the barn-like buildings, leading a saddled brown horse and speckled pony by their reins. He was followed by Butch and a boy, who looked maybe sixteen, with short cropped hair. Dressed for winter weather like the older men and wearing a battered cowboy hat, he looked every bit like a much younger version of Butch. He was leading two horses as well, one dappled gray with a black mane and tail and the other a taller horse, black all over. Butch carried a rifle, which he slipped into a leather scabbard on the left side of the black horse.

Sam looked up. The sky to the west along the horizon was beginning to turn grayer. Handing the reins to the brown horse and speckled pony to Ray, he said, "You all should probably hurry if you're going to ride. Another rough snowstorm is supposed to be rolling through later today." He finished cinching both saddles, then disappeared back into the building.

Butch and Jesse jumped up on their horses. Ray helped his daughter onto the pony. "You've never ridden before, have you?" he asked her.

"No," she answered.

"Not a problem," said Butch from atop his horse. "Jesse can hold the pony's reins and lead her along. All you have to do, darling, is hang onto the saddle horn and keep your feet in the stirrups."

Jesse walked his horse up alongside the pony and grabbed

its reins. He looked at Valeria but didn't say anything. A moment later, her head snapped back, and she was being pulled along behind Jesse at a brisk trot. He led the way with Butch and Ray at the rear.

They rode across the snowy valley to a fence line to the south. There, they went through an old wooden gate and crossed a shallow creek into a forested area where the surrounding land rose and fell more dramatically. From behind her, Valeria heard her father and Butch talk about the cattle business, but Jesse never once turned his head around or said a word. He seemed to know exactly what he was doing, though it didn't look like they were following any kind of trail.

Eventually, at the foot of a mountainous terrain where there were countless stones and boulders to avoid as they rode up several rugged paths, Jesse's trek took them farther east and back south again. Then, without warning, Jesse stopped his horse abruptly and raised his hand. He pointed to an object lying atop the snow in the near distance.

"There it is," he said.

Butch and Ray rode on ahead while Jesse slowly led his horse and the pony to a nearby downed tree limb. After tying them, he helped Valeria down off the pony. "Thank you," she said.

"No problem." Jesse didn't look at her. Instead, he turned and wandered off to where Ray and his father were examining what was left of the dead cow's remains.

It was a grotesque sight, bones, and cartilage stained red with frozen blood, scattered bits of hair, and a skull still attached to the rest of its body. The cow had been devoured. Several ravens stood atop the exposed ribs and vertebrae, standing guard over what was left. They were slow to leave at first but leapt and flew off into a nearby stand of snow-tipped evergreens when the two men and Jesse approached too close to the carcass.

Valeria stood apart from the two men and Jesse, a good distance farther back and well away from the horrific scene. She couldn't hardly look at it.

A light sprinkling of snow began to fall.

Ray walked around the dead cow and inspected the immediate surroundings. "This was wolves for sure," he said. "Based on how much was eaten, I'd say the pack responsible for this is fairly large, maybe ten or more individuals." He glanced up at a nearby ridge. "The Togwolee pack staked out this area a few years ago. We counted a dozen of them last summer. But there's a possibility that either the Lava Mountain pack or Lightning pack have moved into their territory over the winter months out of necessity, looking for food. If these wolf packs run into each other, there's going to be a bloody turf war if there hasn't been one already."

Butch reiterated his sentiment from earlier. "I hate wolves." He was scrutinizing the surrounding area as well. "It looks like yesterday's snowstorm has covered over their tracks." He turned to Jesse. "When you found this two days ago, did you see any wolf tracks?"

"Just around the body," said Jesse. "The wind must have swept away any tracks leading up to it." He reached for a small stone near his feet and hurled it at one of the ravens, then added, "But I did notice someone else had been here before me. There were shoe prints in the snow nearby."

"What do you mean?" asked Ray. "All the way out here?"

"Yes. I don't see them now, but when I got here, there were shoe prints all through this area. They were hard to miss."

"It doesn't make any sense," said Butch. "Who in their right mind would be wandering around in such a remote area this time of year?"

"That's a good question," said Ray. "The closest road is more than four miles away across some pretty rugged wilderness, and the trails are mostly buried under snow. You could die out here, and no one would find your body until spring, and maybe not even then."

Valeria glanced up. The sky had turned a pale gray. The wind had picked up, and the earlier light dusting of snow had turned into a brisk flurry.

"We'd better head back," said Ray. He led Valeria to the pony, untied it, and helped her get on. "I'm sure you weren't expecting all this today." He smiled.

"No," she responded. "But it's kind of exciting."

Just then, a deafening gunshot rang out behind them. The pony was startled and suddenly bolted across the snow, dodging trees and boulders as it ran aimlessly with Valeria on its back, hanging on for dear life. She heard the men shouting, but their voices receded and were quickly gone as the pony sprinted onward through a dense tangle of woods and beyond a rocky hillside. At the edge of a ravine, it stopped and reared up.

Valeria was thrown. Flailing, she screamed as she felt herself tumbling out of control into the ravine. At the bottom, the back of her head hit a rock. She felt a trickle of blood at the corner of her lips. Her legs hurt. She went to cry out, but no sound emerged. The snow was falling softly on her face. She opened her eyes for a moment, then closed them again.

CHAPTER 4

"Everything will be okay. They just want to keep me overnight in the hospital and run a few tests."

"Please, Mom. Please don't leave."

"Stay here with Abuela and be good. Don't give her any trouble."

"Please don't leave me."

"I'll be back to pick you up in the morning."

"But you won't. You're not coming back."

"What are you saying, Val?"

"I love you. I love you, Mom."

Valeria felt a flickering warmth lightly caress her cheeks, then oddly, someone's breath. Feeling woozy, she slowly opened her eyes and shrieked. Just inches above her face, staring back, was a gray wolf.

"Sparkle! Come here." A man's voice came from somewhere close by. "Leave her alone."

The wolf immediately looked up, glanced at Valeria once more, then walked away.

Trembling, Valeria sat upright, terrified and ready to flee, but quickly fell back. An old, tattered sleeping bag was wrapped around her, and a leather knapsack lay under her head. When a minute later, she tried to rise again, the entire world felt like it was spinning. She was having trouble focusing her eyes, and her head hurt.

It was nighttime. A wavering glow illuminated the four

walls of the crude log structure in which she lay. Just outside a doorless entrance to the room, she made out the silhouette of a man sitting cross-legged next to a campfire. The wolf lay beside him.

Valeria couldn't keep her eyes open. Something was wrong with her legs. She felt a sharp pain when she tried to move. Confused and frightened but too weak to fight whatever was happening, she allowed the soothing warmth of the sleeping bag to embrace her, and soon, she slipped away back into a deep sleep.

When Valeria woke up again, a pale morning light streamed through the tiny room. Outside the doorless entrance, it was snowing steadily. The man she had seen earlier was tending to the white-hot coals of the fire and stirring a cast iron pot. She smelled coffee and food. There were also three wolves lying nearby. All but their faces were buried in the snow.

Valeria went to rise and groaned in pain.

The man rushed in, grabbed her arms, and gently laid her back down. "Don't move just yet," he said. "You've fractured both your legs."

Valeria nodded. She studied the man's face. He was much older than her father. His brownish skin had the look of well-worn leather. The area above his brows, as well as around his dark eyes and the corners of his lips, were etched with deep, formidable lines. His long jet-black hair, streaked with gray, was neatly braided into two tight ponytails that hung down both sides of his chest.

The man left, then returned a minute or two later. He lifted Valeria to a sitting position and held a tin cup up to her lips. "Here. Drink this," he said. His voice was firm but also calm and reassuring. Valeria took a sip. It was the best water she'd ever tasted. She tried to gulp it all in one swig and began to choke.

"Slow down and take your time. You've been unconscious

for more than two days," said the man. "It's good you're awake, but you shouldn't try to move around too quickly. Right now, it's important that you rehydrate and eat a little something so you can regain your strength."

Valeria finished drinking and lay back, too weak to respond. She watched the man go back to the campfire, reach into the pot with a ladle, and fill a shallow metal bowl. Whatever was in the pot smelled wonderful. He returned with the bowl and a spoon. After helping Valeria sit up again, he knelt beside her and fed her.

She couldn't get enough. It was some kind of stew with potatoes, carrots, and meat. The man tried to slow Valeria down, withholding the spoon now and then, but she ate ravenously. "What's in this?" she asked with her mouth full.

"Vegetables and a jackrabbit," said the man.

Valeria didn't stop eating, and soon, she had finished it all. Though her head still ached, the world around her began to come into much sharper focus, and she didn't feel quite as dizzy. It was then an entire sea of serious questions flooded her mind. "Who are you?" she asked. "Where am I?"

The man set down the empty bowl and spoon. There was no floor inside the makeshift room, just pebbles and dirt. "My name is Shimmer Wat Madoick Bungu," he said stoically. "It's Shoshone and means Twelve Horses." He paused, then added, "My father called me Bungumobonzi. It means horsefly. He said I was a constant pain in the butt." He grinned. "I loved to torture my father. But anyway, you can call me Philip. And you must be Val."

"How do you know my name?"

"Three days ago, I heard men shouting, 'Val! Val!' well into the night and the next day. It echoed across these mountains and didn't cease until they were forced to stop searching when the worst of the blizzard came."

Philip stood up and disappeared outside. A minute later he was back carrying a crude bench made out of split logs, which he placed near the campfire. He came back in. "You've been lying down too long. We need to get you up. It'll improve your circulation, and you'll feel better," he said. "Do you feel strong enough to sit upright on your own?"

"I think so," said Valeria.

He unzipped the sleeping bag and helped Valeria to her feet. Her badly swollen legs were bound securely by a pair of homemade wooden splints. Both pant legs had been neatly cut along the seams and rolled up. The hard splints ran from just below both sides of her knees to her ankles and were held together by short lengths of rope made from pine needles.

Philip lifted Valeria and carried her to the bench by the fire. He went back inside and retrieved a blanket, which he placed around her shoulders. He sat beside her and stirred the rest of the stew simmering in the pot. Still buried in deep snow, the three wolves nearby never moved. They appeared to be napping, but Valeria could tell all three were quietly observing her.

The cold air was refreshing, and it felt good to sit close to the fire. Valeria saw now that the tiny room she'd been lying in was just an old, weathered log shed. It was tucked away high on a rugged hillside, near a rockface, surrounded by a stand of trees and countless boulders. In the distance, through the dense snowy haze, she made out the faint outline of a vast mountain range.

Philip poked at the coals with a stick. "Your mother is with us," he said without looking up. "She's nearby, watching."

His words startled Valeria. "How do you know my mom?"

Philip reached for a kettle resting on a flat rock by the fire and poured himself a cup of coffee. "Would you like some? It'll warm you up."

"No, thank you. I want to hear more. You've never met my mom. You have no idea who she was."

"As you were lying in the ravine and near death, your mother came and spoke to the wolves." Philip held the cup with both hands and took a sip.

Valeria stared at Philip, disbelieving and speechless.

"When the men searching for you stopped shouting your name, I knew they'd failed," he said. "Something needed to be done quickly, so I asked the Wolf God, protector of all, for guidance, and it told me of your mother's presence." He took another sip. "The snowstorm had come, and your scent was faint, but the wolves were able to track down where you lay with the help of her maternal spirit. Your mother whispered in our ears and led us to you. She hasn't left since."

Valeria listened but said nothing. She wanted to believe Philip but wasn't sure she should. How could he possibly have known about her mom's passing? His explanation of how her mother's spirit had helped him find her sounded too good to be true, but she couldn't think of a reason he might lie about such a thing.

"Thank you for saving my life," she said.

Philip finished his cup of coffee, got up, and walked over to a pile of wood next to the shed. He grabbed an ax leaning against the pile, split several short logs, and brought an armful back to the fire. He carefully placed them around and over the hot coals, then sat down beside her. "There's no need to thank me," he said. "Your mother is the one who saved you."

For a time, both sat by the coals and watched the new logs catch fire and burn. Little more was said. Eventually, Philip rose. He went into the shed and brought out a rifle with a scope attached to it. Hanging at his hip was a large fixed-blade hunting knife in a leather sheath. He walked over to the other side of the fire across from Valeria. The heads of all three wolves perked up. They each stood and shook off the snow.

"I was already running low on provisions when the storm

hit," said Philip. "It's my own fault. I wasn't expecting company." He reached into his pants pocket, pulled out a handful of bullets, and started loading the rifle. "If I don't go now while there's decent light and find us more to eat, we're both going to starve."

"You're not going to leave me here alone, are you?" said Valeria. "What about the wolves? My dad told me wolves are dangerous." She began to panic. "I don't know where I am or who you are. Can't you just take me to someone's house close by and drop me off? Or maybe you can call the cops and tell them where I am? They could come get me."

"Don't worry. I'll be back. And these wolves aren't going to bother you because you're with me. They're not staying here anyway. I need them to come along." Philip finished loading, and lowered the rifle. "If we have time, we might search for one of our pack who's gone missing."

Philip started to walk away but stopped and turned around. "You'll be safe here if you stay near the fire. We're a few miles from any known trails, and they're buried under several feet of snow as it is. The terrain is extremely dangerous. You can easily break your neck or freeze to death if you venture too far into certain areas. We're off the grid, and until this snowstorm stops and the weather clears some, it might be a week or more before I can take you back to your family."

"What about calling someone?" asked Valeria.

"There's no cell service this far out. The mountains block the signals, and I've never owned a phone." He looked over at the wolves and made a gesture with his hand. They immediately came and stood near him. "I want you to wait by the fire and keep warm. I'm sure Search and Rescue will send their helicopter to look for you, but I suspect the bad weather has delayed things. Hopefully, they'll come this way and spot the fire. If you see a helicopter, wave your arms and try to get their attention."

Before Valeria could respond, Philip turned and walked

off. The wolves followed. She soon lost sight of them in the snowy haze.

A few minutes later, Valeria heard a gunshot.

The warmth of the fire was hypnotic as an icy wind howled. The sound was relentless and haunting. The combination of hot and cold had a calming effect on Valeria, and she lost track of time. She felt herself doze off again and again, but the unceasing ache in both legs always snapped her back awake.

Valeria had never been so alone in the world. She missed her friends in California and her grandmother. She thought about her father and Lauren, who had to be worried sick about her. By this time, they probably assumed she was dead. Again, she remembered her mother's last words to her and what Philip had said. Was her mother watching over her like a guardian angel? When he told her, it seemed too far-fetched to ever believe, but now, as she sat by the fire and listened to the sound of the wind, she imagined she could hear her mother's voice whispering within it. She thought to herself, *Maybe the wind is alive with all the spirits who ever breathed.*

Valeria listened for Philip's return, but hours passed with no sign of him. The fire dwindled. Then she heard something. She wasn't sure, but it sounded like the crunch of footsteps approaching in the snow. They were coming from a different direction than the one Philip had taken when he left. Anxious to see his face appear from out of the snowy haze, she sat up a little straighter. A few minutes passed, but no one came. The sound of footsteps stopped.

She called out, "Is that you?"

The wind picked up, and the fire's embers flickered in response. On the other side of the flames, in the near distance, a wolf suddenly appeared, followed by four more. From the ominous gaze in their eyes, Valeria instantly understood these wolves weren't with Philip. With the lead wolf baring its fangs, the group circled the fire and slowly approached her from all sides. Quickly, she grabbed a half-burned log from the edge of the fire with both hands and swung it wildly at them.

"Get back!" she yelled. "Go away!"

The lead wolf stopped for a moment, as did the others. Valeria and the wolf locked eyes. She held the burning log in front of her like a torch and shook it at him. He continued to step cautiously toward her.

"Don't come any closer!" Valeria panicked. She rose to her feet to run, took two painful steps, and fell headfirst into the snow. The log slipped from her hands and was doused.

"Philip! Dad! Somebody, please help!" Valeria rolled over onto her back and looked up. The wolf was just feet away now, staring down at her. She cried out in desperation, "Mom! Help me, Mom!"

The wolf lunged at Valeria. She screamed. There was a sudden flash of white fur. She saw it out of the corner of her eye. It vaulted over her head and caught the wolf in midair, knocking it violently to the ground. A vicious snarling and growling ensued. Valeria sat up, paralyzed with fear. A new wolf, a sixth, was squared off between her and the attacker. Unlike the other wolves surrounding her, this one was nearly all white.

There was a brief respite as both wolves bared their teeth and sized up the other, but it didn't last more than a few seconds. The white wolf tackled and tore into the gray. Valeria saw the blood spill onto their fur as each bit the other and fought savagely. Their fierce growls were unlike anything she'd ever heard. The gray who had attacked her was knocked down onto its back, and the white was quick to sink its teeth into its neck. There was a loud, piercing whimper, and the gray scrambled to its feet. It snarled, but the battle was over. The gray turned and ran off into the snowy haze.

For a moment, there was silence. The remaining four wolves that had come to attack Valeria glared at her. They looked to be frozen in place or thinking, and it wasn't until the white wolf growled deep and low at them that they turned in unison and hurried off in the same direction as their defeated companion.

The white wolf was bleeding. There was blood on its fur and around its mouth. It lay down in the crimson-stained snow. Valeria struggled to lift herself back onto the makeshift bench by the fire, her legs throbbing in pain and body shaking. Once up and sitting again, she remained perfectly still, too weak and frightened to even scream. The two stared into each other's eyes, and neither moved.

How much time passed, Valeria didn't know, but the snowstorm began to lighten a bit, and eventually the white wolf got up and slowly staggered toward her. She held her breath. The wolf sniffed her legs, looked around, and collapsed at her feet. Its eyes closed.

CHAPTER 5

Valeria stayed close to the fire and watched the burning wood gradually turn to white-hot coals as she nervously waited for Philip to return. Shivering, she leaned forward to get warm. An hour or so more had passed since the attack. The white wolf lay on its side in the snow near her, maybe sleeping, but she couldn't tell for sure. The wolf also looked to be dead. Its eyes were still shut, and it wasn't moving.

Then, from somewhere in the distance, not far away, Valeria heard a howl. The mournful cry echoed off the surrounding hills and mountains before disappearing. It was followed shortly after by a noisy chorus of howls. Warily, she listened to what sounded like three wolves, all howling the same melancholy refrain at the same time. The white wolf sluggishly raised its head and sat up, then howled in response. The others, unseen, stopped for a moment as if listening, then began again.

A few minutes later, Philip appeared. He was dragging the dead body of a deer on a crude sled made out of aspen poles lashed together with strips of bark. Trailing behind him were the three wolves he had left with earlier. He laid the sled and deer beside the old shed and immediately came over to check on Valeria.

"What happened?" he asked.

Valeria told him everything.

Slow to respond, Philip inspected Valeria's bound legs

closely for a moment and saw the fire was nearly extinguished. He stroked the white wolf's head before walking over to the woodpile to chop a few logs, returned with an armful, then arranged them over the hot coals. He got down low and blew on the coals until one of the logs sparked and caught fire.

"Wolves hate fire. Most won't come anywhere near it," said Philip. He took the rifle into the shed and brought out an old canteen filled with water. He unscrewed the cap and handed it to Valeria, who drank greedily. "You should've been safe," he added. "But it's been a tough winter. Many animals out here are dying of starvation. And about the time a man thinks he can predict what a wolf will do, he's fooling himself. A ravenous wolf is known to become erratic. It was my fault. I'm sorry."

Meanwhile, the three wolves with Philip rushed over to greet the white one. With expressions of happiness or curiosity on their faces, Valeria couldn't tell which. They each took turns circling and nuzzling the white wolf before returning to their original spots in the snow to rest.

Philip turned his attention to the white wolf. Seeing splashes of blood on the snow near where it had been laying, he carefully reached for the wolf and said, "Lie down for me, Gypsy."

For the first time, Valeria realized each of the four wolves had a name. She watched as Philip's hands lightly touched Gypsy's shoulders. The wolf growled and lay down for him.

"It's okay, dear," said Philip softly. "Now I need you to roll over for me so I can see the other side." Again, Gypsy groaned but did what he asked.

Gypsy's other side was covered in blood. She remained perfectly still while Philip ran his hands over her thick fur. He found and inspected the source of the blood, a gaping wound low on her side, not far behind her front leg. "It's just as I feared," said Philip. "She's been shot."

"Why would anyone want to shoot her?" asked Valeria. She didn't quite know what else to say.

Philip went into the shed and returned with a tin plate and an old rag. He knelt by the fire and scooped some blackened ash onto the plate using a flat piece of wood. He then mixed the warm ash with a bit of snow.

"It was the boy who did this," said Philip. "The one they call Jesse. I saw him take a shot, but I didn't know for sure until now that she'd been hit."

Valeria suddenly remembered the rifle Butch had brought with him when Jesse had led her father to the dead cow's remains and also the unexpected gunshot that had spooked the pony. "If you saw him shoot Gypsy, that means you must have been somewhere close by watching us," said Valeria.

Philip said nothing. He took the rag, soaked it in the wet ash, and pressed it firmly against Gypsy's bullet wound. She let out a muffled growl but didn't move. "Hopefully, this will staunch the external bleeding," said Philip, "but it doesn't look good."

"What do you mean?"

"She's not going to survive."

"How do you know?"

Philip gently rubbed Gypsy's head as he pressed the cloth against the wound. "The bullet is still lodged inside her. From the angle where it entered, it looks to have pierced her liver." He applied more ash to the wound. "If she doesn't slowly bleed to death internally, it's likely the wound will become infected. Either way, I don't think she'll make it."

Valeria had many questions for Philip but couldn't bring herself to ask them yet. She watched him tend to Gypsy. He continued to apply pressure to the bullet wound and began to sing softly. "Fair is the white star of twilight, and the sky clearer at the day's end. But she is fairer, and she is dearer. She, my heart's friend." He repeated the verse several times.

"That's so beautiful," said Valeria.

"My mother used to sing it to me when I was a child," said Philip. "It's an old Shoshone love song. There are more words to it, but I can't remember them now."

Philip got to his feet. With all four wolves looking on, he walked over to the makeshift sled holding the dead deer and dragged it behind him to beyond a line of nearby trees, out of sight. Thirty minutes later, he returned with nothing but large sections of deer meat. He laid a large piece near Gypsy and another on a flat stone near the fire. The rest he hauled to an area about thirty yards away from the encampment. Valeria watched Philip dig a hole and bury the meat in the snow.

He came back, again went into the shed and brought out a large cast iron skillet, several metal utensils, and two potatoes. He sat down next to Valeria. "The others have already eaten," he said. "We were blessed with good fortune, and I let the wolves have the second kill. It should hold them for a few days." He placed the heavy skillet directly atop a pile of hot coals, then peeled the potatoes with his hunting knife.

"Have you ever tasted venison?" asked Philip.

Valeria shrugged. "I don't know what venison is."

"It's what deer meat is called." Philip cut the peeled potatoes into much smaller chunks and tossed them into the skillet. He then carved the venison into two steak-size portions and placed them alongside the potatoes. Everything soon began to sizzle and fill the air with a wonderful cooked aroma. Without looking at her, he added, "You must forgive me. I'm not used to having someone to talk to, and my manners aren't good." He moved and stirred the potatoes in the skillet. "If you'd care to, I'd enjoy hearing you tell me about yourself and the place you're from."

Valeria hesitated at first, but a few words turned into

lengthier descriptions, and before long, her entire life story came pouring out of her like a waterfall along a river. She couldn't help herself. Philip seemed to be listening intently, and she ended up telling him things she'd never told anyone. Nearly every important thought she had about her best friends and the world she knew was laid bare. She also confessed her strong feelings of guilt over her mother's sudden passing. By the time the food was ready, there wasn't much left to say. She even told him about the plane ride to Jackson Hole, meeting Lauren, and her first and only day alone with her father.

Philip cut off a small piece of venison and stabbed it with a large metal fork. "Open your mouth," he said.

"Mmm, that's actually pretty good," said Valeria as she tasted it. "It's different, but I kind of like it."

"I'm glad." Philip removed the skillet from the coals and portioned out the potatoes and venison onto two metal plates. He handed a plate to Valeria along with a fork and knife.

Not much more was said while the two ate. Valeria was hungrier than she thought and soon devoured everything in front of her. Philip, on the other hand, took his time. He ate slowly and methodically. When he was done, he spent several minutes staring at the fire and repositioning a few of the logs. Eventually, he looked up. "You've lived a full and interesting life already for one so young," he said.

Valeria didn't think so. She glanced down at Gypsy. The meat laid for the wolf had been eaten. "After it stops snowing and you take me back to my dad, where are you going to go?" she asked. "Where do you live?"

"This is my home," said Philip.

"Don't you have a family somewhere?"

"These wolves…this pack is my family."

Valeria didn't know quite what to say. She set her plate down and said, "Thank you."

Philip looked out across the wilderness and pointed. "On the other side of these mountains, east of where we're sitting, is a place called Wind River Indian Reservation. I was born and raised there," he said. "Occasionally, I used to come to this spot with my father to hunt. This old cabin or shed has always been here. It was probably erected by white miners searching for gold over a hundred years ago. I'm sure it was never meant to last more than one winter, but look–here it is today, still standing."

Philip got up and went over to where Gypsy lay. He knelt beside her and stroked her back. The bleeding appeared to have stopped. "I returned here some years ago." He lowered his voice. "It was early morning, the tail end of summer, when I first met Gypsy. She and two others from the same litter were down by the Gros Ventre River, trying to catch trout. It was funny. They were too small yet to hunt for bigger game–no longer pups but not fully grown. I watched them for several hours and knew right away that Gypsy was an alpha female. When they failed to catch a meal, I did something I shouldn't have done: I fed them."

"If you knew it was wrong, why did you do it?" asked Valeria.

"There should have been an older wolf or several others nearby watching over them, but I never saw any. Most wolf pups are cared for and guided by the adults in their pack. There's generally six to eight members in a wolf pack...sometimes less, sometimes more. But no pack would have left young wolves their age alone to fend for themselves. So, I assumed the adults had been killed, probably at the hands of hunters or a rival wolf pack." Philip paused. "Their playfulness and youthful innocence tugged at my heart. I'd been living out here secluded for a long time, and I couldn't just leave them to die."

Gypsy looked to be in a lot of pain. As Philip ran his hands gently over the wolf's fur to calm her, she let out a low, sustained growl that sounded a bit like someone groaning.

"Why did she save my life?" asked Valeria.

"Wolves have an incredible sense of smell. If the winds are right, their nose can detect prey over ten miles away. It's possible she smelled my scent on you from a distance, which would have been interpreted as a sign that I'd accepted you as part of the pack. She might even think we're related." Philip sat upright next to Gypsy. "Hand me that canteen, please," he told Valeria. He took it from her and trickled water into the wolf's mouth. "Those wolves that attacked you were probably members of the Togwolee pack. They recently killed two of ours, including Gypsy's mate, Axel. I'm sure Gypsy stepped in to save you because she thought you were one of us."

"How many more wolves are there in your pack?"

"There were eleven as recently as last spring, but since then, several in the pack have been killed, and others have disappeared, which means they're more than likely dead," said Philip. "The pack has been decimated. The wolves you see with us now are all that remain. The two over there, Gypsy's daughter Sparkle and son Titan, are her offspring from several years ago. The third, Romeo, is an outsider wolf that was allowed to join the pack."

All three, Sparkle, Titan, and Romeo, immediately raised their heads when they heard Philip mention their names. They remained alert for several minutes before settling back down in the snow.

Gypsy continued to groan.

"We've got another serious problem," said Philip. He put his arms around Gypsy's neck and tried to lift her. "I need to move Gypsy into the shed so she can use it as a den."

"Why?" asked Valeria. "What's the matter?"

"She's pregnant and going into labor."

"When was she due?"

"I'm not sure. I thought it wasn't for another week, but it

looks like she's ready to have her pups."

"How soon?"

"Now."

Just before the first pup arrived, Gypsy sat up for a moment and howled. The three members of the pack, lying outside in the snow, answered her. She slumped back down onto her side and gave birth soon after. The pup was wrapped in a fetal sac and attached to its umbilical cord. Gypsy quickly severed the cord with her teeth, ate the placenta, and licked the puppy clean. She then lifted the pup with her mouth and positioned it near her underbelly so it could nurse.

Careful not to intrude, Valeria had lain quietly on the sleeping bag across from Gypsy and watched the wolf give birth. The birthing process looked exhausting and painful. It was also exciting. From just inside the shed's open doorway, Philip stood guard and watched as well.

"Normally, she'd find a small cave or dig a hole somewhere nearby to create a den for her little ones," whispered Philip. "But given she's hurt, this old shed will have to do. Until I can get you back to your father, it looks like you're going to have a few roommates."

Soon, six newborn puppies were nuzzling and nursing on Gypsy.

"Since you're going to need to sleep and spend some time in here as well, I want Gypsy to get used to you being near the pups," said Philip. "Just don't make any sudden moves or try to pick them up just yet."

"They're so adorable!" whispered Valeria. "I've always wanted a dog, but my mother would never let me have one. She said the landlord didn't allow pets."

"Wolves are not dogs. They're far more dangerous and nearly impossible to tame. You know that, right?"

"I do, yes. My dad told me the same thing." Valeria smiled. "But just look at how cute they are!"

CHAPTER 6

It continued to snow for ten days and nights.

On the morning of the eleventh day, Valeria rolled over in the sleeping bag and opened her eyes. Bright sunshine streamed in through the numerous gaps in the log walls, where the chink used to seal the room had long ago worn away. Lying on top and nestled against her body were three of the pups. Every night, several of the pups, their eyes still closed from birth, somehow managed to wriggle across the earthen floor to the other side of the room where Valeria was sleeping and cuddled up.

After a few minutes more of prolonged snuggling, Valeria gently lifted each snoozing wolf pup off her and, one at a time, returned them to Gypsy. The three stirred briefly but soon got comfortable and flopped back down next to their mother.

Leaning against the wall beside Valeria were two crude crutches, which Philip had fashioned out of cut Aspen branches. She grabbed the crutches, lifted herself up, and made her way outside. As usual, she found Philip sitting next to the fire, preparing a small breakfast for them both and sipping coffee.

"Good morning," said Philip.

At night, he slept by the fire, covered in animal furs, and each dawn, he could be heard chopping wood. The sound echoed off the surrounding mountains.

Before Valeria had a chance to sit, he set down his cup and knelt in the snow. "Here, let me take a closer look at your legs," he said. She stood there while he inspected them. "Good. This looks good. The swelling is almost completely gone. I think the fractures in your legs are healing well, better than expected." He looked up at her. "It's time to remove your splints. We need to get you walking around."

Philip got out his hunting knife. "Hold still." Starting with the left splint, he sliced through the strands of rope holding both sides together. He gently pulled the splint apart and took it off Valeria's leg. He did the same thing with the right splint.

"How does that feel?" asked Philip.

"That's so much better! My legs feel really stiff but lighter."

"The muscles in your legs are a little atrophied from being held in place." Philip sat back down and reached for his coffee. "You just need to walk around and get some exercise. The more you move about, the faster your legs will fully heal. But first, come sit and have some breakfast. I've made your favorite stew, minus the carrots. We're out of carrots."

Valeria couldn't get enough of Philip's jackrabbit stew. As usual, it smelled delightful. And though she felt a teensy bit bad for whatever rabbit had to sacrifice its life for her meal, after a few mouthfuls, she couldn't think of a convincing enough reason why anything that tasted this good shouldn't be eaten.

After breakfast, Philip retrieved several large pieces of trimmed venison and took them to Gypsy. "While the mother is caring for her young pups in the den, the other members of the pack help out by bringing her something to eat," he had explained shortly after Gypsy gave birth. "Raising wolf pups is a group effort. The success and longevity of the pack depends on everyone cooperating."

Valeria always listened intently to everything Philip said. His knowledge of the wilderness she'd found herself in was vast, and she knew her survival might depend on what he was telling her. Over time, she'd learned Philip was a patient and tolerant man who valued his solitude and embraced silence. When he did speak, it was almost never frivolous. He spoke simply and with a purpose.

According to Philip, Gypsy's condition was worsening by the day. His prediction that her bullet wound would become infected appeared to be coming true. The wolf could barely sit up to eat what food he brought her, and while she was lying down, her breathing was noticeably labored. "When she stops eating altogether, we'll know the end is near," said Philip.

Several times a day, Sparkle, Titan, and Romeo took turns coming into the shed to briefly look in on Gypsy and the pups. Like Philip, they each made sure the new mother had enough to eat, bringing her sizable portions of their own meals and leaving it near her.

When Philip was done tending to Gypsy, he came back out and sat down. His face looked tense. "This is my fault," he said in a low whisper.

Valeria looked at him inquisitively, unsure what he meant. Philip was staring intently at the fire. "What are you talking about?" she asked.

"I never should've fed her and the others that day by the river. I should've left them alone. It's because of me that Gypsy lost her fear of humans, and it's the reason that boy was able to put a bullet in her. She let herself be seen because she didn't fear him. I'm the one responsible. I'm the reason she's going to die. Not the boy. Me."

Valeria reached over and touched Philip's arm. "If it wasn't for you, Gypsy and the others probably would have died young," she said. "She was able to grow up and have some pups of her own because you chose to help. Sparkle, Titan, and those six little pups lying in there with her are alive, and you're the reason they've gotten the chance to live. You might not have done the right thing that day, but you did a good thing."

Philip didn't respond. Instead, he got up and went behind by the woodpile. A minute or so later, he returned holding two large objects made out of what looked like pine branches, cut and lashed together. "I made these for you," he said, "to celebrate the day your legs were better." He placed them next to Valeria.

"What are they?" she asked.

"Snowshoes," he replied. "I know they don't look like much, but they'll work just fine. Wearing these will keep you from sinking into the deep snow as you walk. It's time we took you back to your people."

Valeria threw her arms around Philip and hugged him.

Philip's plan was to give Valeria three or four days more to stretch and strengthen her legs before they set out on the long and dangerous hike across the rugged mountainous terrain, which was still blanketed in several feet of snow. If the weather remained clear, he estimated the trek would take a full day to complete, maybe two if they needed to rest and hunker down somewhere. He'd already scouted the area while out hunting and found the trails were impassable. They'd remain buried for weeks. This meant he and Valeria would need to cut across the backcountry through steep areas he knew were treacherous, but with his years of experience, he was confident they could make the journey.

That was the plan, but the next morning, something happened to change things. Philip had just finished disassembling and cleaning his rifle for the day's hunt and was listening to Valeria go on about how she had woken up in the middle of the night to find all six pups lying on top of her. She was describing the humorous scene in great detail when he stopped her abruptly. He put a finger to his lips. "Shhh," he said. "Do you hear that?"

Valeria nodded. It was the distinct pulsing chop-chop sound of a helicopter flying somewhere nearby. She and Philip listened closely. With the way certain echoes swiftly bounced off the mountainous terrain, it was difficult at first to tell exactly which direction the sound was coming from.

Twice before, they'd heard a helicopter, but on those occasions, the overcast sky had been too impenetrable to see anything. Philip quickly reassembled his rifle, checked the action on it, and slung it over his shoulder. He stuffed a handful of bullets in his pants pocket and grabbed the canteen.

"They'll never see this campsite from a distance. It's too hidden," Philip said hurriedly. "I'll head over to a nearby clearing and see if I can attract the crew's attention. Hopefully, they'll pass by close enough where they can see me."

Sparkle, Titan, and Romeo rose up, ready to go with him. He raised his hand and told them, "No. You guys aren't coming." All three lowered their heads and laid back down. He turned to Valeria. "I want you to stay here, near the fire. I'll be back."

"No," said Valeria. "I'm coming with you."

Philip glared at her. "It's out of the question." He turned his back on Valeria and began to walk away. "You're not strong enough yet. It's not safe."

"No!" she repeated.

Philip stopped and turned around.

Valeria's makeshift snowshoes were leaning against the shed. She hobbled over and grabbed them. Back at the bench, she looped the shoes' leather straps around her feet and ankles like Philip had shown her and tied them off. Once she was upright, it took her a minute or two to find her balance, but soon, she was moving across the snow to where Philip was watching and waiting.

"I'll be okay," she said. "I just can't sit around here by myself. Please let me come along."

By now, the sound of the helicopter was gone.

"There's a chance they'll make several searches this way

while the weather holds up," said Philip. "All right. You can come, but you've got to follow my lead and do what I say. One wrong step, and you might get us both killed. You understand?"

"I promise not to cause any trouble."

Philip went into the shed and returned with a long length of rope. He looped one end around Valeria's waist and tied it off. The other end he tied to himself.

The two headed out. Philip made his way through the snow, pulling Valeria along behind him. About ten feet separated the two. She tired quickly but was able to keep pace for the most part.

This was the first time she had seen sweeping areas of the Teton wilderness since the day she had ridden with Butch, Jesse, and her father in search of the dead cow. The sky was a deep blue. Everything else, the valleys and mountains, was buried under several feet of snow. What lay outside of shadows glistened in the sunlight. A brisk wind blew from the north, hitting them square in the face whenever they stepped out from behind a rocky bluff or stand of trees.

After about a half hour, Philip stopped.

"There's a steep mountain slope nearby where there are no trees over a wide-open area, just snow. It would be hard for the helicopter crew to miss us," said Philip. He stopped, uncapped the canteen, and handed it to Valeria. She took a sip of the cold water and passed it back. "We're making good time and should be there soon."

They sat on the edge of a big rock to rest.

"How do your legs feel?" asked Philip.

"They're a little sore but not too bad," said Valeria.

"That's good, but by the end of the day, the muscles in both your legs are going to throb and feel a lot worse. It would've been better if you'd stayed at the campsite."

Valeria didn't respond. She was looking out upon the

breathtaking scenery before her. For some reason, the sun appeared brighter to her now, the snow-capped mountains more rugged, the abundant forests more mysterious.

After a few minutes, Philip stood and took one last sip from the canteen. "Well, let's see if we can make it the rest of the way without stopping," he said. "We're going to be crossing over some steep cliffs. So make sure you walk behind me and don't veer from my path. The last thing we need is for you to tumble off another ledge." He checked the knot on her end of the rope and his. "This time, if you fall, there's a fifty-fifty chance you'll be taking me with you."

Philip's path took them dangerously close to several sheer drops, then downward through a wooded area that was thick with tall spruce and fir trees.

On the way, Valeria decided to question Philip about something she'd been curious about for some time. "That day I was with my father, why were you and Gypsy there watching us? What were you doing?"

With his back to her, Philip kept on walking and didn't respond.

"Are you going to tell me?"

"It's no accident that cow was found many miles from Goshawk Pass Ranch and in a remote place it shouldn't have been," said Philip. He slowed his pace. "The young boy, Jesse, brought the cow there a few days before."

"I don't understand. Why would he do that?"

"He was using the cow as bait." Philip stopped for a second to check where he was. "And it wasn't the first time he'd done it."

"Bait for what?"

"For wolves. It's been a rough winter. Food in the wild is scarce. The boy knew a wolf pack would eventually come and take down the cow to eat it. The poor thing was defenseless. He'd tied the cow to a tree, knowing the wolves would pick up its scent. Then he lay in wait with his rifle, ready to shoot and kill any wolves that came around. I heard him bring the cow to where you found its remains and saw him."

"Couldn't you have stopped him from doing it?" Valeria was angry. "You were right there watching and could've done something."

Philip didn't stop walking. "I prevented Gypsy and the others from walking into the trap and going after the cow, but wolves are smart, and we weren't the only ones around. The Togwolee pack waited until the boy left and attacked the cow while he was gone." He paused to help Valeria through an uneven area covered in rocks, where the footing wasn't good.

"I don't own a horse, and the distance on foot to the ranch was too great," he added. "And anyway, if I'd been caught returning the cow, they would've accused me of trying to steal it and had me arrested. It's a long story, but I've been warned to stay out of the area before, and I couldn't risk it for a cow. I'm sorry, but it wouldn't have stopped Jesse from sacrificing another one. I'm sure his father doesn't have a clue."

They came to the edge of an enormous mountain slope covered in snow.

"To protect Gypsy and the others, I made it a point to monitor the boy's movements. The day I heard your father's group making their way to the kill, I came to observe and listen. That's all. I didn't want Gypsy to come with me because I knew there'd be trouble if she was seen, but I couldn't stop her.

Valeria didn't know what else to say about what happened. She was still fuming about what Jesse had done but decided not to bombard Philip with any more questions. His answers made sense.

"I hope the helicopter comes back this way," she interjected.

"Me too." Philip adjusted the rifle's strap on his shoulder and stepped onto the slope. "Around this part of the mountains, this is the widest expanse with no trees. From the air, the crew should be able to spot us easily."

"I've never skied, but it looks like a ski slope."

"You're right. It does. But this slope isn't accessible to the average skier. It's too far off the grid, and there are no trails to it. But I'm sure over the years, it's been skied on more than once by a few of the locals."

Philip began trudging across the snow slope with Valeria in tow. "We need to make our way out to the middle and wait," he said. "If the helicopter doesn't fly over us within a couple hours, we'll head back to the campsite."

A few minutes later, they were both sitting in the center of the slope, resting and glancing periodically up at the sky, waiting.

They heard the helicopter in the distance not long after, but it didn't fly anywhere near them. After an hour or so more of waiting, both were ready to give up and head back home.

The disappointment was visible on Valeria's face.

"Well, it was worth a shot," said Philip.

He helped Valeria to her feet, took a few steps, then heard something–a sudden loud rumble that sounded like thunder.

Philip looked up. The top of the slope had collapsed.

"Avalanche!" he yelled.

In the blink of an eye, a deafening roar that sounded like a jet engine flying close to the ground barreled down the slope. Still tethered to Valeria by the rope, Philip scooped her up in his arms and began to run, but by then, it was too late. The wall of churning snow, higher than their heads, had descended upon them.

Swallowed whole, they were taken on a violent ride and buried.

CHAPTER 7

Valeria couldn't breathe. Disoriented, she opened her eyes and struggled to find a way out from under the snow that was pressing her down. How far she was below the surface, she didn't know. Her arms were pinned. Not sure which direction was up, she wriggled her fingers and frantically clawed at the snow. Finally, after a minute or so, a wisp of cold air brushed against the palm of one of her hands, and she knew which way to go. Gasping for air, she freed her face and dug herself out.

She immediately looked around for Philip, but he was nowhere to be seen. The rope, which had tethered them together during their trek to the slope, was still firmly tied to her waist. Her end of it was buried more than a foot or so under the snow. Valeria stood up and tugged at the rope with all her might. When it didn't budge, she got down on her hands and knees and desperately dug again. A short length of rope eventually gave way. She kept pulling at it and digging up the rest until she came to the other end. There, she found Philip's body, face-up under the snow.

His eyes were closed. Valeria quickly removed the snow from around his head and off his chest and arms. Philip lay motionless. Placing her hand near his mouth and nose, she felt for a breath. There was none. She felt his wrist for a pulse. Nothing. In a panic, she knelt beside Philip and pounded her fists against his chest. She didn't know CPR and guessed at what to do.

"Wake up!" Valeria screamed, trembling. "Don't die! Don't you die on me!"

When he didn't respond, she waited a few seconds and began pounding and doing compressions on his chest again as strongly as she could. Her arms soon weakened, but she kept at it for what felt like forever.

Tears streaming down her cheeks, Valeria called out his name again and again. "Philip! Wake up! Philip!"

Then, just when she was ready to give up, Philip coughed. His head moved slightly, as did his arms. Valeria felt again for a pulse and found it. Philip was alive, but his eyes remained shut.

"Thank God!" Valeria looked down at him. "Are you all right?" she asked, but Philip didn't respond or move.

Valeria began removing the rest of the packed snow from Philip's body. The rifle was still strapped over his shoulder and lying under his back. She lifted him to a sitting position, took the rifle off him, and tossed it aside. Then, she laid Philip back down. Once his legs and feet were uncovered, she got behind his shoulders and pulled as hard as she could. She struggled to drag him out of the hole he was in. It took a lot of effort, but eventually she succeeded. He was lying face up, still unconscious.

Unsure what to do next, Valeria sat beside Philip and waited for him to awaken. Although the sun was now high in the sky, its warmth was thwarted by an icy wind from the north that blew continuously across the slope. After about thirty minutes, she decided he needed to be moved someplace else where they were less exposed to the fierce wind and where they'd be safer. Briefly, she searched for her snowshoes, but they were nowhere to be found. Gone too was Philip's canteen.

After sitting Philip upright a second time and leaning his body forward, Valeria undid the rope from around his waist. She looped it higher on him, across his chest and under both arms, before tying it off again. She then laid him back down softly, stood up, and, pulling on the rope as hard as she could, attempted to move Philip off the slope.

The undulating snowpack, now broken apart and terribly uneven after the avalanche's unexpected wave of destruction, made dragging Philip's heavy body off the slope more difficult. Valeria tried to follow the chaotic depressions in the terrain, where it was easier to slide his body along the snow's surface without having to lift him over a crest. Several times, she had to stop to catch her breath.

At last, Valeria reached a vast wooded area that ran down the mountainside, parallel to the slope. There, she spotted a cluster of large boulders amid the trees. She dragged Philip to an area just behind them, where the wind was partially blocked and not as biting.

Valeria untied the rope on both ends, which bound them together, and went back to the slope to retrieve Philip's rifle. When she returned, she set it upright against a rock and knelt beside him.

Philip was still unconscious. *What if he had a concussion or is in a coma?* she thought. She wasn't sure how long she should wait for him to wake up. *Maybe he's hurt or bleeding somewhere internally.* If so, he would need a doctor. There was no way to know how bad he was injured. *I should go find help.* But how? She had no idea where she and Philip were in the mountains and also remembered what he had told her earlier: the hike they were planning on taking to return her home was dangerous and would require at least one or two days.

Should I stay with him or go get help? What if he's dying? Her mind raced back and forth about what to do.

When another half hour passed and Philip still wasn't awake or moving, Valeria made a decision. Somehow, she needed to find help. The afternoon sky was beginning to turn cloudy and gray. If she didn't set out on her own soon, she and Philip might both succumb to the elements or, worse, die of starvation.

Valeria repositioned Philip's body as close to one of the boulders as she could to get him out of the wind, raised his head a little, and stood up. "I'm sorry, but I'm going to leave you here," she said, looking down at him. "I don't know what else to do. I'll be back for you as soon as I can."

She glanced around, making a mental note of the area. Then she turned and walked away.

The most logical thing Valeria could think to do was hike down the mountainside toward a lower elevation where the chance of accidentally tumbling headfirst off some precipice was less likely. Without the makeshift snowshoes, however, taking steps proved to be more difficult. Where the snow was compact, she could walk fine, but where the drifts were softer, she'd sometimes sink up to her hips. A few minutes in, she found a slender dead branch she could use as a walking stick and prod to see how deep the snow was in front of her.

Carefully, Valeria made her way through a maze of snow-covered trees and boulders, and before long, the rolling terrain she found herself in gradually became less steep. Just as Philip had predicted, her legs began to throb and ache badly, but she didn't let the pain stop her from moving forward slowly, one cautious step at a time. Instead, she let her mind wander to more pleasant things. She thought about her mother, who somehow had spoken to Philip and the wolves from the beyond when she was hurt and near death, lying in the ravine. Her mother had never left and was watching over her. That's what Philip had said. Was her mother watching now? Valeria's eyes welled up, and she smiled.

It'll all work out, she thought. And even though she was lost in an immense wilderness with no idea which way to go, for the moment at least, she didn't feel scared.

Valeria lost track of time as the once bright sun gradually fell and then disappeared altogether behind an overcast sky, turning the world around her a much gloomier shade of gray.

Other than the tiresome crunching of her footsteps in the snow and the occasional rustling of tree branches, an eerie silence surrounded her. There was no howling wind, no sign of other life anywhere. More than an hour passed before she heard something different, a faint noise coming from somewhere in the distance to her right. She stopped to listen. It sounded like water trickling.

She decided to make her way toward it. As she trekked through a particularly dense part of the forest, the sound steadily grew louder and more distinct. Some fifteen to twenty minutes later, she stepped into a small clearing and came upon a meandering creek, partly iced over and strewn with rocks and snow but still flowing.

Exhausted, hungry, and dying of thirst, Valeria knelt next to the creek, scooped some water into the palms of both hands, and took a sip. The water was ice cold. Soon, she had her body hunched over a snowy embankment and was drinking directly from the running stream.

Against the whiteness of the sky above her, Valeria saw her reflection in the water. It was the first she'd seen her face since the day she was reunited with her father, and she didn't recognize herself. The person in the crystal-clear water staring back at her had a dirty face, scraggly hair hanging down in twisted clumps, and much browner skin.

With her thirst quenched, Valeria stood and took a moment or two to think about what to do next. She knew she needed to keep moving or risk dying alone in the wilderness. The small creek, not more than ten feet across, gave her an idea. She could walk alongside the winding stream and follow its natural course to a lower elevation off the mountainside. It might lead to a larger body of water, possibly a lake or river, maybe a road, or somewhere else where she could find help.

Valeria rested for a few minutes, then set out again, anxious to see where the creek led. In many places, the snow-covered trees and brush were too thick, and she had to veer off course to avoid getting entangled, but for the most part, she was able to keep the flowing stream within sight. Using the walking stick she'd found earlier, she carefully prodded the depth of the snowdrifts in front of her to avoid accidentally stepping into hidden voids underneath the snow's surface.

A light snow began to fall. It wasn't long before Valeria felt herself weakening. Her legs, not yet fully healed, were beginning to throb. Out of necessity, she stopped now and then to sit on a rock and rest, but she was afraid if she sat for too long, she'd never get back up. So, she forced herself to stay upright despite the pain and kept pushing.

Another hour passed, and Valeria began to stumble. She tripped on a jagged rock concealed under the snow and fell. The persistent pain in her legs had become too intense, and despite her best efforts, thoughts of lying down somewhere in the snow and giving up crowded her mind. Physically drained to the point of delirium, she could barely take another step, but somehow she kept moving. Then, just when she didn't think she could go on, the ground beneath her feet leveled off, and she came upon a narrow valley. There, she spotted a small half-frozen lake beyond the trees.

Nestled at the base of a rockface, the lake was littered on all sides by huge boulders that had tumbled down from the surrounding mountains. *How long have these stones been here?* Valeria wondered. *Maybe millions of years.* There was a serene stillness that was breathtaking. She knelt at the edge of the lake and drank from it, not sure why she was asking such questions. This place was unlike anything she'd ever seen.

Valeria allowed herself time to soak in the surrounding

splendor and rest, knowing she'd soon have to rise once more. She lay atop one of the boulders, felt the snow falling gently on her face, and closed her eyes.

Within moments, Valeria passed out and silently slipped into a dream. Her mother was sitting next to her by the lake. Together, they gazed up at the sky. Snowflakes without end, no two ever alike, were falling…

"Everything will be okay. They just want to keep me overnight…"

"Mom. I'm sorry. I should've told you I love you."

"Stay here…and be good."

"I love you, Mom."

"I'll be back…in the morning."

"I love you."

Valeria might have stayed asleep longer, but she was stirred awake by a faint rustling. She sat up and looked around. The noise seemed to be coming from behind a line of trees beyond a bend in the lake off to her right. She remained very still and waited for whatever it was to show itself, but the sound stopped.

She spotted several suspicious looking shadows that appeared to come and go, swaying and moving along the edge of the woods. Maybe they were just tree limbs catching the wind. Valeria couldn't be sure, but it was enough to get her back on her feet. Keeping a wary eye on the shifting shadows in the distance, she knelt by the lake for one last drink of water.

Valeria drank as much as she could and then turned to leave. Opposite the creek, which had led to the lake, the valley appeared to continue on between a narrow gap in the mountains. She headed off in that direction and soon reached a small rise overlooking where she'd been. She glanced back

"Oh, my God!" She didn't mean to shout it out loud but couldn't control what sprang from her mouth. "Oh, my God!" she repeated.

Near the same boulder where she'd been lying down,

Valeria counted five wolves milling about. She knew right away they were picking up her scent. Were they after her? There was no way to know, but she wasn't going to hang around to find out. Frightened and unsure what to do, she quietly made her way over the rise until the wolves were out of sight, then started to run. Her legs were so weak that she staggered and fell several times, but still, she kept going.

Never once looking back, Valeria ran as best as she could until she reached a wooded area at the foot of a rocky bluff. She stopped to catch her breath behind some trees. That's when she heard what sounded like footsteps approaching in the snow behind her.

Valeria turned and screamed.

She recognized the wolves immediately. They were the same five from the Togwolee pack that had attacked her at the camp. With his head held low, and fangs bared, the lead wolf crept toward her while the others stayed just behind him on either side.

Maintaining eye contact and jabbing at the wolf with a dead branch, Valeria slowly backed away until there was nowhere to go. Trapped by the face of the bluff, she knelt and felt around in the snow with her hand. Finding what she was looking for, she slowly rose. Suddenly, the wolf leapt, and she caught him between the eyes with a rock the size of a baseball. Stunned, the wolf fell at her feet.

Valeria turned and ran through the woods. The other wolves, taking a moment to check on their fallen mate, were slow to give chase but soon did.

Looking back over her shoulder to see where they were, Valeria tripped over her own feet and tumbled head over heels down a steep hill. Arms and legs flailing, she rolled and rolled, eventually coming to an abrupt stop beside a lone tree in a clearing beyond the woods. She slammed into the tree so hard that all the snow on its lower branches shook loose.

The wolves were closing in fast.

Valeria was trapped with nowhere to run. Quickly, she grabbed a fistful of snow and scrambled to her feet. She raised the snowball. "Get back!" she yelled. "You saw what happened to your friend!" The pack stopped but was now within ten feet of her. Seconds later, they were joined by their bruised and growling leader. Together, with their fangs bared, they formed a semicircle around their prey and cautiously approached.

One of the pack lunged at her legs. Valeria threw the snowball, striking the wolf harmlessly in the face. It confused and stopped the wolf just long enough for her to reach above her head and grab a limb, which she wrapped her arms around. Snarling, the others attacked. She kicked the leader in the mouth and, with every ounce of strength she had, pulled herself up, kicking and screaming.

Her heart racing, Valeria frantically climbed higher and didn't stop to look behind her until she was fifteen or so feet off the ground. When she finally did take a look down, the wolves were agitated, pacing anxiously around the tree and peering up. Several of the wolves attempted to climb after her but lost their footing on the first few branches and fell. It was only then Valeria breathed a sigh of relief. She realized that as powerful and agile as the wolves were, their bodies weren't built for climbing trees.

The good news was the pack couldn't reach her. The bad news was they weren't leaving. All five wolves eventually lay down in the snow around the tree and kept watch, occasionally wagging their tails and gazing up.

By now, it was late afternoon. The overcast sky was beginning to darken as the sun descended beyond the mountains. It would soon be nightfall and much colder. The wind was already whipping through the branches, giving Valeria chills. Although she desperately wanted to close her eyes and rest, she knew she'd almost certainly fall and either break her neck or be eaten.

Then, Valeria heard something. It sounded like low-pitched bellowing and footsteps crunching in the snow. The wolves' heads perked up. They heard it, too. From her perch high in the tree, Valeria looked out across the valley. Near a treeline in the far distance, she spotted a small herd of elk on the move. They appeared to be heading toward the lake.

Valeria could tell the wolves were contemplating their options. They could wait for her to come down or take their chances with the elk. When their leader got to his feet and jogged slowly toward the herd, the decision was made. The other four wolves chased after him.

It was still snowing lightly. The moon already had come into view on the horizon, though the sun had yet to set behind the mountains entirely. With daylight waning, Valeria lost sight of the elk herd over the rise of a hill in the distance. She kept her eyes fixed on the wolves through the emerging haze of evening until they, too, disappeared over the same rise. Not willing to make a run for it too quickly in case the wolves returned, she let another ten to fifteen minutes pass before climbing down the tree.

Valeria picked up a dead branch to help with her footing and headed off as fast as she could across the snow in the opposite direction of the wolves. Unlike earlier, there was no creek to follow. The terrain in the valley rose and fell but wasn't nearly as steep as the surrounding hills and mountains, which made walking a lot easier. The creek had been somewhat reassuring, and without it, she felt less confident regarding which direction to go. Based on where the moon was in the sky, she believed she was heading north but wasn't sure.

After the sun went down, the air became frigid. The snow glistened in the moonlight. Shadows deepened. Exhausted almost to the point of being numb to the stabbing pain she felt in her legs, Valeria staggered forward, allowing the natural ebb and flow of the land guide her. She avoided the higher elevations and dense woods, except where there were no other options.

Several more hours passed.

The snow flurries stopped, and afterward, the stars shone brightly. Valeria felt their presence above her but could hardly look up at them. Each step had become a struggle. She only had enough strength to gaze at the ground in front of her to see where to place her foot next. Although she desperately wanted to stop, thoughts of Philip lying unconscious in the snow kept her moving. She couldn't bring herself to quit, knowing he might be dying and needed her help.

Then, rounding a bend between two lines of trees, Valeria came upon a sharp rise in the land that looked insurmountable. She fell to her knees and cried.

I can't do it. I can't take another step.

Tears streaming down her face, she looked up. In all directions, the darkness was like a vast ocean, brimming with glittering stars, more than she'd ever seen in her life.

And in the midst of the stars, somewhere beyond the difficult ascent, was white smoke, delicately rising and twirling before vanishing forever into the night sky.

Smoke? Maybe it's coming from a chimney.

CHAPTER 8

A short-lived gust of snow kicked up from under the search and rescue helicopter as it lifted off the ground from a meadow behind the log home of Celeste and Quinn Pollock, the ex-hippies and retired couple who had found Valeria on their doorstep the night before.

Celeste and Quinn were joyfully waving to Valeria as the chopper rose higher. Valeria waved back. She'd only spent one night and part of the morning with the two and already she loved them. The Pollocks, who claimed to be distant relatives of Jackson Pollock, the famous painter, raised horses for enjoyment and sold custom-made jewelry at weekend flea markets and local festivals. Their gift to her, a long handmade silver necklace, with several turquoise gemstones interwoven and dangling from it, hung around Valeria's neck. Beside her was a large thermos filled with herbal tea, a secret blend only Celeste knew the exact ingredients to, and one of her many specialties. A perennial favorite at festivals, the tea was guaranteed to soothe the mind and heal whatever ails you, according to Quinn.

From the air, Valeria saw the Pollocks' entire homestead, their stables, everything. Unlike others who owned property deep in the Teton wilderness, the couple refused to erect a fence line or anything that would create a barrier between them, their horses, and the outside world. Valeria remembered something Quinn said about living the way they did at the breakfast table that morning: "The wall that protects you also imprisons you."

Valeria's father was sitting next to her.

"I promised to come back and stay with Quinn and Celeste so they can teach me how to ride a horse," said Valeria, still taking in every inch of the breathtaking scenery passing by her window.

"We'll definitely take them up on their offer," said Ray. "They're good people."

Earlier that morning, when Valeria's father showed up with two helicopter crewmen, there had been a long tearful embrace, a flurry of unending questions, as well as a blissful thankfulness that only comes when a loved one, once thought to be lost forever, is found. It took a little while, but eventually, the questions ceased, replaced with a kind of warm emotional stillness that's nearly impossible to describe in words.

The two experienced search and rescue crewmen in the helicopter, wearing official yellow-and-black uniforms and white flight helmets, were Tyler, in the front seat behind the controls flying the chopper and, beside him, his copilot Dean.

Valeria and her father were both handed headsets, which they put on.

Tyler radioed into their command center. "We have the Cortez girl." He paused while the operator on the other end acknowledged the report. "When we land, she needs to be taken to the medical center to be checked out." Another pause. "Yes, let them know. We plan to return ASAP, but first, we need to search for a second person, a man she says is hurt, possibly dead. We need the girl's help in finding the location."

The helicopter hovered high over an area just south of Celeste and Quinn's property.

"Tell us again everything you remember about the terrain you hiked across yesterday," said Dean, through the headset. "What were the landmarks, if any, that stood out?" He and Tyler were surveying the ground below as the chopper moved steadily along on a more or less southerly course.

"There was a creek and then a lake. There were a lot of boulders around it," answered Valeria. "Snow and trees. Big rocks and so much snow and so many trees. The wolves. That's mostly what I remember. There was the slope where we were hit by an avalanche..."

From the air, everything looked different. Valeria peered out her window, searching for details in the landscape that might help the men retrace her steps, but the new perspective was disorienting.

After a few minutes, Dean nudged Tyler. "Look! Over there to our left," he said. "I see some tracks in the snow along that treeline. Rotate around so I can check them out." Dean put a pair of high-powered binoculars up to his eyes.

"What do you think?" asked Tyler.

"I'd say we're heading in the right direction," Dean answered. "The footprints look fairly fresh. So unless we have someone else wandering around way out here, which I doubt, I'd say those are hers."

The lower the helicopter hovered, the more the snow on the ground kicked up, obscuring the tracks. "I'm taking us up a little higher," said Tyler. "Keep an eye out for the lake."

A few minutes later, Valeria recognized something and pointed. "Over there. I know that tree. It's the one I climbed to get away from the wolves." The lone tree stood out near the bottom of a hill.

Dean peered through his binoculars. "She's right. I see footprints leading away from it."

"Then the lake is probably off in that direction," said Tyler, motioning straight ahead. "I have a better idea now which mountain slope they hiked to." He adjusted his flight controls and picked up speed.

They soon spotted a lake to the east and crossed over a

long, meandering creek that flowed down a snowy mountainside. The surrounding terrain turned steeper and rockier. The chopper climbed higher.

"There's the slope," said Ray, through his headset.

The jumbled mounds of snow, which lay across the entire slope's surface from top to bottom, were a clear sign that a recent avalanche had occurred.

Tyler hovered over the area, searching for a safe place to land. He chose an open spot beyond some trees a few hundred yards away from the steep slope. "This is as close as I can get," he said after they touched down. He shut off the engine and waited for the rotor blades to stop turning before letting everyone out.

Dean grabbed a medical kit backpack out of a metal storage bin attached to one of the helicopter's landing skids. Tyler retrieved a rolled length of nylon rope and some other gear and handed a few things to Ray. The last item to be unloaded was a long basket stretcher for use in the wilderness. They were bringing it in anticipation that Philip, dead or alive, would need to be transported back to the chopper. Dean put on the backpack while Tyler securely placed the other essentials on the rescue stretcher to be carried up the slope by all three men.

"For your own safety, Val, I'd normally insist you wait for us here in the helicopter," said Ray, "but we're going to need you to show us where you left Philip. Do you feel strong enough to walk on your own? If not, we can carry you."

"My legs feel sore, but I'm okay, I think," she answered.

The four proceeded to trek through the woods over to the bottom of the slope.

Seeing the extent of the avalanche's devastation firsthand, Dean turned to Valeria and said, "You're lucky to be alive, young lady."

"Show us where you left Philip," said Tyler.

Valeria pointed to a wooded area to the left of the slope,

halfway up. "Over there, behind some boulders. I'll know the spot when we get closer." She gazed up at the mountain's lofty snow-covered incline and felt a shiver of fear run through her. Somehow, just one day later, the slope seemed steeper and more intimidating.

With Dean leading the way, they maneuvered up the slope along its left edge with the stretcher and the cache of rescue equipment and medical supplies. Where possible, they stepped around and avoided the worst of the uneven sections in the snow where the footing was particularly bad.

Eventually, they came to approximately the midway point of the slope. "How much farther, Val?" asked Ray. "Does any of this look familiar?"

Valeria glanced around. Everything looked different. "No," she answered. "None of this looks right."

The wind on the slope wasn't nearly as fierce or cold as it had been just the day before. The skies were a deep blue.

They continued on. Another fifty yards or so up, Valeria stopped. "This is it!" she said. "I remember those trees." She pointed to an area beyond them. "The boulders are going to be over there. I laid Philip down behind some big rocks so he wouldn't freeze."

"I see them," said Dean.

Stepping off the slope and into the adjacent woods, the four hurried over to a group of large boulders that were located right where Valeria said they'd be. Tyler and Dean were the first to reach the other side of the rocks.

"He's not here," said Tyler. "Are you sure this is the place?"

"Yes. I swear it," answered Valeria. "I left him right here. His rifle was laying against this rock."

Like Philip, the rifle was also missing. There were no footprints or an indentation in the snow of a body, nothing to indicate anyone had ever been there.

"You've got to believe me," said Valeria. "He was here. Maybe Philip woke up, and when he couldn't find me, he left."

Ray placed his hand on her shoulder. "We believe you," he said. "The question is, where did your friend go, and is he still hurt?"

"Based on how long Val says the guy was knocked out, it's reasonable to assume he suffered a concussion at the very least," said Dean. "And if he did receive a hard blow to the head, he might also have an epidural hematoma."

"What's that?" asked Valeria.

Tyler answered for Dean. "A condition where the blood pools into the lining between the brain and skull. Out here, it often happens when a skier doesn't wear a helmet and falls, hitting their head against hard-packed snow. Often, the skier will get up and shake things off like nothing happened, and they'll mistake the pain they feel for a headache, only to die a few hours later."

"That's terrible," said Valeria.

"They're talking worst case scenario," said Ray. "Philip might have walked away from the avalanche mostly unscathed or with just a few busted ribs or other broken bones. He was lucky to have you around to dig him out and revive him. So, let's just hope for the best."

The four made their way back to the edge of the slope. The day's warmer spring weather seemed to be holding, with few clouds gathering overhead.

"Where do you think this guy went?" Dean asked the others.

"Let's take a second to review what we know," said Ray. "We have no idea when Philip awoke, but when he did, he found himself behind the rocks with his rifle next to him. Right then, he realized Val had survived the avalanche. How else would he have gotten behind the rocks? He probably called her name over and over, and when she didn't answer, he went searching for her. My guess is he hiked back to his campsite, believing she'd try to return there."

"That makes the most sense," said Tyler. "Given what Val told us about Philip's condition when she left him, I think, at a minimum, we need to find this camp, see if he's made it there, and offer to airlift him to the medical center for x-rays."

"How are we going to do this?" asked Ray.

"Philip's tracks should still be intact from yesterday when he and your daughter hiked here to the slope," answered Dean. "His footprints will lead us to the camp. You and I can follow them. Tyler, meanwhile, can take Val and the stretcher back to the chopper and wait for us to radio him with our location."

Valeria interrupted the men. "I'm coming with my dad," she announced forcefully, leaving no room for argument.

"Well then, let's get rolling," said Dean.

Tyler headed back down the steep slope with the stretcher while the others set out in the opposite direction to search for Philip and Valeria's tracks in the snow from the day before. Near the top of the slope, they found them.

Valeria stood next to the cold ashes lying in the fire pit and called Philip's name again and again.

"He's not here," said Ray.

The three wolves, Sparkle, Titan, and Romeo, were also gone, as were the makeshift sled, rope, ax, pots, skillet, and all the cooking utensils and supplies. Near the campsite, there was a large hole in the snow where the stored venison had been dug up and taken.

Dean poked his head inside the old log shed. "Hey guys," he said. "You need to come and see this."

Valeria rushed inside the shed ahead of her father. She

fell to her knees and was immediately greeted by the six wolf pups. They swarmed her, knocking her down onto her back. Whimpering, the pups nuzzled her face and neck and licked her excitedly.

Gypsy lay in the far corner by a wall, her eyes open but not moving. Ray knelt down and examined her. "This one's dead," he said softly. He stroked her white coat. "That's too bad. What a gorgeous animal."

On the verge of tears, Valeria closed her eyes and let the anxious pups overwhelm her senses. She said nothing because there weren't words for what she felt. Philip had been right about how things would end for Gypsy. For a moment, she hated him for predicting it, though she knew it wasn't his fault. He had expressed a deep regret for having fed Gypsy and her young siblings that day by the river and blamed himself for the wolf's death. How could she stay mad at someone with so big a heart? She wasn't able to and soon found herself smiling despite the cascade of tears and sadness welled up inside her. Gypsy had saved her life.

Dean stepped outside the open doorway. "I'm going to radio Tyler and have him come get us. It'll be faster than hiking back down," he said. "I'm forwarding our GPS location to him. He'll need to lift us out of here. I don't see a safe place anywhere to land."

Ray knelt next to his daughter and put his arms around her. "I know this is going to be hard, but we need to leave the wolf pups behind," he said.

"No!" cried Valeria. "They're too little. And they have nobody but me now. I won't leave them!"

"Val, you have to understand…even though I'm a game warden and my main job is to help wildlife in the area coexist with the local people and thrive, there are many laws governing what we can and can't do. We're simply not allowed to take young wild animals into captivity, no matter how much we might want to help the injured and little ones."

Ray stood up. "Nature can seem very unfair," he added, "but it's not for us to decide what's right and what's wrong when it comes to the natural laws that determine the ebb and flow of life."

Valeria wiped away her tears. "Dad, I don't care about your stupid laws," she said, sniffling. "Can't you see? I'm the only family these pups have now, and you're going to help me take care of them despite your job. You owe me."

"It's not right. I can't let you do it."

"And what about Mom? How do you explain what happened to her? Are you going to give me the same lecture about the natural laws and ebb and flow of life? Mom was alive and was taken from me. I didn't get a chance to save her or do anything. But now, don't you see? I can save these wolf pups. They're just babies."

"Please, Val. Let's not do this. What happened to your mother was a tragedy. You're not being fair."

"Well, Dad, you said it yourself. Life isn't fair. And nature is life. It's all the same. Whether it's animals or people, aren't we supposed to help save those who are innocent?" Valeria stood up, clutching two of the pups. The others immediately whined. "There's no way I'm leaving here without them."

Ray stared at his daughter and, ever so slowly, broke into a smile. He called out to Dean, "Radio Tyler, and tell him we're bringing along six more passengers."

"You know we're not allowed to use the helicopter to airlift or transport wildlife," said Dean.

"I know, but some rules were meant to be broken," said Ray. "If anyone at the sheriff's office questions you about it, blame the transport on me. I'll take the heat for it."

A few minutes later, Tyler had the helicopter over the

campsite, hovering. "I don't see anywhere around here to land," he radioed to Dean.

"There isn't any. The area's too rocky and steep," said Dean. "Go ahead and set the controls on automatic pilot and send me down the rappel rope. I'll secure Val and Ray in the harness one at a time."

"And who are the other six?" asked Tyler.

"You'll see."

With its rotor blades noisily whipping the air, the helicopter hovered directly overhead. The rescue line was lowered. Dean secured Valeria and two of the wolf pups in the safety harness and gave Tyler a thumbs-up. Moments later, they were resting safe and sound in the chopper, the two pups on her lap.

Ray was next to be fitted in the harness and raised, followed by Dean. They each brought up two more pups and held onto them in their seats. Dean put on his flight helmet and handed Valeria and her father their headsets.

Tyler closed the doors. "Everyone okay?"

Valeria nodded. She was staring out the window at the old log shed and camp as the chopper hovered in place for a time, then gradually lifted straight up, higher than it had before. Soon, everything on the ground below looked like specks.

Tyler radioed the command center. "We're on our way back." He paused to listen to the flight operator's response. "No. We weren't able to locate the other person." Another pause. "Roger that. We'll be there shortly."

He checked his instruments, and off they flew.

CHAPTER 9

"Good morning," said Dr. Kennedy with a broad smile. He came into the hospital room holding a computer tablet, clipboard, and a handful of x-rays. "How are you feeling?"

Valeria had been rushed to the local medical center the day before to be checked out and admitted. The doctors had insisted she undergo a complete physical evaluation, including blood tests, x-rays of her legs, and more. She took a hot shower and washed her hair for the first time in weeks, and was hooked up to an IV line to rehydrate her body.

"I feel good, Doctor," answered Val. She was sitting up, enjoying breakfast in bed.

Ray, unshaven and wearing the same game warden uniform he had on from the day before, was also in the room, standing near a window. He refused to leave his daughter's side and had spent the entire night dozing on a chair beside her bed.

"Good morning, Doc," said Ray.

Dr. Kennedy held up one of the x-rays for a better look, put it back with the others, and pulled out another one. "I have some good news," he said. "I've shown these to an orthopedic specialist this morning, and he's in agreement. You suffered multiple fractures in the tibia and smaller fibula in both of your legs as a result of the hard spill you took. But remarkably, they appear to be healing well." He paused to inspect Valeria's legs. "How do they feel?"

"A little sore," answered Valeria. "But not too bad. They feel a lot better now."

"Whoever set your legs out in the field did a remarkable job." Dr. Kennedy stood up. "The initial swelling is gone. We don't think casting them will be necessary, but I'd avoid running or doing anything too strenuous. Your legs are still healing."

"When can I leave the hospital?" asked Valeria.

"I don't see any reason to keep you here any longer. All your other vitals look good," said Dr. Kennedy. "I'll let the front-desk nurses know to discharge you."

"Thank you," said Ray. He shook the doctor's hand.

"Stay safe, both of you," Dr. Kennedy said warmly. He began to leave, then stopped at the doorway and turned around. "Remember, no matter how tall the mountain is, it cannot block the sun." He laughed. "I read that somewhere." He left, closing the door behind him.

As soon as he left, there was a knock on the door. It was Lauren, holding a bouquet of daffodils in one hand and a duffle bag in the other.

"Val!" shrieked Lauren, tossing the flowers and bag onto the foot of the bed and giving Valeria the most enthusiastic hug of her life. "It's so wonderful to see your beautiful face!" Lauren wiped a couple of stray tears welling up in her eyes. "Oh, yes! It's really you! Everyone was praying for your safe return, but when they didn't find you after a few days, we thought we'd lost you forever." Eventually, she stood back and gave Valeria some space. "When are they going to release you?"

"Thank you for coming and bringing me flowers," Valeria replied. "I thought about you and Dad a lot. The doctor says I can leave today."

"That's great!" said Lauren. "I brought you a change of clothing." She gestured to the duffle bag. "You can go into the bathroom and get dressed. You'll feel better. And as soon as they let you out of here, you and I are going to celebrate. I want to take you shopping for new clothes and—"

"You don't need to do that," Ray interrupted.

"Shush!" said Lauren. "Why don't you go home, Ray, take a long shower, and get some rest? You look like you haven't slept in a month. You can meet us somewhere later. I'll call you." She gave Ray a quick hug and a kiss on the cheek. "This will give Val and me a girl's day out. You can have her to yourself after we've had some fun."

"I guess, okay," said Ray. "I do need to contact dispatch and let them know where I am." He kissed Valeria on the forehead. "Is it all right with you, Val, if I go regroup and meet up with you later today?"

"Sure, Dad," said Valeria. "It's okay."

"All right then." He kissed Lauren's cheek. "Enjoy yourselves. Let me know when you're done."

Before Ray left the medical center, he went to the admissions office and signed all the necessary documents needed to discharge his daughter. Shortly thereafter, an elderly nurse came to Valeria's room with a wheelchair. "Are you ready to go home?" she asked.

True spring had finally arrived. All the streets in Jackson were wet and muddy with warming snow that was quickly turning to slush. People everywhere were peeling off their sweaters and jackets when they stepped outside.

Lauren drove Valeria to the town's main shopping district and took her in nearly every clothing boutique there was. Everywhere they went, the shopkeepers and staff already knew Valeria's name.

"Hasn't anyone told you yet?" asked Lauren, standing at a register, paying for a new pair of shoes.

"Tell me what?" answered Valeria.

"You're front-page news." Lauren thanked the store owner and handed Valeria the shopping bag with her shoes.

Outside the store, she continued, "Jackson is a small town, and the locals who live here year-round all know your story." They were walking to a salon to have their hair done, their arms overflowing with bags. "Most everybody knows your dad. He's well liked. So when he lost you in the mountains the way he did, the whole town felt terrible. And now everyone's excited to have you back among the living." Lauren laughed. "You'll maintain your celebrity status for a little while until something else newsworthy happens around here."

They stepped into the hair salon. "Good morning, Miss Lauren," said an attractive woman at the front counter. "And a good morning to you, Val. What can I do for you ladies?"

A half dozen or so customers were sitting in chairs near the front door, waiting their turn.

"I'm long overdue for a trim," said Lauren, grabbing at a lock of her hair and frowning. "As for Val, it's whatever this angel wants. I'm sure she has some ideas as to how she likes to look, but in addition to getting her hair cleaned up and styled, she could use a manicure."

"Very good," said the woman. "Come this way. We're ready for you." She turned and addressed the other customers who'd been waiting. "None of you mind, do you?"

"No!" they all said at once, smiling.

"You go ahead and take care of them," added one older lady, sweetly.

An hour or so later, Lauren and Valeria emerged from the salon, each feeling properly pampered. They carried their trove of shopping bags to the Jeep and tossed them in the back.

The two got in, and after pulling down the sun visors to briefly admire their new hairdos in the mirror, Lauren started up the car and pulled away. "I'm sure you're anxious to see your babies," she said.

"Oh, yes!" said Valeria. "Do you know where they are?" For some odd reason, as she watched the streets and buildings pass by, she felt both content and restless. She couldn't remember ever feeling such an intense, heightened awareness of the world around her. "When we landed yesterday, an ambulance was waiting. They took me straight to the hospital, and Dad said he wasn't sure what to do with them. He looked so tired. I didn't want to bother him about it this morning."

"The pups are safe. You'll see. But first, we've got one more stop to make. I've arranged a little surprise for you." A few minutes later, Lauren pulled up next to the Silver Beaver Eatery. Hanging in the window was a colorful banner that read, WELCOME HOME, VAL!

Inside, Valeria was greeted with cheers. Her father was there with her grandmother, Abuela, who threw herself upon Valeria, showering her with kisses and hugs. "My grandbaby! My lovely grandbaby!" she repeated loud enough for everyone to hear.

Celeste and Quinn were also there, as well as dozens of other people whom Valeria had never met, including some of Ray's coworkers. Her father led her around the dining room and politely introduced her to the various individuals. All nodded approvingly or took her by the hand and said, "It's so nice to meet you."

After a time, Hazel came out and ushered Valeria to a table near George the buffalo, joined by Ray, Lauren, and Abuela. Everyone took a seat, placed their orders, and enjoyed a most delightful lunch. Abuela had many questions for her granddaughter, but for the most part, they were lighthearted inquiries as to what happened to her in the wilderness, nothing too heavy-handed.

"Weren't you scared?" asked Abuela.

"Yes, Grandma. I was at first," answered Valeria.

For some reason, Valeria found herself not wanting to elaborate too much about what happened to her. She withheld essential details and, at times, pretended not to remember. Her answers to the various questions were mostly of the one-word variety. But truth be told, no one gathered in the room to celebrate her life, pressed her for better explanations, or asked her to put her harrowing experience in any kind of context.

After dessert was served, Ray rose from his seat and, turning to face all the guests, tapped his water glass with a spoon. "May I have everyone's attention?" he announced. He waited a few moments for things to quiet down before continuing. "Thank you all for coming today. I know we're not drinking wine or champagne, but I'd like everyone to raise their glass in a toast to my daughter, Valeria, who was lost but has somehow returned to us safe and sound. I couldn't be prouder of her. Cheers!"

A joyous celebratory "Cheers!" went up throughout the room, followed by the sound of glasses clinking all around.

Valeria stood up and thanked everyone. Her father threw his arms around her and, with a few tears in his eyes, gave her a big hug.

Then, just as things were settling down, the front door to the Silver Beaver opened, and in walked two familiar faces, both wearing cowboy hats: Butch Hardin with his son Jesse beside him. They tipped their hats to Hazel and several other women before making their way across the dining room to where Ray and Valeria were standing.

"Hello, Ray," said Butch.

"What are you doing here?" asked Ray, his voice tense.

"We heard about the party and wanted to come and personally apologize to you and your daughter for what happened out there that day." Butch extended his hand.

"Thank you," said Ray. "I appreciate you taking the time."

He took Butch's outstretched hand and shook it. Ray then went to shake Jesse's hand, but before he could, Valeria stepped between her father and the boy.

"You killed her!" yelled Valeria.

A hush fell over the room.

"What are you talking about?" asked Jesse.

"Gypsy! You shot her."

"Who's Gypsy?" Jesse looked genuinely puzzled.

"The white wolf."

"Oh!" Jesse wasn't able to hide a sly smirk. "For a moment there, I thought you were accusing me of murdering someone. Wolves don't count. They're fair game whenever they trespass onto private property and kill livestock."

Ray tried to intervene by stepping between Jesse and his daughter, but she shoved him aside.

"She didn't raid your cattle," said Valeria, angrily. "You led that poor, frightened cow into the mountains and used it as bait! You sacrificed the cow… just so you could pick off the wolves with your rifle and call yourself a man." She started to curse but stopped short.

"What is she saying, Jesse?" asked Butch.

"She's talking nonsense," Jesse lied. "I don't know where she came up with this."

"You shot and killed Gypsy!" yelled Valeria. "It's true. I know it! She was so beautiful…so special and good."

Jesse straightened his back and puffed out his chest more. "I know you're new around here, so I don't expect you to understand," he said, glaring at her. "But out on the farms and ranches, we have a saying: the only good wolf is a dead wolf. If I did kill one of your precious wolves, so what? All I have to say about it is good riddance! I did the world a favor."

Valeria lunged at Jesse, shoving him backward onto a table, knocking it over, and sending him along with all the plates, glasses, and silverware crashing to the floor. The people sitting at the table jumped out of the way as she leapt on top of him and pinned his chest with her knees. Valeria's two fists were a blur, pounding Jesse's face again and again while the boy desperately tried to block the flurry of blows without striking her back.

Ray went to lift Valeria off Jesse, but Lauren put her arm out and stopped him. "Let it go," said Lauren, holding him back. "He deserves a good beating."

Eventually, Jesse freed himself out from under Valeria and got to his feet. Butch grabbed him by the shoulder and, without saying a word to anyone, led his son outside. They could be seen getting into a truck and leaving.

Leaning over to clean up the broken dishes and spilled food, Hazel said, "Well, that was something."

For a moment or two, everyone else was silent, but then someone at a table began to clap. Another yelled out, "Yes!" Soon, the entire room was cheering and applauding. It went on and on for several minutes.

CHAPTER 10

In the coming days, Valeria thought about Philip often. Why did he abandon the wolf pups? Maybe he was hurt and physically unable to take them with him. He'd taken all his personal possessions and deserted the old shed and campsite in a hurry. Where did he go and why? She considered various explanations, but in the end, there was simply no way to know why Philip had left the newborn wolves behind. One thing was clear, though: it was now her responsibility to raise and care for Gypsy's pups.

Abuela spent some time with Valeria and Ray before returning to Los Angeles. She tried to convince her granddaughter to make the flight and come live with her–she'd apparently received special permission from the association that ran her retirement center–but Valeria turned her down. Despite missing her old friends, school, and neighborhood, Valeria wanted to remain in Wyoming with her father. She couldn't imagine ever going back except perhaps to visit. She didn't want to be separated from her dad, the pups, or this rugged new world she now found herself a part of.

Her grandmother agreed to ship the rest of Valeria's belongings to her, as well as some of her mother's personal effects, old photographs, and keepsakes. Rosa had enjoyed buying out-of-fashion designer purses at yard sales and flea markets. She loved to haggle over the price and also had a thing for vintage costume jewelry and nice shoes, which she hardly ever wore. It all would be sent to Valeria.

As required by the Wyoming Game and Fish Department, Ray lived in a state-provided game warden home in the center of Jackson. It was a modest house, but Valeria found it to be warm and pleasant. She had her own bedroom, and most everything in town was within walking distance. Her father bought her a secondhand bicycle to use if she wanted to ride over to Lauren's veterinary center, which was too far away to walk to, or get somewhere faster. A follow-up visit to an orthopedic specialist had confirmed her fractures were nearly fully healed.

Given her recent ordeal and unique circumstances, Valeria was given special permission to resume school full-time in the fall. Between now and then, she'd need to complete some of her California classes remotely, report to a local counselor once or twice a week, and attend summer school in Jackson, scheduled to start in a few months, to make up for all the classroom time she had lost.

Ray dropped off Valeria at the veterinary center on his way out of town; his first stop, to follow up on an anonymous tip he'd received as to the whereabouts of two poachers who'd been trapping and killing animals illegally. His agenda might change depending on the events of the day, but he was eager to find whoever was responsible for the poaching and make arrests.

"I hope you find them," said Valeria.

"So do I," Ray said. "But to be honest, though, this part of my job can be frustrating." He leaned over and gave his daughter a quick kiss on the cheek before she got out of the truck. "Once they're caught and arrested, the poachers are required to appear in court, but most of the time, they just get a slap on the wrist for their crimes. The judge usually makes them pay a small fine and suspends their hunting license for a season or two. It's a joke, really, that killing protected wildlife, around here at least, isn't considered a worse offense. But still, it's important I arrest those responsible. Poaching is illegal, and catching the culprits will at least serve as a warning to others."

Outside the front door of the Teton Pass Veterinary Center, Valeria turned to wave goodbye and watched her father drive off, his truck's brake lights reflecting off the road's surface when he came to a stop at the next intersection. Almost all the roads in and around Jackson were wet with spring snowmelt.

"Good morning, Val," said Kimberly from behind the front counter. A young married woman in her mid-twenties, she doubled as Lauren's receptionist and one of her assistants. Kimberly was looking at a computer screen and sipping a cup of coffee. "You can go on back. The pups haven't gotten any exercise yet today." She handed Valeria six nylon dog leashes. "Dr. Ross is busy seeing her morning patients. So, if you can, try not to make a lot of noise while she's working."

Three people were sitting in the waiting area with their dogs by their feet. An older woman was holding a large tabby cat on her lap. The cat stared at Valeria warily.

"Okay," said Valeria. "Thank you." She opened the door that led to the various examination rooms and kennels.

"And oh, yeah," said Kimberly. "They haven't eaten anything yet this morning. I was waiting for you to get here because I know how much you enjoy feeding them. I'll bring you the bottles in a few minutes."

Valeria didn't learn about it until after the party at the Silver Beaver, but Lauren had promised Ray she'd look after the six wolf pups. Caring for the young pack at the veterinary center wasn't ideal and was a temporary solution at best, but thus far, it had worked out.

Somehow, with their keen sense of smell, the pups immediately detected Valeria's presence and whined loudly before they could even see her. She made her way down the hall to the large room-size dog kennel where the six were being kept. Careful to close the door behind her, Valeria was mobbed the second she stepped inside.

"My babies!" she exclaimed, with arms open. She knelt and allowed herself to be overrun, nuzzled, and licked from head to toe.

Gypsy's litter had produced three sisters and three brothers. Their coloration and markings, though similar, were distinctive from one to the other, making it fairly easy to tell them apart. As yet unnamed, the girls were wearing matching pink collars to identify them at a glance, and the boys, blue. The new collars were Lauren's idea.

Valeria tried to keep the laughing and giggling down to a minimum, but it was difficult. She got down on the floor with the rambunctious pups, lay on her back, and let them swarm over her. When one or more of them accidentally nipped her during their romp, she patted the guilty party's nose with her finger and said, "No! Play nice."

About fifteen minutes or so later, Kimberly came into the room clutching six large baby bottles. "Who's hungry?" she asked lightheartedly.

The second the pups spotted the full bottles, they all jumped off Valeria and sat up, tails wagging.

"Until we figure out an easier way to do this, you guys will need to take turns," said Kimberly. She left for a moment and returned with two metal folding chairs. Sitting across from Kimberly, Valeria grabbed one of the pups, cradled it in her arms like a nursing baby, and fed it a bottle while Kimberly fed one of the others. The two pups eagerly gobbled the blended homemade mixture of one cup of warm goat's milk, two raw egg yolks, and one cup of plain yogurt. The formula was a nutritious substitute for their mother's milk.

"Dr. Ross says the pups will be gradually weaned off the

bottles over the next ten days to two weeks or so," Kimberly stated. "After that, they'll need to start eating solid foods. In the wild, the mother and other members of the pack chew up the meat they bring back for the pups and regurgitate it into their mouths, like some birds do."

"Gross!" said Valeria.

Kimberly laughed. "Don't worry. We'll be using dog bowls. We just need to make sure their meat is soft enough for them to chew. Until they're a little older, any solid food we give them needs to be moist."

After Valeria and Kimberly finished feeding the first two pups, they gently massaged their swollen bellies to stimulate a bowel movement before setting them back down on the floor and lifting the next pair of puppies onto their laps. Before long, all six were resting on top of one another in a loose pile near Valeria's feet, their eyes half closed as they sleepily digested their meals.

The young wolves paid no attention when Kimberly got up to leave. She needed to resume her duties at the front counter. But when Valeria rose to stretch her legs, all six sat up, and several whimpered. One of the boys grabbed her pant leg with his teeth.

"Relax, my little angels," said Valeria. "I'm not going anywhere."

She leashed up the pups and led them to an enclosed area behind the veterinary center. There, she let them off their leashes so they could frolic and burn off some of their pent-up energy. At first, the six were hesitant to leave Valeria's side, but soon, they were playfully chasing and pouncing on one another. Valeria got down with them and joyfully took part in all the fun.

Eventually, Lauren took a short break from seeing patients and came outside for a few minutes to monitor things. "How's it going?" she asked.

"Great! I love them so much," answered Valeria, holding one of the pups. "They've accepted me as their mom. I never want to leave them, not ever."

Around 4:00 p.m., Ray returned for Valeria.

She took a moment to pick up and embrace each pup individually before reluctantly saying goodbye and making sure the door to the kennel was shut behind her.

Kimberly was at her computer, checking in a dog owner at the front counter. "See you tomorrow, Val," she said.

Lauren came out of an examination room and gave Valeria a quick hug. "Good night, dear. We'll see you in the morning," she said. "Kimberly and I will feed the pups their last bottle of formula for the day before we close." She chuckled. "I don't know if Kimberly's told you, but the pups have taken to howling for you whenever you leave them. It's adorable how attached they are to you, but thankfully, their cries don't last too long." Smiling, she returned to the exam room.

Ray was standing out front, talking on a two-way radio. He greeted his daughter, and Valeria climbed into the truck. Behind her in the backseat were two unshaven thirty-something-year-old men dressed in matching camouflage caps, jackets, and pants. Both were handcuffed, their hands in front resting on their laps. Ray finished talking and got in.

"Say hello to Oscar and Percy," said Ray, pointing to each man so she'd know who was who. "These are the two men I was telling you about this morning. Guys, this is my daughter, Val."

Everyone said hello. "Nice to meet you," added the one named Oscar. "I have three daughters of my own. One is around your age."

"Why are they here?" Valeria asked.

"I'm escorting Oscar and Percy to the sheriff's office and detention center to be processed," answered Ray. "I was close by and thought I'd drop you off at home on my way. There's always a lot of paperwork, so it's likely I'll be tied up for a while dealing with these two and getting home a little later than usual. In the freezer, there's a pizza you can heat up if you get hungry."

Just then, a call came in on Ray's two-way radio. He picked up, listened to the woman's voice on the other end, and responded, "Okay. I'm on my way." He hung up and quickly backed out the truck. "Change of plans, everyone." He turned on the flashing emergency lights mounted in the truck's grille and raced down the road at a high rate of speed.

Less than five minutes later, Ray pulled over close to a two-lane bridge crossing the Snake River, on the near side, and got out. "Wait here," he said.

There were four bicycle riders on the bridge, standing beside their bikes. When they saw Ray walking toward them, they all pointed to the river. "It's down there," said one of them. Ray leaned over the edge of the bridge and looked. He came back to the truck at a trot and popped open the tailgate.

Ray returned to the side of the truck with a large roll of yellow nylon rope draped over his shoulder and holding a pair of PVC chest waders. He unlocked the truck remotely and opened the rear passenger doors.

"Come on. Get out," he told Oscar and Percy. "I'm going to need your help." The two men did as told and held out their arms. Ray removed a key from his pocket and unlocked their handcuffs.

"What's going on?" asked Percy.

"A newborn moose calf is stranded in the middle of the river," answered Ray. "It's in danger of being swept away. Let's go."

Valeria got out of the truck and followed her father and the two other men down a steep embankment north of the bridge to the rock-strewn shore of the Snake River. The rough grayish water was swift and churning with new snowmelt. Out in the center of the river, on what looked like a shallow rise, stood a moose calf, no more than a few days old, struggling to stand in fierce current up to its belly. It was frozen in place, scared to move. On the near side, some distance away, the calf's mother, clearly distraught, was running back and forth along the shore.

After kicking off his boots, Ray quickly stepped into the waterproof wader, slipping it on over top of his game and fish uniform. The chest-high wader, held in place by straps looped over his shoulders, looked a lot like overalls. He handed the nylon rope to Oscar and Percy and, clutching the end of it, stepped into the river.

With the water swirling around his waist, ice-cold and unrelenting, Ray carefully made his way toward the moose calf. Several times, he paused and fought to remain upright in the turbulent current. Then, roughly a third of the way, he unexpectedly reached a deep area in the river, where the bottom suddenly dropped away. Ray disappeared underwater and popped up moments later, fifteen to twenty yards farther downstream, off course and treading water.

"Hang on!" shouted Oscar, letting out a little slack in the taut rope. "We've got you."

Still grasping the yellow rope, Ray got his bearings and swam hard in the general direction of the stranded moose calf until he reached the same submerged ridge in the middle of the river and was able to stand again.

The moose calf stood trembling a few yards away. Not wanting to startle the animal, Ray approached it slowly from behind, but when he extended his arms to grab hold of it, the calf's instinct was to flee. It leapt into the churning water with Ray lunging after it. He managed to tackle the moose and wrap one of his arms around its neck, but once again, he was in freezing water over his head. The strong current was trying to carry them downstream, and several times, their heads vanished underwater, only to resurface moments later.

Ray struggled to tread water and maintain his tenuous hold on the young moose at the same time; somehow, he managed to do both while also hanging onto the rope. With Valeria yelling words of encouragement to her father, Oscar and Percy braced their feet against several large rocks along the shore and tugged on their end of the lifeline with all their might.

Together, they were able to pull Ray to shallower water, where his feet could touch the uneven river bottom. He staggered the rest of the way back to shore, shivering but still holding the moose calf.

"Where's the mama?" asked Ray, wrapping the rope loosely around the calf's neck and tying it off.

"Over there," answered Valeria. The calf's agitated mother was nervously pacing back and forth near the river's edge, about fifty yards away.

"The rest of you wait here," said Ray.

Using the rope as a lead, Ray walked slowly and cautiously toward the huge adult moose, careful not to make any sudden moves as he brought the baby to her. When he was within twenty yards or so, he knelt next to the calf and patted its head. "You're safe now," he whispered.

Ray undid the rope from around the calf's neck and let go. The baby immediately darted off to be with its mother, who, in turn, took a moment to nuzzle and comfort her offspring before hurrying off with it to hide in the nearby woods.

Back at the truck, Ray thanked Oscar and Percy for their help. He changed out of the wader, grabbed some cans of soda from an ice chest, and handed everybody one. Afterward, he handcuffed the two poachers and took Valeria home.

CHAPTER 11

"Did you remember to bring the picnic blanket?" asked Ray.

He locked the truck, adjusted his backpack, and set out on a secluded trail near the foot of the Teton mountains that ran along the north end of the range. Beside him, he had three of the wolf pups on leashes.

Valeria fell in behind her father with the rest of the pups. She also had on a hiking backpack, a brand new ultra-lightweight one he'd bought for her.

"Yes," she answered. "I've got everything."

It had been a little more than a month since Valeria's return and Ray's first day off in weeks. The pups had nearly doubled in size. Their once-floppy newborn ears were beginning to stand erect, and their feet and heads had grown much larger. All six were increasingly more agile, energetic, and curious.

The trail began over level terrain and, after a quarter mile or so, gradually climbed higher. They hiked until Ray reached an open area with a magnificent view of both the mountains and valley below.

He took off his backpack and set it beside a large boulder. "One of the perks of being a game warden is you learn over time where all the best places are," he said. "The general public doesn't come to this spot. It's not highlighted on GPS or any of the tourist maps."

"It's awesome here," said Valeria. She laid down her

backpack, took the three pups' leashes from her father, and tied them off with hers to the low limb of a spruce; then, she helped lay out all the food on the picnic blanket. A small blue-gray bird with a distinct cinnamon-colored underbelly flew down from a nearby tree to watch.

"What kind of bird is that?" she asked.

"A red-breasted nuthatch, a male," answered Ray. "There's likely a nest nearby. They eat insects, spiders, and seeds."

Valeria grinned. She'd come to admire her father's broad knowledge of the ecosystem in and around the Teton National Park, Yellowstone, and elsewhere in Western Wyoming. Try as she might, she hadn't yet been able to stump him with a specific question about any animal or plant.

Smelling food, several of the pups tugged at their leashes and whined.

"Don't worry," said Ray, reaching into his pack for a sealed extra-large bag of finely chopped meat. "We didn't forget about you."

Hazel at the Silver Beaver had insisted on donating all her restaurant's unused and leftover meat scraps to the pups, and gradually, with Lauren's help, Valeria was able to wean the young wolves off the substitute milk concoction. As soon as Ray unsealed the bag of meat, its tantalizing aroma had their full attention. All six heads perked up.

Ray carried the bag to an area between two trees, about ten yards or so away from the picnic blanket and other food. "Go ahead and let them off leash," he said.

"Are you sure it's safe?" asked Valeria with a look of concern. "What if they run off? They're still young and might get lost chasing something. We'd never be able to find them way out here."

"They're not going to stray far. You're their mother, and the pups won't want to be where they can't see or hear you." Ray knelt and scattered the meat on the ground over a small area. "It's important they be introduced to natural habitats like this and take part in group meals with the grown wolves in their pack."

Valeria walked over to the pups. "I'm going to be watching you close," she warned, trying to sound stern. "If any one of you takes a single step where I can't see you, all of you will be punished." She unhooked their leashes. They hesitated to leave her side, but as soon as she broke eye contact with them, they rushed to where Ray had laid out the meat and began to eat.

Ray and Valeria sat down on the picnic blanket, took in the picturesque vistas surrounding them while they relaxed, and enjoyed the coleslaw, sandwiches, and chips they had packed. The world around them felt so idyllic that, at first, little was said. It seemed neither of them wanted to disrupt the fragile perfection that enveloped them. All felt right. When the young wolves had devoured every scrap before them, they returned to Valeria and lay on the ground beside her, next to the blanket. Their eyes looked drowsy. Several yawned, and soon, all six were asleep atop one another in a loose pile.

Valeria enjoyed her father's company. He was easy to be around. But often, in moments like this, when they were alone together, and everything was peaceful and quiet, she'd look at him and couldn't help but think about her mother. For too many years, he'd been absent from her life, and she still had lots of questions she wanted to ask him. Her parents' relationship had ended when she was just a baby. Were he and Rosa ever in love? Why did he leave them? She wanted to ask, but somehow, such questions now seemed irrelevant. *Let the past be,* she thought.

After a time, she broke the stillness. "Philip said Mom's spirit spoke to the wolves." She leaned back and glanced up at the sky. She counted three clouds overhead; they didn't seem to be moving. "That's how he was able to find me in the snowstorm. Mom guided them to me." She looked at her father. "He told me she's still here, watching us."

Ray didn't respond immediately. A minute or more passed; he appeared to be thinking. "I believe him," he said almost matter-of-factly.

He picked up a pebble that had made its way onto the blanket and nonchalantly tossed it aside. "When the first fur trappers and early settlers came to this land, the Shoshone people were already here and had been for hundreds of years. These mountains were theirs." He paused. "I don't doubt what your friend said is true. How else can we explain how he found you?"

Again, Ray went quiet for a moment. "I've seen ancient petroglyphs etched on rocks by ancestors of the Mountain Shoshones. If you want, I can take you to see them sometime. Most are simple drawings of animals and hunting scenes, but others depict powerful spirits we know very little about." He tossed another stray pebble. "The Shoshone people have great respect for this land's spiritual presence and for wolves. They see the wolf as a creator God."

One of the young female wolves stirred and sat up. Not long after, it wandered away from the pile to an area about fifteen yards away, looked back at Valeria, then disappeared behind some trees.

"Oh, no, you don't!" said Valeria.

She went to get up and go find her, but Ray grabbed her arm. "Wait. Give her a minute or two," he said. "Trust me. She won't venture too far."

Valeria stared at the wooded area the young wolf had strayed off into and watched intently for her reappearance.

When the pup didn't return after a few minutes, Ray added, "I know you've become extremely attached to them, Val, but these pups won't stay pups for long." He grabbed a thermos, took a sip of water, and set it back down. "They're going to grow up faster than you want and become adult wolves in just a matter of months, not years. Before that happens, we need to let them explore and learn what it means to be a wolf."

Despite what her father said, Valeria stood up. She didn't want to risk the young wolf becoming lost and was more anxious than before to retrieve it.

"Wait," Ray repeated. "Be patient."

"How much longer?"

Just then, as if she had been listening, the young female pup poked her head out from behind a rock. She sniffed around a little longer, then came scampering back to the picnic blanket and lay down with the rest of her littermates to nap.

Valeria breathed a sigh of relief and sat next to her babies. She knew everything her father said was true, that she would need to let the pups go off on their own one day, but she didn't want to think about the future just yet, not today. It was too nice out. So, she closed her eyes and allowed herself to rest.

On the ride back to Jackson, Ray played some music through the truck's speakers using his smartphone. It was a collection of lovely and mournful tunes sung by a mature woman in a foreign language Valeria didn't recognize. The singer sounded as if she were wiping away tears, her heart breaking. The melancholy songs were mesmerizing and unlike anything she'd ever heard.

"What kind of music is that?" asked Valeria. "And what is she saying?"

"It's a traditional Portuguese music called Fado," answered Ray. "I once took a job on a cargo ship, and one of my shipmates was from a seaport in Portugal. In the evening, after supper, he'd play songs like these over and over until I couldn't get them out of my head. I don't know what she's singing about exactly, but my friend told me the lyrics speak to the harsh realities of everyday life. Fado melodies are about fate, the sea, being poor, coming to grips with loneliness, and hope."

Valeria listened to her father's Fado. The music had a soul, and it didn't much matter that she didn't know the words. "I can tell by the tone of her voice that she lost someone very dear to her," she replied.

She was looking out the window and seemed to be talking to herself. "When I heard the wolves howl in the mountains, it was like they were reaching out for something they could never touch. Their voices soared far above everything. It was kind of a sad sound and so deep and moving at the same time. I still hear them at night, in my dreams."

CHAPTER 12

The house phone rang more than twenty times before Valeria finally staggered out of bed to answer it. Awakened from a sound sleep and still in a daze, she mumbled, "Yes. Okay. I'll get him for you," and brought the phone to her father.

Without opening his eyes, Ray rolled onto his back, coughed twice, and took the phone from Valeria. He put it on speaker.

"Ray. We've got trouble." It was Lauren. "You need to get over here right away!"

"Where's here?" Ray sat up in bed. "And what time is it?"

"Six a.m." Lauren's voice sounded tense. "I'm outside the veterinary center."

"Okay. I'm on my way." He hung up and called out to Valeria, who was already back in her bed, under the covers. "Get dressed! We're leaving in the next few minutes."

Less than fifteen minutes later, they were pulling up to the veterinary center. The morning sky was just beginning to brighten. There were two vehicles parked out front, a black SUV with a US government license plate and, beside it, an animal control transport vehicle, custom outfitted with a row of steel cages in the back. Lauren stood near the transport, gesturing and arguing with two men. One was large and wearing what Ray recognized to be an army tactical uniform; the other had on civilian clothes.

"The plate on that transport truck says Wisconsin," said Ray. He parked sideways behind the two vehicles, effectively blocking them in.

They got out, and Lauren rushed up to Ray. "Thank God you're here!" she said.

Just then, two soldiers, dressed in camouflaged army fatigues, came out of the front door to the center, dragging the litter of young wolves by their necks using ropes. All six wolves were resisting being taken; several were growling menacingly at the men. When a female pup stubbornly dug in her heels and refused to move any farther, one of the soldiers kicked her. The wolf yelped and bit the man's leg.

"Ow!" the soldier bellowed, booting it off him. "The damn thing got me."

Valeria screamed, "Get away from them!" and took off toward the soldiers. "What are you doing?" After running up to one of the men and grabbing him by the arm, she attempted to force the ropes out of his hands, but he maintained a firm grip and shoved her out of the way.

Ray rushed back to his truck and returned, holding a rifle at his side. He calmly walked up to the two men whom Lauren had been seen arguing with. "Now then, which one of you two fellows is going to explain what the hell you're doing here?" he asked firmly.

The civilian, a trim middle-aged man who was going bald, extended his hand. Ray ignored the offer to shake hands. "I'm Dr. Theodore Irwin with the Food and Drug Administration," he said. "And this is Sergeant Norris, whose men are acting as my escort—"

Lauren interrupted him. "These goons in uniform showed up unannounced at my home in the middle of the night and forced me to come and open the center," she said angrily. "They threatened me with legal action if I didn't cooperate."

"We're sorry for any stress or inconvenience we may have caused, Dr. Ross," said Dr. Irwin. "As I've already tried to explain several times, we simply didn't want to attract attention to ourselves by showing up at your practice during the day and are trying to avoid any unnecessary confrontation as we speak. We've come for the wolf pups and will leave quietly once we have them."

"Do something, Dad!" yelled Valeria.

One of the two soldiers, coming out of the center, opened a latched compartment on the animal transport vehicle, grabbed one of the snarling young wolves roughly, and tossed it hard, rope and all, into the cage. He then reached down for another.

Valeria heard a click.

"Let go of the wolf," said Ray, his rifle pointed at the soldier's head. "And stand back up slowly." The rifle was cocked.

With the others looking on, the soldier obeyed his instructions. At Ray's request, he retrieved the second wolf from the cage and gently set it down on the ground with the others. The task completed, Ray lowered his rifle.

Valeria grabbed the rope leads from both soldiers and knelt with the wolves to reassure them. They all swarmed her, took turns licking her face and neck, and seemed to calm down at once.

"You've got some explaining to do, Dr. Irwin. Tell me who the hell you and your cronies are," demanded Ray. "And what does the FDA want with a litter of wolf pups?"

"I don't know who you think you are," Sergeant Norris said, "but my men have orders to appropriate these wolves, and we're not leaving without them." He took a step toward Ray. "So, I suggest you move out of the way and let us do our job."

Ray stood his ground. Pointing to the badge pinned to his shirt above his left pocket, he said, "You see this, Sergeant? I'm the game warden in these parts, and you boys are off your base and outside the limits of your authority." He shoved the sergeant backward. "Am I making myself clear? I have legal jurisdiction over these six orphaned wolves, and they're not going anywhere with you, not today, not ever."

His voice lower and sterner than before, Ray turned his attention again to Dr. Irwin. "Unless you want me to arrest you for harassment, kidnapping, and grand theft, you're going to answer my questions. Why are you here? And what do you want with these wolves?"

At first, Dr. Irwin glared at Ray; then his expression softened until he looked to be a bit amused. "What's your name?" he asked in a friendly tone. "To whom am I talking?"

"My name is Ray…Ray Cortez, but you and your buddies here can call me Officer Cortez." Ray wasn't smiling. "And let's get one thing straight: I'll be asking the questions."

"There's no need for everyone to get upset. I'll be happy to explain things," said Dr. Irwin. He walked calmly over to where Valeria and the wolves were and stooped down to pick one up. "May I?" he asked Valeria politely. But the pup wouldn't let him touch it, growled viciously, and threatened to bite. The doctor abruptly stood up and retreated back to Ray.

"I'm the chief officer and scientist for a company that specializes in cutting-edge animal research." The doctor paced back and forth a little. He then crossed his arms and continued. "The organization I represent works closely with the US government and the FDA, doing advanced research for the military."

"In other words, you'd like to confiscate these pups while the litter is young and vulnerable so you can run neurological experiments on them," said Lauren. She was angry, her voice rising as she spoke. "You want to train and weaponize wolves on behalf of the army for use in war games and combat. Is that it? You intend to turn these pups into lab rats to test out your ideas."

"You're putting words in my mouth," Dr. Irwin responded. "But yes, there is a military component to the research we want to conduct, but not exclusively." He paused and whispered something to the sergeant, who, in turn, motioned for the two soldiers to back away from Valeria and the wolves.

Dr. Irwin continued, "It's important to understand that if it weren't for federal grant money provided by the United States government, we wouldn't have the financial support needed to conduct much of the vital animal research done in this country, most of which involves testing new drugs to see if they're safe and effective for humans." He paused. "There is a slight catch, of course. In return for supporting new scientific research, the various branches of the government have the power to choose and oversee what research we do. In this case, the Department of Defense has expressed an interest in wolves. That's why these men are with me."

"Why wolves?" asked Ray.

"It's their extraordinary sense of smell," Dr. Irwin responded. "For well over a hundred years, various foreign armies and police forces around the world have tried to train wolves and wolfdog hybrids to track the enemy and criminals, but every attempt has failed. The prevailing conclusion is, genetically speaking, wolves simply cannot be trained. They lack certain essential connections in their DNA that dogs possess." The doctor smiled. "But we have reason to believe we can alter the wolf's response to training, and we'll be the first to succeed."

"Lab rats!" Lauren repeated. "How are you going to accomplish this? Do you intend to pump them full of mind-altering drugs or cut them open and splice their DNA? Whatever you're planning to do to these wolves is wrong on so many levels and morally bankrupt. I don't care what your end goal or other reasons are."

"Based on the license plate I see on that transport vehicle of yours, you must have, I'm guessing, a top-secret lab somewhere in Wisconsin," said Ray. "If I'm right, it means you and your army friends here drove more than a thousand miles to get your hands on this particular litter of wolf pups. Tell me why."

"We've been on the lookout for a healthy litter of newborn wolves ever since the federal government took them off the endangered species list. But, in truth, wolves are still quite rare, and we don't have the manpower or resources to search for an entire litter in the wild on our own." Dr. Irwin again paused. "When we heard the news about your daughter finding her way out of the wilderness, and she'd brought back the babies with her...well, what more can I say? It attracted our attention."

Sergeant Norris stepped in. "My men have orders to return with these six wolves. This is the last time I'm going to say this to you: we're not leaving without them. Our directives were handed down directly from the Pentagon and cleared by your game and fish bosses at the state level." He shoved his way past Lauren and the two men and stood between Ray and Valeria. He then turned his back to Ray. "With all due respect, Officer Cortez, we don't have to justify our presence or give you any further explanations. You've already been told more than you need to know." He motioned to the two soldiers to grab the wolves.

The two men reached for the wolves. Blocking them with her body, Valeria quickly rose and kicked the closest man to her in the shin. Then suddenly, from somewhere behind her, she heard a loud pop, followed by a brief hissing sound. She and the men, as well as Sergeant Norris, all stopped and turned around.

In his hand, Ray was holding a large and very sharp, heavy-duty survival knife, which he carried with him in his pocket at all times. He'd punctured and flattened a rear tire on the transport vehicle.

Ray ran his hand lightly over the sidewall of the tire and felt the damage. "That's really too bad," he said calmly. "If you had just run over a nail with your tire, the tread on this thing could've been patched; this tire could've been saved, but this can't be fixed." With the four other men staring at him, he walked behind the truck to the opposite side. There was another loud pop and a hissing. He came back. "And I might be wrong, but these truck tires look to be an odd size and will need to be special ordered." He walked up to Sergeant Norris. "In the meantime, there's several towing companies in Jackson you can call, and if you need to stay for a while, we have some nice lodges in the area. Some even serve their guests breakfast and whatnot."

At the same time, Lauren rushed over to help Valeria take control of the pups. Sergeant Norris and the two soldiers didn't try to stop her. They glared at Ray, dropped the leads, and stood aside.

"What do you think you're doing?" asked Dr. Irwin. His face looked flushed.

"You'll see," said Ray. "Wait here." He walked over to his truck and returned, holding a pair of handcuffs. "Turn around, Doctor, and give me your hands. You're under arrest."

"You can't do this."

"Well, you're wrong." Ray snapped the cuffs on the doctor's wrists. "As a law enforcement officer, I'm duty-bound to respond to any and all criminal activity I stumble across in the field. And if I'm not mistaken, your attempt to abduct these wolves is also wildlife related, wouldn't you agree? Let's see... Attempting to steal protected wildlife and transport it across state lines with the intention of torturing and abusing the animals, threatening and kidnapping Dr. Ross, and assaulting my daughter." Ray paused. "Those are some serious charges, Doctor–more than enough, I think, to take you into custody on."

Still standing where they were nearby, Sergeant Norris and the two soldiers looked on and said nothing.

CHAPTER 13

Dr. Irwin posted bail and was released the same day. A temporary restraining order was issued, prohibiting him from coming within one hundred feet of Lauren, Valeria, or the young wolves. But the criminal charges against him were soon dropped as part of a plea deal with the Food and Drug Administration.

As a result of the confrontation, the wolves were moved to Ray's small three-bedroom home in town. During his short stint in jail, Dr. Irwin had threatened to bring a lawsuit, and Ray didn't want Lauren or her veterinary practice to be affected by any legal action the FDA might pursue.

In truth, though, plans to move the young litter had already been in the works before the recent threat of a lawsuit. The pups had quickly outgrown the veterinary center's kennel and dog run and needed more space to spread out and roam. Ray had a six-foot-high privacy fence installed around his backyard, and one of the bedrooms was cleared of furniture so it could be used at night as a temporary den. But from the day they first arrived at the house, the wolves insisted on sleeping with Valeria on her bed and being near her and wouldn't use the spare bedroom. Of course, she didn't mind and let the pack tag along with her wherever she went.

As news of the wolves spread through the community, many conservation-minded and longtime residents stepped forward with offers to help. Hazel continued to bring the wolves fresh meat, most of it leftovers from the restaurant, but also large bones and other portions of bison and elk from a local butcher–items that normally would be discarded. Another person, an elderly man with a long gray beard, showed up unannounced with several castoff deer and rabbit hides for the wolves to play with and fight over in the backyard.

One sunny morning, two weeks into the move, there was a knock on the door. When Valeria opened it, she was greeted by a smiling young couple in their thirties and their three kids, a boy no more than seven and his two younger sisters. Valeria could tell right away by the way they were dressed that they were tourists.

"Excuse us, miss, but is this where they keep the wolves?" asked the father. "We were given directions and told you wouldn't mind if we stopped by. We'd really love to see some wolves before we fly home."

With Valeria and Ray's permission, one of the local online newspapers arranged a poll and contest, asking their readers to suggest names for the six wolves. Prizes were to be given out to those whose names were selected. The contest was briefly mentioned during a news-hour segment on a regional television station, then rebroadcast by other media outlets. Soon, name submissions poured in from all over the country.

For hours on end every day, the adolescent wolves tussled one another, either over control of favorite chew bones and hides or for no good reason at all. Between long naps, there was always a lot of playful goading, nipping, and harmless rolling around on top of one another. Considered fair game, Valeria was often lured into their persistent mischief. Occasionally, the wolves' roughhousing got a tad out of hand, resulting in an unintentional bruise or scratch here and there, but before things got too chaotic, Valeria would assert her control as mama and break up the fun.

Also, with each passing day, the wolves' need to expand their horizons and explore beyond the confines of the yard seemed to grow stronger. Whenever she was able, Lauren would drop by to check on things and assist Valeria in taking the wolves on lengthy walks around town. Although it helped burn off some of their youthful energy, it wasn't enough. They were perpetually curious and began to dig holes under the fence, looking to escape.

Around noon one day, Valeria went into the house to fix herself a sandwich, and when she came back outside, two of the wolves were gone. A quick inspection of the surroundings revealed a large hole under the fence, partially hidden behind a shed.

Valeria started to panic, then remembered what her father had told her earlier about the wolves not wanting to be too far away from her. *They have to be nearby somewhere,* she thought. *But where?* She hurried the other four wolves into the house and rushed out the front door to look for the two runaways.

She didn't have to go far. A block away, she heard a commotion just down another street. "Get away from here! Go! Get!" a woman yelled. Valeria ran and found the two wolves in somebody's front yard, under a tree, looking up at a hissing cat.

A woman stood nearby with a broom in her hand, brandishing it like a weapon at the two wolves, who, for their part, appeared unfazed.

When she saw Valeria rush up to the wolves with two leads in her hand, the woman asked angrily, "Do these two hooligans belong to you?"

"Yes! I'm very sorry, ma'am," answered Valeria. "This is my fault. I was supposed to be watching them, and they got loose when I wasn't looking." She secured the leads. "But there's no reason to be afraid. They like to play and would never hurt your cat."

"You can't know that," said the woman, still upset.

Valeria quickly took control of the two wolves and headed back to the house. On her way, she thought about the incident, and her eyes welled with tears. The woman was right.

When Ray came home that evening, he was in a somber mood. Valeria told him what had happened, but he didn't comment on it or ask any questions. He took a shower, fixed dinner, and said very little while they ate at the table. After doing the dishes, he came into the living room and sat next to her on the sofa. She was watching TV. Quietly, he picked up the remote and turned it off. Most of the wolves were lying on the floor, sprawled out around the room, and half asleep. One of the girls was on Valeria's lap, getting her head and neck rubbed.

"They found him," said Ray.

"Found who?" asked Valeria, a puzzled look on her face.

"Your friend, Philip. His last name is Wakska."

"Oh my God! That's so great!" Valeria lit up with excitement. "Where is he? When can I see him?" she asked, practically bouncing up and down and smiling.

"Well, we could go see him tomorrow, maybe, but just for a few hours. He's being held at the Wind River Indian Reservation."

"Held? Why is he being held?"

"Philip's in jail." Ray reached down, lifted one of the wolves off the floor, and gently placed it on his lap. "I don't know all the details, but apparently, there's been an outstanding warrant for his arrest that dates back several years. It might explain why he was living way out in the mountains by himself." He paused as he rubbed the wolf's head. "Very few people, even if they knew the terrain, would've been able to do what he did and survive."

Early the next morning, they packed a lunch, dropped off the wolves at the veterinary center for the day, and began the two-and-a-half-hour drive east to the adult detention center on the Wind River Indian Reservation. Little by little, with each passing mile, the grandeur of the Teton mountains and Bridger-

Teton National Forest gave way to a rolling and barren prairie grassland engraved with immense vistas, undulating hillsides, and rocky bluffs in the distance.

"The Wind River Reservation is home to two tribes, the Eastern Shoshone and Northern Arapaho," said Ray. "It's a vast land, thirty-five-hundred square miles of mostly prairie and mountains, and along this stretch of road, there are no trees of any kind anywhere in sight, not a single one as far as the eye can see. But it's still quite spectacular, don't you think?"

"I don't know. It has kind of a wide-open, dead look to me," Valeria responded. "But it's pretty in its own way."

Thus far, they'd had the highway almost entirely to themselves. Ray whizzed around a truck that was hauling cattle, the first eastbound vehicle they'd come upon in nearly a half hour. As they went by, Valeria pumped her arm to entice the trucker to honk his air horn, and he obliged. She and her father grinned.

"There aren't any houses or gas stations. There's nothing out here," said Valeria, after another forty minutes of the same desolate scenery. She yawned. "Where are all the people?"

"The entire Native American population on the reservation is less than fifteen thousand, and most of them live in a handful of small towns to the south and east of here." Ray sat up a little straighter and passed another slower-moving vehicle. "It's tragic, really, but the reservation has suffered from high unemployment for years. Seventy-five percent of working aged adults can't find a decent paying job. It also has a reputation as being one of the most dangerous places to live in the United States. The isolation and unrelenting poverty have led to a lot of substance abuse and violent crime."

Eventually, Ray turned right onto another two-lane highway, which cut through more rolling prairie land, not much different in appearance than the first stretch. Not long after, they crossed a narrow river and came upon a tiny rural community and the detention center.

Inside, they stepped through a metal detector after emptying their pockets, signed in at the front desk, and made their visitation request. A half hour or so later, they were ushered back to a large open room with high-resolution security cameras strategically placed throughout. There were tables and chairs spread out in the center of the room and a number of people sitting across from handcuffed inmates in bright orange jumpsuits, talking quietly. At one table, a woman held a newborn. At another, a distinguished-looking older Native American dressed in a suit and tie was pointing to a stack of documents and shaking his head as an inmate nodded. Nearby, an armed female guard with a stoic expression watched over everyone.

Valeria and Ray were escorted to a table and asked to sit. Soon after, a guard brought Philip into the room from behind a thick security door that buzzed when it opened. His feet were shackled, and hands cuffed. He wore an orange jumpsuit like the other inmates. The guard led Philip by the arm to the opposite side of the table and then told him to sit and not move.

"Remember, there'll be no shaking hands, hugging, or physical contact of any kind," instructed the guard. "Understood?"

Valeria and Ray nodded. Seemingly indifferent, Philip stared at his cuffed hands and didn't respond.

Philip raised his head to look at Valeria, and ever so slowly, his serious expression was replaced with a meek smile. "I've missed you, Val," said Philip. "Is this your father?"

"Yes," answered Valeria. "I've missed you too."

"I'm Ray Cortez. I want to thank you for saving my daughter," said Ray. "It's a miracle you found her."

Philip shook his head. "There's no need to thank me. It was her mother, truly, who led us to her," he said softly. "Val is a joy. She blessed me with her presence and, in the end, saved my life. I am forever indebted to her."

"When you were unconscious, I went to find help," said Valeria. "We came back for you in a helicopter, but you were gone. Where did you go?"

"I woke up dazed and in a lot of pain. It was night. I opened my eyes and lay there in the dark for a while, wondering where you might be. It hurt to breathe. When I finally could stand, I found your tracks nearby in the snow. It was then your mother's spirit came and whispered to me. She told me you were safe, that she'd watched over you and guided your path."

Valeria and her father exchanged glances.

Philip continued, "I struggled to make my way back to the campsite. At first light, I gathered my things and set out to find a doctor. Gypsy must have passed away while we were gone, and there was little I could do for her pups. Transporting a litter of pups isn't easy, and I was too hurt. I had no choice but to leave them behind with Sparkle, Titan, and Romeo." He looked down again at his cuffed hands. "I didn't know when I'd be able to return, if at all, and since the pups were still very young and not yet weaned off milk or ready for solid foods, it was likely they weren't going to survive anyway."

"We found them, looking for you," said Valeria. "When we got to the camp, they were still lying next to Gypsy, but Sparkle, Titan, and Romeo weren't there. I was allowed to bring the pups home, and we've been raising them ever since. It's been in the news. Did you know the pups were with me?"

"No." Philip's eyes lit up, and his face brightened. "I've had feelings of guilt over leaving them to starve ever since. It's haunted my dreams. Thank you both for coming here and sharing this. I didn't know."

"They've grown a lot bigger," said Valeria. "Maybe you can come and visit us and them someday." She paused for a moment, looked around, and lowered her voice. "I mean, when you get out of this place."

"How did you end up in jail, if I might ask?" said Ray.

"It was one of the most difficult things I've ever done, but I made my way out of the mountains to a highway. I hitched a ride on a truck to the reservation. There's a doctor out here who I've known all my life. I showed up on his doorstep, and he took me to a medical center for x-rays. My ribs were broken, and I had a collapsed lung. It had been punctured."

Philip paused to look around the room. "I couldn't catch my breath, so I had no choice but to stay at the center for treatment. I was there for a couple weeks, recovering," he added. "The world out here on the reservation, it looks so big, doesn't it? So much open land, so much sky, but when you live here all your life, it can start to feel so small in many ways. There are no secrets. Everyone knows everybody else's business. While I was being treated, one of the nurses, who's also Shoshone, recognized me and turned me in to the police for the reward. They came and arrested me."

"Why was there a warrant for your arrest?" asked Ray. "What did you do?"

Valeria interrupted. "If you don't want to say, it's okay. I just wanted to see you again and thank you for all you did for me."

"Thank you for coming into my life. You mean more to me than you know, Val," said Philip softly. He looked into Valeria's eyes. A moment later, he closed his and sang in a gentle whisper, "Fair is the white star of twilight, and the sky clearer at the day's end. But she is fairer, and she is dearer. She, my heart's friend."

Philip opened his eyes. "I had a daughter your age. You remind me of her." He leaned forward a little and lowered his voice. "She disappeared six years ago."

"What's her name?" asked Ray.

"Minsi." Philip's expression turned serious. "The police

on the reservation don't have the manpower or resources to do a proper search for longer than a few weeks. When she didn't turn up, I went looking for her myself. It took me more than a year, but eventually, I was able to learn she'd been taken by a member of a small drug gang."

Philip's hands were clenched.

"That's terrible," said Valeria. "Were you able to find her?"

Philip looked away and shook his head. "No," he said. "Minsi's still out there…somewhere…

"I tracked the drug gang to a safe house on the reservation, showed up with a shotgun, and made them to tell me what they knew. They claimed not to know who my daughter was, had never met her, and as for the guy accused of abducting her, none of them had seen him for months. I searched the place from top to bottom, and there was no sign of her having been there." Philip paused. "I was in my truck, about to leave, when I heard a screen door slam and spotted someone behind the house, running off into the prairie. It was him."

"What did you do?" asked Ray. "You must have been enraged."

Philip glanced at the security guard still standing nearby, watching everyone, and lowered his voice. "I kept my head down and pretended to leave. I drove to just beyond a bend in the road, walked back through the brush, and waited. It wasn't long. The kid came back. The thing I remember most was he was smiling."

Valeria was trying not to tear up. "Oh, my God," she blurted under her breath.

"I came out of hiding and confronted him," Philip continued. "I didn't intend to kill him; I needed him to tell me what happened to Minsi, where he'd left her. I needed to know whether she was alive, but he pulled a pistol out of his waistband and pointed it at my head. I already had my shotgun raised, and I didn't give him a chance to pull the trigger."

"I don't see you had a choice," said Ray. "It sounds like a clear case of self-defense."

"I was arrested and charged with second-degree murder because I showed up to the property already armed. I was the aggressor, they said. The other members of the gang continued to deny knowing anything about my daughter and gave statements that incriminated me. The police also charged me with arson."

"Why arson?" asked Ray.

"I torched the safe house and burned it to the ground."

"I'm so sorry all that happened to you," said Valeria. Her eyes were red. A tear streamed down her cheek. "I had no idea. Is that why you came to the mountains?"

"Yes." Philip looked into Valeria's eyes and smiled. "You remind me so much of her." He paused for a second, then continued, "Because I'd never been in trouble and had a clean record, a judge let me post bail until the trial, but I never showed up to court. I was certain I'd be convicted by a jury and sent away to prison for years."

Philip again looked down at his cuffed hands. "For a while, I kept a low profile and lived in remote areas of the reservation, but when a cash reward was offered by both the bail bondsman and police for information to my whereabouts, I left for the Tetons."

For a few moments, there was complete silence.

Valeria wanted to express her sympathy and sorrow but felt overwhelmed. She didn't know what to say to Philip. She instinctively understood the depths of his grief and realized it might be better to say nothing. She thought, *No matter how heartfelt they're spoken, sometimes words are pointless. They'll never make him feel whole again or put things right.*

"Is there anything we can do to help?" asked Ray.

Slow to respond, Philip glanced again at the guard. He appeared to be thinking. "When the wolf pups are old enough, take them to the mountains where they were born and release them." His eyes again met Valeria's. "Set them free."

CHAPTER 14

"Please kneel with the wolves and look over this way," instructed the cameraman. "It'd be nice to have a group shot with you in the middle."

"Okay," said Valeria. With the help of Ray and Lauren, she gathered the six wolf pups close to her, got down on one knee, and posed for a short video clip as well as some still photos.

A small crowd of tourists had gathered to watch. "Are those real wolves?" asked several. Some were taking snapshots with their phones.

It was a dry, bright, sunny morning. They were standing in front of the Yellowstone Justice Center, located about four hours from Jackson in the town of Mammoth, inside the national park. A female news reporter and cameraman from a Wyoming-based television station had arrived to interview Valeria and Ray for a ten-to-fifteen-minute human interest story. Everyone had agreed to meet up at the justice center prior to the father and daughter's hearing with a US District Court judge.

At stake was custody of the wolves. The Food and Drug Administration, on behalf of the army and federal government, had filed a lawsuit six weeks earlier, challenging the authority of Ray and the state of Wyoming over the wolves and demanding the litter be handed over to Dr. Irwin and his team of researchers.

The reporter stepped in front of the video camera with a handheld microphone. "I'm here with Valeria Cortez, the girl who was lost in the mountains and ultimately saved these wolves," she replied, smiling. "I understand there was a recent contest to name the wolves." She held the mike near Valeria's face.

"Yes, there was."

"And what are their names?"

Valeria stood up, holding their leashes tightly. "The girls are Tess, Yoko, and Roxie." She smiled for the camera. "And the boys are Diesel, Scout, and Zeus."

"Lovely names," commented the reporter.

Though technically pups, the litter had reached a stage of rapid growth. They were gaining weight, more than a pound a week, and resembled adult wolves in nearly every way, except they were slightly smaller in stature. Their appetites had increased significantly as well, and it was becoming increasingly more difficult to curb their natural urge to hunt, both alone and as a pack. As a precaution, Ray put radio collars on the six wolves, monogrammed with each wolf's name, in the event one or more of them got loose.

The reporter walked over to Ray, who was standing off to one side. "This is Ray Cortez, Valeria's father and a game warden in Teton County," she said. "Officer Cortez, you're here today because the United States government wants to take possession of these wolves. Can you tell us why?"

"We've been told why, but I don't want to divulge that information until after the judge makes a decision. The bottom line is we're fighting for custody of these wolves. For us, personally, they're an extended part of our family. Valeria has helped raise them since they were born, and their bond with her is unbreakable."

Ray glanced at his daughter. The cameraman panned his lens over to Valeria and then back to him.

"This lawsuit is an unwarranted intrusion," Ray continued. "It's the same as a guardianship case involving children. We want to be the ones to shape these young wolves' lives going forward, not some agency of the US government."

Lauren interrupted the interview. "It's time, Ray." She gathered the leashes from Valeria. "The wolves aren't allowed inside the courthouse. So, I'll wait out here with them until you're done." She gave Ray and Valeria kisses on the cheek. "Good luck."

Ray and Valeria went inside and took the elevator to the second floor. They waited a few minutes before being invited to step into the courtroom by a uniformed officer, who then led them to a table facing the judge's bench. Seated at another table to their right and also facing the bench were Dr. Irwin and two other men dressed in suits.

"They must be lawyers for the FDA," whispered Ray, leaning over to Valeria.

As they waited for the judge to arrive, folks from Jackson filed into the courtroom and took seats on the benches in the back, including Kimberly, Hazel, and others, some of whom Valeria knew and others she didn't. Soon, every seat available to the public was filled. It was then Valeria saw Butch Hardin enter the chamber. With him was a weathered-looking elderly woman she didn't recognize. Wearing a denim shirt and blue jeans, the lady walked using a wooden cane; Butch gently supported her arm as she shuffled along. The two made their way to the front row, where Butch said something under his breath to a couple of other guests, who nodded and politely gave up their seats to Butch and the woman.

A short time later, a female court reporter came in from a door to the left and sat at a small desk just in front and to one side of the judge's bench. She opened a stenotype machine and rested her hands on the keys, ready to type a transcription of the hearing.

The bailiff, dressed like a police officer and wearing a

badge over his left shirt pocket, followed her into the room. "All rise," he announced.

Everyone in the room stood up. The judge, a tall, gray-haired black man wearing a dress shirt, tie, and a long dark robe, strode to his bench. "Please be seated," he said. A nameplate atop the bench read, "Judge Jack Dupree."

The judge took a moment to glance through some documents and then looked up. "I'd like to remind everyone involved that this is a custody hearing, not a trial." He paused to pull out several papers from the stack in front of him. "Both sides will be given an opportunity to argue the facts, and at the end of this hearing, I will make my decision."

He then turned his attention to Dr. Irwin and the two attorneys. "I must say, this is one of the more unusual lawsuits I've seen, and I'm curious. Why is the United States Food and Drug Administration seeking legal custody of six wolves?"

Dr. Irwin rose to his feet. "Your Honor, we're in the process of doing cutting-edge animal research that requires a litter of young wolves," he said. "As outlined in the documents we've submitted to you, the US government has empowered our agency with sweeping authority, eminent domain if you will, over domestic animals and wildlife of all kinds. We have the legal right to make compulsory acquisitions of any species of animal for a public purpose."

"The power of eminent domain, as stated in the Fifth Amendment, can only be exercised if you compensate the owners of the property you're taking from," Judge Dupree responded. "Do you intend to pay the state of Wyoming or the Cortez family for these wolves?"

Valeria jumped to her feet. "We don't want their money!" she yelled. "They're not for sale."

"Order!" said Judge Dupree, forcibly. "Sit down, young lady. You'll have your chance to speak."

Ray grabbed hold of his daughter's arm. She was visibly upset. "Do what he says and sit," he whispered to her. "Stay calm."

Valeria reluctantly sat back down.

"Wolves aren't pets that anyone can lay claim to," Dr. Irwin responded. "And the six wolves in question are neither the private property of the Cortezes nor the state of Wyoming. They're a national asset and should be treated as such. We've submitted a written plan to you explaining the importance of these wolves to our mission. We're doing vital scientific research that, in the end, will benefit all Americans."

Judge Dupree turned to Ray and Valeria. "Why have you resisted the US government's demands for these wolves?" he asked. "You were asked to submit your own written plan of action in response to the FDA, Officer Cortez, but I don't see that you've done so. It's obvious you and your daughter have been caring for this orphaned litter up to now, but what do you intend to do with them going forward?"

Ray stood up. "If I may, Your Honor, I'd like to first talk about the FDA's plan. It's a facade," he said. "Dr. Irwin has cleverly omitted a few details regarding his agency's intentions. In regard to the six wolves, he's left out key words that apply to his so-called research, words like 'manipulation,' 'unnatural,' and 'pain.' He's not forthcoming as to what kind of experiments he intends to do or how he intends to house the wolves."

One of the attorneys next to Dr. Irwin sprang to his feet. "I object!" he said loudly. "The Food and Drug Administration is not on trial here, and Officer Cortez's remarks are pure nonsense."

"Are they?" asked Judge Dupree. "I agree with the officer that the reasons you've submitted for why you want these wolves are short on specifics. Have a seat, sir." He again turned to Ray. "You didn't answer my question, Officer Cortez. You were asked to submit your own plan to the court prior to this hearing today.

Where is it?"

"Our goal is to reintroduce the wolves back into the wild," answered Ray. "We'd hoped to have a more detailed plan worked out beforehand, but we've run into a few snags—"

"What kind of snags?" interrupted the judge.

"For a while now, the wolves have been living with my daughter and me. This was done out of necessity until I could find someplace more suitable near the mountain range where they were born. Ideally, we need a ranch or someone who's willing to take in the wolves for a time while the pack is gradually familiarized with their natural surroundings."

"So...what are you telling me?"

"I haven't been able to locate anyone around that part of Teton County who's willing to help us. The ranchers and other people I've talked to either don't want to be bothered or are fearful of wolves in general. There's a great deal of mistrust of wolves that's sadly the result of ancient myths and legends. It's been hard to overcome some of the unfounded misconceptions folks have, especially among the cattlemen and sheepherders, who see them as a threat to their livelihood."

Dr. Irwin stood up. "If I may interject, Your Honor."

"Go ahead," said the judge.

"The latest census indicates there are more than enough wolves already roaming the area in question," said Dr. Irwin. "And it's clear Officer Cortez's plan has failed already because the people who live in the region don't want them and—"

"Your Honor, there are only eleven breeding pairs and less than a hundred and fifty wolves outside Yellowstone, south of the national park," interrupted Ray. "In the area where these pups were born, there are currently only three known wolf packs, whose territories sometimes overlap. I don't think any reasonable person would construe numbers like these to mean there are too many wolves. If anything, it means they're still extremely rare.

"I should also add that the biggest threat to the wolf population in the Tetons and elsewhere continues to be man. As an apex predator, the wolf plays an important role in keeping the natural world's ecosystem in harmonious balance. We need to learn to live among the wolves, educate the public, and protect wolves from the kind of shameful government experimentation and exploitation Dr. Irwin and his colleagues have in mind."

"Officer Cortez was asked to provide this court with a written plan, and he didn't do it," said Dr. Irwin. "Your Honor, our team of research scientists can make much better use of these wolves. They'd be invaluable to helping advance our understanding of wolves in general."

Judge Dupree again turned to Ray. "Dr. Irwin is correct when he says you failed to provide a detailed plan or anything in writing regarding how you intend to reintroduce these wolves back into the wild. Based on what you've told me just now, it sounds like you've reached a wall, and you're still unsure how to solve the problem." He paused. "Officer Cortez, it's clear to me you don't have the necessary resources to properly care for these wolves much longer. They're going to outgrow your home in Jackson if they haven't already. It saddens me to say this, but the time to have figured out a workable solution was prior to arriving here today. You've run out of time."

Valeria stood up. "Can I say something?"

"Yes, you may," the judge responded.

"These wolves belong to me, and they're not pets," said Valeria. "They're family."

"She means they've bonded to her," said Ray. "When their mother died, the pups became attached to my daughter. She and the six wolves have been nearly inseparable."

Judge Dupree went to say something, but Valeria interrupted him. "Their mother, a beautiful white wolf named Gypsy, saved my life, and when she later died, I made a promise to take care of her pups," she said. "What's in my heart for them doesn't need to be put in writing. I love them, and they love me. My father and I are trying hard to do what's best for them, and it's not fair that the government and army want to take a piece of our family away from us. They're interfering with our lives, and I don't care what their reasons are–it's just not fair."

A number of onlookers whispered back and forth. When their voices merged and suddenly grew louder, the judge banged his gavel. "Order!" he said sternly. "Order in the court!"

Once the commotion settled down, Judge Dupree addressed Valeria directly. "I sympathize. I truly do, but my job is to listen to all sides and evaluate the various facts as they're presented to me. I can see you're very attached to these wolves. That's understandable, given the unique circumstance in which the animals came into your life, but I'm required by law to be objective and follow certain criteria. I cannot make decisions based on matters of the heart."

Judge Dupree took a few moments to glance through some papers in front of him. The courtroom was dead quiet. Then he looked up. "Officer Cortez, you were asked to submit a workable proposal to this court regarding how you intend to deal with these six orphaned wolves going forward, and you've failed to provide one. For that reason, I have no choice but to rule in favor of the FD—"

From somewhere in the room, a voice cried, "Wait!"

Valeria, Ray, and everyone at the other table turned to see who it was. The judge paused.

The interruption had come from the elderly woman sitting beside Butch Hardin. With help from Butch, the lady stood up. "May I approach the bench?" she asked loudly.

A noisy murmuring erupted in the courtroom. Judge Dupree hammered his gavel several times. "Order!" he yelled. When things again quieted down, he glared at the woman and asked, "And who might you be?"

"My name is Eleanor Hardin. I own Goshawk Pass Ranch in Teton County," she answered. "I have the land and resources the Cortez family needs to finish what they started." She looked at Valeria and Ray and gave a little smile. "May I approach, Your Honor?"

"Yes, you may."

CHAPTER 15

On the front steps outside her house, Valeria finished lacing her new pair of rollerblades and stood up. She skated over to Lauren, who was standing on the sidewalk, wearing old-fashioned roller skates and holding the wolves' leads.

"Here you go," said Lauren. "Why don't you take the girls today? I'll take the boys." She separated three of the leads and handed them to Valeria.

"Okay," said Valeria. "I can't believe this is the last time we'll be doing this."

It was now mid-August, more than a month since the court hearing. A few stray clouds hovered in the early-morning sky, which otherwise was a deep, vivid blue. There wasn't a trace of a breeze anywhere.

The wolves took notice of who had whom, and down the sidewalk, they went at a brisk pace, pulling Valeria and Lauren along behind them like they were sled dogs. The pack knew the preferred route by heart, stopped at intersections when told to, veered off into the street to avoid people blocking the sidewalk, and, in general, followed verbal commands and firm tugs on the leads, though there were times when one or more of them wouldn't.

Out front, leading everyone, was Roxie, the largest of the three females. Roxie insisted on being first in most everything the pack did and could be stubborn and a bit aggressive if she didn't get her way. Her dominance over the other five wolves–she ate first, won every tussle over favorite playthings like bones and pelts, etc.–seldom wavered. The young wolf was emerging as the female alpha in the pack's hierarchy.

Valeria and Lauren crisscrossed downtown Jackson, stopping now and then to talk to shopkeepers, who'd come out to say hello and pose for pictures and selfies with tourists. Families with children were always excited to see the wolves, whose celebrity in the area was on the rise.

"Can I pet them?" asked one little girl, standing beside her mother and father. According to the girl's father, they'd been told by a receptionist at the hotel where they'd been staying when the wolves would be passing by on their morning jog, getting exercise.

"No, sorry," said Valeria. "I wish you could, but these are wild wolves, and I'm not sure how they'll respond. I don't want you to get hurt."

"They're a lot bigger than I thought they'd be," the mother commented.

Valeria's father had been right. In a relatively short time and much quicker than Valeria had expected, the pups had matured to the point where they were now nearly indistinguishable from adult wolves. They were taller and had gained a significant amount of weight. Their thick and lustrous gray coats, interspersed with white and tan markings, shimmered in the sunlight.

Valeria, Lauren, and the wolves continued on. After an hour-and-a-half or so jaunt through the town, they circled back to Jackson Town Square, where they passed under one of the four magnificent arches made of elk antlers and stopped to rest beside the Veterans Memorial Monument, located in the center of the park.

More tourists approached with questions and took photos. A few of the townspeople out for a stroll also waved and said hello as they passed near the square.

Hazel pulled up in her car and got out. "I dropped off some fresh meat at the house, hoping to catch you there before you left," she said, walking toward them. After everyone exchanged hellos, she added, "Your father told me where I might find you. I just wanted to say goodbye to the wolves in case this is the last time I get to see them."

The wolves recognized Hazel immediately as "the lady who brings meat" and responded enthusiastically to her presence. They took turns sniffing Hazel's hands and nuzzling her legs. She adored the pups, and it was clear they felt the same way about her. From the day they'd first arrived on the scene, Hazel had lent a helping hand and established her own special bond with them. She was one of the few people still allowed to come in close contact and interact with the pack.

After giving each wolf a quick hug, Hazel said, "Ray asked me to tell you both that he's loaded up the trucks and ready to get rolling." She turned to Valeria and gave her a hug as well. "I packed sandwiches for everyone in case you get hungry and stop somewhere on your way."

"Thank you," said Valeria. "You're the best."

Hazel smiled. "You're most welcome. Well, I really don't have a lot of time to chitchat today and need to get back to the Silver Beaver. Take care."

Valeria and Lauren waved to her as she drove off, then got back up on their skates.

"We'd better head to the house," said Lauren.

Fifteen minutes later, they arrived. Ray was waiting for them out front.

"I loaded up your suitcases, Val, and most of the wolves' supplies. You need to go in the house, and after you change out of your skates, do me a favor and look around to see if I missed anything," he said. "Since the wolves are too big to all ride in one vehicle, half can ride with me, and you and the others can ride with Lauren. I'll lead the way. You two can follow me in the Jeep."

It was a little past noon when they passed under the decorative archway and onto Goshawk Pass Ranch. Valeria closed the wrought iron entry gate behind them and got back in the Jeep. She hadn't seen the ranch since that fateful wintry day in March, and it looked much different. The air was warm, and the fields were green. There were large herds of cattle, busy eating the lush grass, dispersed over a broad area, and men in cowboy hats milling about near the outbuildings and barn.

Lauren parked next to Ray's truck, close to the ranch house. The wolves were left in the vehicles for a minute while they got out.

A booming voice called out, "They're here!" It sounded like Butch Hardin, but when Valeria looked up, he or whoever it was had gone into the house. She heard a screen door slam shut.

"Let's get the wolves out of the trucks," said Ray. "It's too hot to leave them in there for long."

He helped Valeria and Lauren tie off the wolves by their leads to a couple of nearby fence posts.

The screen door again slammed. "Hello there," called out another voice. "It's good to see some new faces around here." Everyone looked up from what they were doing. It was Eleanor Hardin walking toward them with her cane.

Butch had a hold of his mother's arm. "Let go of me!" she yelled at him. "I'm not an invalid, damn it!"

Ray walked over to her and extended his hand. "Good afternoon, Mrs. Hardin," he said. "How are you doing today?"

"I'm doing fine, Officer Cortez. The only thing I have a little trouble with is getting up and down," she answered. "But you should see me ride a horse." She turned to Lauren. "It's good to see you, Dr. Ross."

"You, too," Lauren responded, smiling.

Eleanor turned her attention to Valeria. "I must say, Ray, you have the most extraordinary daughter." She extended her hand to Valeria. "I've been so looking forward to spending time with you, dear. You're one impressive young lady."

Valeria couldn't help but smile. She softly shook the elderly woman's hand. "Thank you, Mrs. Hardin."

"My friends call me Eleanor. Use that, okay?"

"Yes, ma'am."

Eleanor motioned to Butch to come stand closer to her, and when he did, she punched his arm. "Did you even bother to tip your hat and show some proper respect?"

"I'm sorry," said Butch. "I forgot." He took a step forward, bowed slightly, and tipped his cowboy hat to Lauren and Valeria. "Greetings, and my apologies."

Eleanor glared at her son and frowned. "I swear," she muttered, "just when you think you raised them right."

Ray went to the back of his truck and popped open the tailgate to retrieve Valeria's suitcases and bags. "We appreciate you doing this," he said.

"You're more than welcome," said Eleanor. Then, turning to Butch, she added, "Make yourself useful and go help Ray take Miss Val's things into the house."

Butch walked over to where Ray was standing with the cases. On his way, he came within a few feet of the wolves lying near the fence posts, and two of them sat up and growled at him.

"Damn rotten wolves," groaned Butch half under his breath, just loud enough for everyone to hear.

While Ray and Butch were busy taking Valeria's things into the house, Eleanor said, "Ladies, gather up your beasts and let me show you to their five-star accommodations."

Valeria and Lauren untied the wolves and hurried to catch

up with Eleanor, who was headed toward several outbuildings, moving along at a quicker pace than they expected. They quietly walked behind her.

Without looking back, Eleanor said, "I know the wolves have been sleeping with you for some time now, Val. Your father explained the routines you and they are accustomed to." She paused for a moment and looked Valeria in the eyes. "You've been the one constant in these wolves' lives, but if we're going to succeed in reintroducing this pack back into the wild, we need to wean them from your presence. It won't be easy, but it must be done."

Valeria listened but didn't respond. The idea that she'd soon be separated from the wolves and no longer a part of their day-to-day lives was difficult to think about. She was more than just a little attached to them, and they to her. She loved them with all her heart.

Some distance beyond one of the outbuildings, where several men were working, Eleanor stopped at a large pen with a tall welded wire fence around it. There, Valeria saw a good-size lean-to made of wood inside the pen with a sloped tin roof.

"This was an old pigpen, which I had some of the men convert," said Eleanor. "A few years ago, we decided to add pigs to our rotation of livestock. I don't remember whose idea it was, but we stopped raising them after a couple of seasons because I could never get used to the wretched smell.

"I had the pigpen renovated for the wolves." She paused and pointed at a number of details. "The old wood fence was replaced with this new one, which is much higher, and a layer of coarse rocks was poured around the perimeter, under the fence, to prevent the wolves from digging their way out. There's also a new trough, which I had installed close to the fence, so it can be filled with fresh drinking water, using a hose or bucket, without anyone having to step inside the pen with the wolves."

Butch approached with Ray following a few steps behind.

Ray leaned over the fence to the converted pen and took a look around. "Very impressive."

Just then, the ranch hand named Sam and another man, both a bit dirty and wearing cowboy hats, showed up, pushing two wheelbarrows filled with sections of a carcass. Valeria recognized the cuts of meat–it was venison from an adult elk. Sam opened the gate, and they went inside and dumped the meat in an open area of the pen.

After the two men finished the task and walked back out, Eleanor looked at Valeria and said, "This is a necessary step. The wolves will be fine here." Seeing Valeria's hesitation, she placed her hand on the girl's shoulder and added, "Go ahead, dear. Lead them in and take off their leashes."

Lauren helped Valeria get the wolves settled in their new surroundings. The leads were removed, and after a few minutes, the two quietly left the pen. The gate was closed, and the wolves, led by Roxie, rushed to the venison and began eating.

Everyone turned to leave, all except Valeria, who stood peering through the fence, transfixed. This was going to be much harder than she imagined. She called to the wolves, and one of the boys, Zeus, got up and came over to nuzzle her hand before returning to his meal, followed by Scout. They were the same two who'd growled at Butch. Soon after, each of the others did the same. The last was Roxie.

"Have you seen Jesse?" asked Eleanor.

She and the others were walking back to the ranch house.

"No," said Butch. "I haven't seen that boy all day."

"Well, have one of the men go find my grandson," she replied. "We're getting ready to have lunch, and I want him back here on the double. Tell whoever you send looking for him, I said so."

As they approached the house and their vehicles, Lauren said, "I really should be heading out."

"Nonsense!" said Eleanor. "I insist you sit and dine with us, Dr. Ross, before you leave. You too, Ray."

They followed her into the rustic-looking ranch house and were led through its main rooms, which had lovely open spaces with lofty exposed beams and high ceilings and were filled with the most elegant western decor. The huge kitchen looked to have been updated in recent years with expensive high-end appliances, and in the center of the home was a magnificent stone fireplace.

Valeria noticed one other detail right away. There were no preserved animal skins draped over any of the furniture or on the floor, and no stuffed heads on the walls such as elk, deer, or other wild animals like she'd seen in some shops and homes around Jackson. A very beautiful chandelier fashioned out of elk antlers hung from the ceiling of a large dining room, but since elk, deer, and moose shed their antlers annually during the winter, it couldn't be construed as offensive to the sensibilities of animal lovers, like herself, who disliked the hunting and killing of wildlife for sport.

The rear of the home had floor-to-ceiling windows looking out over a wide expanse of lush grazing land and rolling mountains in the distance. Eleanor led them through a pair of French doors and onto a veranda, where a long table was stylishly set with fancy crystal glassware and sterling silverware for lunch.

"Come sit next to me, Miss Val," said Eleanor.

Everyone was seated, with Eleanor at one end and Ray at the other. Directly across from Valeria was a place setting for one more person and an empty chair. Knowing who it was for, she cringed.

"You have a lovely home," said Ray.

"Yes, it's absolutely gorgeous," added Lauren. "And what a nice view this is, too."

"Thank you," Eleanor responded. "It's not what most people expect, I think, especially way out here in the hinterland..."

The French doors opened, and out walked Jesse, his cowboy hat in his hands and hair ruffled. He looked sweaty and a little out of breath.

"The house has been remodeled and expanded several times over the years," Eleanor added. Turning to her grandson, she asked, "Where have you been?"

"Out riding," Jesse answered. He threw his cowboy hat, like he was pitching horseshoes, in the direction of two old rocking chairs sitting side by side about fifteen feet away. The hat came to rest on one of the rocking chair's seats.

Jesse sat across from Valeria, glanced at her, and smirked.

Valeria became angry the minute she laid eyes on him. She'd discussed staying with the Hardin family with her father for weeks beforehand and understood the reality of the situation. For the sake of the wolf pups' lives, it was imperative that she squash her deep-rooted negative feelings toward Jesse, at least for a while anyway. Otherwise, her babies, the wolves, would be turned over to the FDA and government per the judge's orders. She didn't have any choice but to accept the arrangement and had thought she could go through it, but now she wasn't so sure. Just the sight of Jesse made her blood boil. She hated him…*hated* him.

Valeria's hands were clenched in her lap. Glaring at Jesse and his smug expression, she wanted very much to reach across the table and punch him in the face like she'd done at the Silver Beaver, or get up and leave. Then she felt someone reach over and gently touch her arm. It was Eleanor who must have anticipated there might be trouble.

Eleanor leaned over and whispered to Valeria, "Be patient, dear. I know what he did." She smiled, then added, "Something like that won't happen again."

A clean-cut cowboy wearing a white apron came out and placed two large plates of fresh sourdough rolls and homemade whipped butter on the table. He then stood next to Eleanor.

"The rolls smell heavenly," said Lauren.

"Thank you," said the cowboy. "Is everyone ready?"

"Yes, we are," answered Eleanor. Turning to Ray and Lauren, she added, "Giuseppe hails from Denver. He's a trained professional chef who gave up cooking in fancy big city restaurants to become a cowboy."

"It was my dream," said Giuseppe, smiling.

Giuseppe went back into the house and returned with a pitcher of ice water. After filling all the glasses, he announced which cuts of steak were available, the various vegetables, and other gourmet side dishes he'd prepared. Then, starting with Eleanor, he went around the table, taking everyone's individual order, thanking each person, and committing it to memory, much like a waiter would do in a more refined restaurant.

Valeria opted for a simple cheeseburger, seasoned fries, and a soda.

"An excellent choice," Giuseppe responded.

Before long, the meal was served, and at first, not much was said other than small talk about the current price of cattle, the warm weather, and speculation about the coming autumn and winter. Valeria continued to glare at Jesse, who seemed to be ignoring her completely.

Afterward, while Giuseppe cleared the dishes and readied the table for dessert, Ray turned to Eleanor. "We can't thank you enough for offering to help with the wolves," he said. "I know I speak for Val also when I say it means a great deal to us."

"You're more than welcome."

"I don't understand why we're doing it!" interrupted Jesse. "I mean, why? There's already plenty of wolves around here, causing trouble. Instead of dumping more of them bastards right outside our back door, we should be getting rid of the ones still close by."

"I have to agree with Jesse," chimed in Butch. "It's hard enough to run a successful cattle ranch without having to constantly worry about wild predators killing off part of the herd and cutting into our bottom line.

"I've only agreed to go along with this madness out of respect for my mother," he added. "It was entirely her idea, not mine. I'll make the best of it, Ray, but if I had my choice, there wouldn't be a wolf near our ranch for a hundred miles, not a live one anyway."

For a moment, everyone went silent. The only sound was the clanking of plates and silverware being cleared from the table.

Then Eleanor said calmly, "Will you excuse us, Giuseppe?"

"Yes, ma'am." The cowboy chef quietly went into the house and closed the French doors behind him.

Eleanor reached for her cane, which was leaning against her chair, laid it on the table in front of her, and rose to her feet. Once up, she grabbed the cane and smacked Jesse hard across the chest with it.

"How infuriating!" she yelled. "It's not enough that you almost got this young lady killed, but you have the nerve to sit before her with that stupid rotten attitude of yours!"

Jesse looked stunned. He stared at his grandmother somewhat blank faced. The smirk was gone. He didn't move.

"Now, before another word comes out of your mouth, boy, you'll apologize to Valeria for what you did and the harm you caused her."

"What happened was an accident," Jesse stammered. "It wasn't my fault…"

"Shut up!" Eleanor shouted. She jabbed Jesse in the chest with her cane. "Not another word! Apologize!"

"I didn't—"

"Apologize!" Eleanor shook her fist at him. "Stand up! You're going to accept responsibility for your foolishness like a man. I said, stand up!"

Jesse pushed his chair back and stood. Without looking directly at Valeria, he muttered, "I'm sorry."

Eleanor slammed her cane on the table. "Like you mean it! Ask her to forgive you."

Jesse glanced at his father with pleading eyes as if silently asking for help, which didn't come, then down at his feet before raising his head and looking directly into Valeria's eyes. He took a deep breath. "I apologize for any harm I've caused you," he said. "I didn't know the pony would bolt. I didn't know you were up on its back, but it's no excuse. I was careless and not thinking about what might happen if I took a shot." He stopped.

"And?" said his grandmother.

"I apologize for what I said about the wolves," he added. "I didn't realize how much they meant to you, especially the white one you call Gypsy. We don't name wolves around here, but I should have stopped to think about your feelings before I spoke." He hesitated for a moment. "Please forgive me."

Everyone was quiet for a moment.

"That was a little better," said Eleanor. "Not the best apology you could've done, but much better." She turned to Butch. "And you!"

"What did I do?"

"Madness? Madness! You're as big a fool as your son!" she said, her voice rising several octaves. "Our family has worked this land since the late eighteen hundreds, and our livelihood isn't the least bit in jeopardy because of wolves! The only time we've had an issue is during the winter months when their natural prey in the wild is in short supply. Even so, you can count on one hand the number of cows we've ever lost in any given year.

"And damn it all, Butch! The state reimburses us, like

some kind of charity case, for any cow or other animal we lose to the wolves." Eleanor paused. "So here's what I have to say to you, son, about wolves and our so-called bottom line. If the wolves kill a few of our livestock now and then out of necessity, so what?"

A few moments later, the veranda now very quiet, Giuseppe opened the French doors and came back out, smiling. "Is everyone ready for dessert?" he asked.

Outside by the Jeep and truck, Valeria gave Lauren a hug.

"Stay safe, okay?" said Lauren. "And good luck."

"I will, and thank you."

Ray kissed Valeria's cheek. "Remember, we have until roughly the end of October to reintroduce the wolf pack into the wild," he said. "It's up to you now to see that it happens. If we fail, Judge Dupree has made it clear he'll allow Dr. Irwin and his researchers at the FDA to confiscate them."

"I understand, Dad," said Valeria. "I'll do my best."

"I'm afraid it might be more difficult than we think to get the pups to return to the wilderness. Let's hope they'll cooperate for their own sake," said Ray. "I'll be by regularly, two or three times a week, to check on things and shuttle your schoolwork back and forth.

"And remember, the Hardin family didn't have to do this for us. It's their home and their rules. Keep that in mind," he added. "So, stay calm and try to get along with everyone. When you can, be sure to thank them for their hospitality and effort. And promise me you'll do whatever they tell you to do."

"Okay," said Valeria. "I promise."

After a few more hugs and kisses, Ray and Lauren got into their vehicles, waved goodbye, and drove off.

CHAPTER 16

The wolves took turns howling well into the night, keeping Valeria wide awake as she tried to fall asleep in the charming guest bedroom that had been readied for her stay. She tossed and turned fitfully. When, at last, the morning sun poked its bright head above the horizon, she climbed out from underneath the soft bedsheets, groggy. It was the first time in months she'd slept alone, separated from her babies, and her mind raced with uneasy thoughts about them having to remain outdoors in the converted pigpen without her near.

Valeria got dressed, anxious to go check on them, but was stopped at the front door by Giuseppe, who ushered her to a breakfast bar near the kitchen.

"Come sit and have breakfast," he said. The smell of bacon, sausage, and eggs was in the air. "I've made you a citrus smoothie to start off with."

"I'm not very hungry," said Valeria, hesitant to sit down before checking on the wolves.

"I have my instructions," Giuseppe countered. "Mrs. Hardin made it clear that I'm not to let you leave until you've eaten something."

Valeria hopped up on a stool. "Where is she?"

Giuseppe set the smoothie, complete with garnish and a straw, in front of her. "She's gone to tack up a couple of the horses." He walked over to the stove. "How do you like your eggs?"

"Scrambled." The smoothie was delicious.

Valeria devoured everything Giuseppe put before her, then headed outdoors, straight to the wolves' pen. She was halfway there when Eleanor came riding up beside her atop an attractive Appaloosa, mostly chestnut with white markings.

"Good morning, Val," said Eleanor.

Before Valeria could respond, the horse whinnied. "Ah yes, this is Annabelle," Eleanor added. "She wants to say hello too, or maybe she thinks you might have an apple. She likes treats."

Valeria returned their greetings. "Good morning."

"Whoa," said Eleanor, bringing the horse to a stop. She extended a hand to Valeria. "Be a dear, will you, and help me get down."

Valeria assisted Eleanor off Annabelle. The two then walked side by side the rest of the way to the pen, with Eleanor leading the horse behind her by its reins.

"I know I'm repeating myself, but I must say again how very impressed I am," said Eleanor.

"How do you mean?" asked Valeria, perplexed.

"Nothing says 'I miss you, I need you, I love you' like a pack of wolves howling," Eleanor replied, then laughed. "I've never heard such sheer devotion for someone in my life. Clearly, this litter has elevated you to a kind of surrogate alpha presence in their lives."

They reached the pen, where Eleanor wrapped the horse's reins loosely around a corner post of the fence. "Thank goodness the wolves eventually wore themselves out," she continued, smiling. "For half the night, nothing short of allowing you to sleep in the pigpen with them was going to quiet them. I didn't think the howls would stop. Just so you know, we have quite a few grumpy cowboys wandering around in a daze this morning, as well as some skittish cows." She laughed hard. "It'll take a little time for everyone to adjust."

Valeria opened the gate to the pen and went in. The first to nuzzle her legs were Scout and Zeus, followed by two of the girls, Tess and Yoko, then Diesel. Not surprisingly, the last to greet her was Roxie. Soon, though, all six were swarming her.

"I've missed you guys too," said Valeria, sweetly.

A half hour passed. With Eleanor looking on just outside the fence, Valeria showered each wolf with as much one-on-one attention as she could, until two ranch hands arrived with another butchered elk carcass. The moment the young wolves smelled its approach, they turned their backs to Valeria, and she quietly retreated from the pen as the large sections of venison were being laid down.

The men had just closed the pen's gate behind them when Sam came walking up. He tipped his hat to both women. "'Morning, ladies," he said before turning to Mrs. Hardin. "The other horse has been saddled up like you asked, ma'am."

"Very good," said Eleanor. "We'll be there in a few minutes."

Sam, along with the other two men pushing their wheelbarrows, headed off in the general direction of the main barn.

From the other side of the fence, Valeria, with Eleanor beside her, lingered for a time and watched the wolves eat. There was an occasional growl and baring of teeth over choice pieces of meat, but for the most part, the siblings cooperated, the carcass was divvied up, and everyone ate.

"They're incredible, don't you think?" said Valeria.

"Yes. Wolves are glorious creatures–intelligent, powerful, and feared," Eleanor responded with a sigh. "I've always had great respect for them, ever since I was a young girl."

"Is it true, years ago, hunters killed all the wolves in

America?" asked Valeria. "My father tells me there weren't any, not a one, in Jackson Hole and the Tetons until sometime after nineteen ninety-five, when a few were brought back to Yellowstone National Park from Canada."

For a moment or two, Eleanor appeared to be lost in thought. She was slow to answer. "Long before I was born right here on this ranch, Wyoming passed a law. Anyone caught freeing a wolf from a trap was fined three hundred dollars." She again paused. "This is the world I inherited and understood. Wolves were despised by everyone who raised livestock.

"History books say the last gray wolves in the area, two pups found in Yellowstone, were killed by park rangers in nineteen twenty-six. The fact is a few stray wolves, now and then, continued to wander through this area for many years afterward, but the encounters were short-lived and not important enough to report to the authorities."

Eleanor gazed at the wolves, eating, and stopped for a moment. "I remember the first time I heard a wolf howl. It was early one evening in April, not far from here. I was still quite young, and it gave me chills. Then, a few days later, I saw him. It was a foggy morning. I'd finished some chores and was coming out of the barn. He was standing there, not more than ten feet away, staring at me with those amber eyes. I froze, and we both looked at each other for the longest time. I didn't shout or say a word. He was huge, but for whatever reason, I wasn't scared. After two or three minutes, he ran off and disappeared into the mist. He never came back, and I never told anyone. The men would've hunted him down with traps, and I didn't want him hurt."

"That's a wonderful story," said Valeria.

"For years, I listened for the wolf's return, and there were times I thought I heard him moving through the forest or howling in the distance, and I'd get excited. But it was only ever the wind blowing across the mountains, the leaves on the trees rustling, and the streams flowing." Eleanor turned to Valeria and smiled. "You're the first person I've shared this with."

"Thank you for telling me." Valeria returned the elderly woman's smile.

They continued to watch the wolves for a few more minutes. Then Eleanor grabbed the horse's reins and said, "Come! We've got a lot of work to do if we're going to succeed in reintroducing your wolves back into the wild where they belong."

One of the ranch hands brought a quarter horse from the main barn to a field, free of cattle, near the house. He also fetched a mounting block, which was a kind of stepping stool designed to make it easier for a young or inexperienced rider to get up on the horse's saddle.

He handed the horse's reins to Jesse, set the mounting block on the ground beside the horse, and headed back to the barn.

Jesse motioned for Valeria, who was standing nearby, to come over to the horse and step up on the block. Seeing she was hesitant, he said, "Well, come on. He's saddled and waiting for you."

Close by, Eleanor watched from atop Annabelle. "This is one of the more laid-back horses we have," she told Valeria. "His name is Zeke. He's getting up in years and prefers to go slow. He doesn't much like to race around anymore like some of the younger stallions."

Valeria couldn't get out of her head what had happened to her that fateful day in March when the pony threw her into the ravine, and she nearly died. As a result of the fall, she'd developed a strong distrust of horses.

Ray had tried to help his daughter prepare for the fear she'd inevitably face. "You'll need to learn to ride a horse like

Jesse and the others at the ranch. Otherwise, there's little chance we'll be able to return the wolves to the wild," he explained. "The pups' original territory is a good hour to two hours' ride on horseback in one direction, too far away to hike back and forth on foot to every day, and unfortunately, there are no roads of any kind to facilitate transporting them in and out of the area. Getting the wolves acclimated back into their natural environment will be a process, and they have the stamina to trek such long distances over and over, if necessary, but you won't be able to. And we both already know the surrounding terrain is too vast and dangerous, especially if the weather turns ugly."

Valeria walked over to the mounting block and stood on the top step.

"Put your left foot in the stirrup, stand up, and swing your leg over," said Jesse.

Gripped with fear, Valeria felt her whole body trembling. She couldn't move. "I don't think I can do it."

"Just take a deep breath and relax your mind," said Eleanor. "We won't let anything happen to you."

"I can't do this."

"It's okay." Eleanor maneuvered Annabelle a little closer to Zeke. "Take your time."

Valeria closed her eyes for a moment and thought about her mother, who somehow, through the wolves, had saved her and the promise she'd made to Philip that she'd return the wolves to their birthplace. She looked over at Jesse, whose annoyed expression reeked of arrogance, and Eleanor, always tough, wise, confident, and calm. Valeria took a few breaths, placed her foot in the stirrup, and swung her leg over the horse. Zeke didn't flinch.

Jesse handed Zeke's reins to Valeria, and Eleanor brought Annabelle up alongside her.

"I'm proud of you," said Eleanor. "The next time your father comes, we need him to bring you a better pair of boots and some more jeans." She reached over and adjusted Valeria's hold on the reins. "Loosen your grip a little, sit more upright, and relax. Jesse and I will teach you everything you need to know about riding and controlling a horse. How do you feel?"

"I'm still nervous," said Valeria.

Eleanor stroked Zeke's nose, then moved her horse a few feet farther away to give him space. "Good boy," she said. "Now I'll explain and show you the basics on how to walk, stop, and steer him while we walk our horses together at a slow pace."

For the next few hours and with Jesse looking on, Valeria followed Eleanor's instructions. Eventually, she was able to get Zeke to walk, turn, and stop on command, simply by using her legs and reins properly. She even worked her way up to a steady trot and kept up with Annabelle and Eleanor all around the field. As time wore on, her confidence increased, and gradually, she felt more and more comfortable riding until she'd all but forgotten that she'd ever been afraid.

CHAPTER 17

That night, Valeria had a dream. Eleanor's wolf had been trapped by hunters. Somehow, they'd learned of her encounter outside the barn. The hunters, a ragtag-looking group of local men, approached the snarling wolf cautiously, its leg caught in a snare, and encircled it. Grinning, they raised and cocked their rifles in unison like a firing squad. Just as they were about to pull their triggers, Eleanor emerged, a young girl surrounded by morning mist. She'd secretly followed the hunters deep into the mountains. When she saw the wolf lying on the ground, weak and defenseless, its leg bleeding, and its amber eyes staring up at her, pleading, she screamed and threw herself in front of it. The men fired.

There was a deafening boom that echoed across the heavens and then absolute stillness.

From somewhere in the forest, Philip could be heard singing softly, "Fair is the white star of twilight..."

Valeria woke up sweating.

The hired men who worked on the ranch never seemed to be in much of a hurry, though they never stopped moving. They herded the cattle, rotating them to different pastures in order to give the cows and calves fresh grass to munch on and fertilize the soil. When need be, they provided basic veterinary care to sick or injured cows and aided heifers during the birthing process. There were fences to be mended, hay bales to be gathered, horses to be shod, and equipment that needed to be maintained and repaired. The work was often strenuous, demanding good stamina and perseverance. For most of the ranch hands, their days began before sunup and ended long after dusk.

In addition, Eleanor had assigned two men to hunt elk and keep a refrigerated stockpile of venison on hand for the wolves.

When Valeria wasn't busy spending time with the wolves, doing her schoolwork remotely, or learning to ride a horse, she enjoyed observing all the activities on the ranch. As a rule, she kept her distance so as not to interfere with the men and their duties, but she helped out with certain things like brushing down the horses and cleaning their stalls if Eleanor asked her to or said it was okay.

On his days off and whenever he could, Ray came to visit his daughter. He brought Valeria a more durable pair of riding boots and shuttled her school assignments and tests back and forth. The wolves' progress was discussed with Butch and Eleanor, as well as various strategies that might help hasten the pack's return to its native habitat. In general, though, there was little he could do but offer his opinions and advice. No one had ever attempted to reintroduce orphaned wolf pups back into the wild before, and there were no proven ideas they could replicate. The only useful research information he was able to find involved the capture and relocation of wild wolves by biologists. These had been mature wolves that already knew how to hunt and interact.

One unexpected problem soon arose, however, that had the potential to derail everything. The wolves had yet to be allowed to venture anywhere outside the pen. The reason: whenever anyone other than Valeria came near the pack, one or more of the wolves growled and showed clear signs of agitation and aggression. The young pack only tolerated the two men who brought them fresh venison each day.

Valeria and Ray were inside the pen, spending time with the wolves during one of his visits, while Eleanor and Jesse looked on from outside.

"It's been nearly three weeks," said Ray. "When was the last time the wolves were allowed to roam around freely with Val and able to get some exercise?"

"They haven't been outside this old pigpen since the day you first brought them here," Eleanor answered. "We've been afraid if any of them got loose, someone might get hurt. We're not sure what to do next. I was going to have Jesse assist Valeria in leading the wolves out into the mountains, but they bare their teeth at him every time he tries to step into the pen or comes near."

"That suits me just fine," said Jesse. "I don't want anything to do with them either."

"Hush!" said Eleanor.

"I don't understand it. They never displayed this type of intimidating behavior in Jackson," Ray responded. "I do agree with your need for caution, though, because it's a bit disturbing. The last thing we need is for anyone to be mauled or worse. I wish I had an easy answer for this, but I don't, and we can only speculate as to the reasons for the change; maybe the sudden move out here to a new environment was too fast and created heightened anxiety collectively within the pack, or perhaps it has something to do with their attachment to Valeria being threatened. I'm not sure."

Valeria listened to what Eleanor and her father were saying but didn't initially add her own thoughts for fear she'd only make matters worse. She'd seen firsthand the marked change in the wolves' temperament toward nearly everyone except those who'd helped raise them and had become increasingly alarmed by their behavior. She'd ignored it up to until now, mostly because their antagonism was never meant for her, but she was starting to realize if the pack didn't stop, it would jeopardize any chance they had to live free in the wild, free from confinement, free from the men who'd exploit them…free…free… With all her heart, she wanted them to be free.

She made her way over to Roxie and stroked the strong-willed wolf's back, feeling the coarse texture of her thick fur. Then the answer came to her, a simple way to defuse the wolves' hostility toward others. Valeria remembered something Philip had once told her and immediately knew what to do.

"I think I've figured it out," Valeria announced.

"What is it?" asked Ray. "What have you figured out?"

"I know why the wolves are scaring off other people and how to stop them from doing it." Valeria walked over and opened the gate. "Let's leave them alone for a few minutes, Dad. I want to try something."

They both left the pen. Once outside, Valeria turned to Jesse and said, "You're going to be my guinea pig." She looked him in the eyes and smiled. "Since we know the pack dislikes you, you're the perfect person to help me prove a point."

"What the hell are you talking about?" asked Jesse. "Prove what?"

"You'll see." Valeria unlatched the gate. "Step inside and just stand there."

Backing away, Jesse raised his voice, "There's no way!" He glanced at his grandmother, who came and stood stoically by his side but said nothing. "I'm not going anywhere near them. They'll tear me apart."

"Are you afraid?" asked Valeria, unable to hide the sarcasm in her voice. When Jesse didn't answer, she added, "Don't worry. I won't let them kill you."

Eleanor nudged Jesse. "Go on, boy. Man up."

Jesse glared at Valeria and then, brushing her aside, went and stood just inside the gate. She closed it behind him. "What now?" he asked.

"Wait," she answered. "Don't move. Let's see what they do."

The wolves reacted almost immediately. As soon as the gate was shut, several of them raised their heads, stared ominously at Jesse, and snarled. When Roxie, followed by Zeus and Scout, got to their feet and took several steps toward him, Jesse turned and jiggled the gate. "Let me out," he said.

Valeria unlatched it, and Jesse rushed out. Seeing he'd retreated, the three wolves paced the perimeter of the pen for a bit, still roused, before returning to their preferred spots in the dirt and lying back down.

Once the wolves appeared to be settled, Valeria again turned to Jesse. "Now, let's see if I'm right," she replied. "Put your arms around me."

"What?" blurted Jesse, confused. "Why?"

"Just shut up and hold me."

"No thanks. I'm not holding you."

With Ray and Eleanor looking on, Valeria stepped closer to Jesse. "I just want to test out my theory, and like it or not, you're going to help me," she said. "So, stop being a jerk and give me a hug." She leaned forward and wrapped her arms around his neck.

Grudgingly, Jesse gave in. He opened his arms and awkwardly embraced Valeria around her waist. "I don't understand," he muttered.

"You will." She laid her head against his shoulder.

Almost immediately, Jesse attempted to pull back, but Valeria held tight. "Don't be so quick to let go," she said.

Valeria glanced at her father, whose bewildered expression made it clear he had no clue what she was doing. "Are the wolves paying attention?" she asked.

"They don't appear to be," Ray answered.

"Good. It's better they don't see."

Eleanor chuckled. "Well, I wasn't expecting this."

"Me neither," said Ray.

Valeria held onto Jesse for two or three minutes. When she finally let go, he stumbled backward and nearly fell. He looked dazed.

"What the hell was all that about?" sputtered Jesse.

Quietly, Valeria went to the pen and cracked open the gate. "Now back in you go," she said with a smile. She was having fun watching Jesse squirm.

"No!" said Jesse. "Are you crazy? I'm not putting one foot back in there."

Valeria started to say something flippant, but her father interrupted, "I'm not sure exactly what's going on or what point you're trying to make, Val, but we shouldn't be asking Jesse to put himself in harm's way." Ray paused for a moment to glance at the wolves. "It's not safe for him to go in there alone. You're placing him at great risk of getting seriously bit or mauled. The wolves have made it clear they don't want Jesse anywhere near them, and things for the boy could turn deadly if the entire pack gangs up on him. They've already warned him."

"Trust me, Dad," said Valeria. "I know what I'm doing." She turned to Jesse. "You owe me, and you also owe these wolves. When you pulled out that rifle and shot and killed Gypsy, you made this day happen. These are her babies, and I ought to let them eat you, but you're safe from them now. I made sure."

"I don't owe you anything," Jesse replied. He turned his back to Valeria, took two or three steps to leave, and felt her tap his shoulder.

"Yeah, you do!" said Valeria. She grabbed Jesse by his shirt and yanked him back around. Her hands were clenched. "You either get back in that pen and help fix things, or I'm going to bloody your face with my fists and embarrass you in front of your grandmother."

This time, it was Eleanor who interrupted, "I have to confess, I'm at a loss, dear. What makes you think the wolves will react to Jesse any differently?"

"They will," answered Valeria. "You'll see."

Slapping Valeria's grip off his shirt, Jesse looked first at his grandmother, then Ray. He groaned and, without uttering another word, walked back to the gate and stepped inside. Valeria closed it behind him.

Nearly all the wolves instantly raised their heads. Jesse froze. Like she had earlier, Roxie was the first to jump to her feet, but the wolf's intentions were hard to read. She appeared to glare at him fiercely but didn't growl, nor was the hair on her back and neck raised.

"Be ready to let Jesse out," said Ray.

"Listen to me, Jesse," said Valeria. "You'll be fine. Just try not to freak out. You're too tense. Don't make any sudden movement and pretend the wolves aren't there. They need to know you're not afraid of them."

Jesse didn't move.

A minute passed, maybe two. At first, it appeared Roxie might lie back down, but then the large female slowly walked toward him. The other five stood and joined her.

"They're going to rip me apart," said Jesse, his voice shaky, his eyes fixed on Roxie. Reaching back for the latch on the gate, he turned to leave.

"Wait!" said Valeria. "Don't move!"

In the next breath, Roxie rushed at Jesse with the others close behind. There was no time to react.

Jesse screamed. His arms went up to try and block her.

"Somebody, save him!" yelled Eleanor, covering her eyes. "I can't look."

For a few moments, there was a struggle, followed by a bit

of confusion, and when it was over, Ray began to laugh. "Well, now, will you look at that?" he said.

Roxie had her front paws draped over Jesse's shoulders and was curiously sniffing his face and neck. The other wolves were taking turns circling his legs and brushing up against him.

Eleanor looked on in amazement. "How in the world do you explain that?"

"My scent is all over Jesse," said Valeria. "As long as he doesn't shower or do something else to get rid of my odor for a few days, he should be okay. From now on, they'll treat him like an honorary member of the pack."

Jesse remained very still and let the wolves finish sniffing.

CHAPTER 18

"Here she comes, the hugger," teased one of the ranch hands, an older man with a scruffy gray beard whose nickname was Big Duke.

Valeria dismounted Zeke, walked him to a fence line, and looped his reins over a rail. She patted the horse on the nose and laughed. "I'm not here for you," she said with a smile. "I'm after a couple of your buddies." A brisk morning wind whipped her hair.

"Aw, shucks," said Big Duke, tipping his hat to her. "Can I have another hug anyway?"

"Sure, you can." Valeria went over and gave the old cowboy a warm embrace. "I like hugging you, too."

Big Duke and several other men were separating calves from their mothers into a large corral, where the youngsters were to be vaccinated, branded, and ear tagged. Several skilled ropers waited nearby on horseback for the calves to be sorted so they could start the process of catching and getting them to the ground. In two to three hours, there'd be a shout of "all done," and the freshly branded calves would be released into a pasture to be reunited with their anxious moms.

Eleanor had asked Valeria to find and hug all the ranch hands as a precaution now that the wolves were being allowed out of the pen. As a result, the men had given her the nickname "Hugger."

"I know Santiago's been expecting you, Hugger," said Big Duke. "He's right over there with that grin on his face, ready and waiting." He chuckled. "I think you've hogtied everyone else."

Valeria cornered Santiago, a bushy haired, middle-aged man with a deep natural tan, and moved in to give him the required marathon hug. Afterward, he thanked her, "Gracias, señorita." He reached for her hand and gently kissed the back of it. "Till we meet again."

The other ranch hands laughed.

With the task finished, Valeria mounted Zeke and headed back to his stall. She was almost there, walking him along the dirt road leading to the barn, when she suddenly had to duck to the side of the road to let a speeding truck whiz past. It nearly hit them. Zeke reared up, but she held onto the reins, and he settled down quickly. The truck left them in a cloud of dust and came to a stop in front of the ranch house.

Valeria's first instinct was to chase after the driver and give him a piece of her mind, but since she was a guest at the ranch, she decided against making a scene. She dismounted Zeke outside the barn and started to lead him to his stall but stopped. Jesse was standing near the truck, talking to two rather large men dressed from head to toe in camouflage. She'd never seen the truck or men before.

Too far away to hear what was being said, Valeria lingered for a bit beside Zeke and watched. Jesse and the men took turns gesturing and pointing; she wasn't sure to where, but it looked to be in the direction of the Gros Ventre River and nearby mountains. After several minutes, the men smiled and shook Jesse's hand, and one of them handed him an envelope. Then, they climbed back into the truck and sped off.

Valeria took Zeke on into the barn and stall, where she untacked and groomed him before letting him out to roam in a nearby field.

"How much farther?" asked Valeria.

"It should be close by," answered Jesse.

An elk had been shot, and its carcass lay three to four miles from the ranch, but unlike previous days, its exact location wasn't revealed to Valeria or Jesse beforehand. Instead, they were told only which trails to take, particular landmarks to look for, and general directions from there to the elk's whereabouts. It was the first real test to see if the wolves could find a meal on their own by its scent.

Since Jesse was an experienced tracker and had great knowledge of the surrounding countryside, his grandmother had assigned him to act as Valeria and the wolves' guide in and out of the remote wilderness. He'd protested vehemently but to no avail. Few others on the ranch knew the neighboring federal land quite as well as Jesse, and the Hardins could ill afford to allocate any more of their hired men to the plan.

Meanwhile, around the ranch, fear of the wolves had largely disappeared, and the gate to the old pigpen was finally left open. Soon after, Jesse and Valeria began the process of gradually acclimating the wolves to their natural habitat. First, they set out on relatively easy half-day hikes through the nearby hills and valleys, leading the young pack to fresh elk and mule deer kills laid for them close to the trails. Once the routine and expectations of finding food were firmly sown in the wolves' minds, the two then took to horseback.

The wolves, as always, were unwaveringly devoted to Valeria and seldom let her out of their sight. It didn't seem to matter whether she was on foot or riding a horse. They kept pace behind Zeke and followed her wherever she went, seemingly oblivious to the fact they were slowly but surely being shepherded farther and farther into the wild.

"Let's stop for a moment," said Valeria. "Maybe they'll be

able to pick up the scent from here."

"Okay," said Jesse. He brought his horse, Cutter, to a stop. He'd been riding out front, as usual, leading the way down a particularly narrow path that ran along a rocky hillside strewn with boulders.

The day's ride had been fairly pleasant up until about a half hour earlier when a fast-moving shower unexpectedly pushed through, soaking everyone to the bone and leaving the trail wet and extremely muddy in places. Since rain wasn't in the forecast, neither Jesse nor Valeria had thought to bring along ponchos.

Both jumped off their horses to rest and shivered. They tied off their horses to the limb of a small spruce, walked to a nearby boulder, and sat. The wolves approached Valeria, tongues hanging out and panting, and immediately lay on the ground beside her.

Valeria leaned down and stroked several of the wolves' heads. Their fur was damp from the rainstorm. "They're going to need to drink some water soon," she remarked.

Jesse didn't respond.

Valeria had grown weary of Jesse giving her the cold shoulder and his terse reactions to whatever she said. She couldn't discuss anything with him because he wouldn't talk to her. His mulish arrogance and aloof nature, bordering on rude and almost always tinged with indifference so thick you could cut it with a knife, annoyed her, but there wasn't much she could do about it. He refused to treat her any other way, and she needed him in order to fulfill her mission.

"Where can we find water?" she asked, trying hard not to overreact.

"There's a creek not far from here."

Although Valeria desperately wanted to lash out, she bit her tongue. She knelt and gave each of her pups some attention, kissing them on the face, running her hands over their fur, and letting them nuzzle her in return. Her babies were almost fully grown now, and for the first time, an indescribable sadness descended upon her mind and enveloped her heart. Her relationship with the wolves would soon be coming to an end, and she couldn't bear the thought. It was all happening too fast, just as her father had predicted.

After a few minutes, Valeria got to her feet. She retrieved Zeke, mounted him, and headed down the trail. The wolves rose and followed her.

"What do you think you're doing?" asked Jesse, still sitting on the boulder.

"Taking them to the creek." She didn't bother to look back.

"You don't know where it is!" shouted Jesse, his voice receding behind her.

"I'll find it!"

When Valeria was out of Jesse's line of sight, she stopped. She closed her eyes and listened closely to the sounds emanating around her: the leaves on trees whispering, the caw of two nearby ravens gossiping, twigs snapping under the weight of something unseen beyond a rise in the hill, and there…there it was…faint, so faint, the sound of water trickling.

Valeria signaled Zeke with her leg to turn right off-trail, then led him down a steep rolling hillside through a dense maze of low brush and rocks, carefully picking her way toward what looked to be a dense forest in the distance.

It felt good to be riding and exploring the wilderness alone with just her babies next to her, free from the incessant weight of Jesse's demeaning presence. She glanced back at them, nimbly avoiding obstacles and keeping pace behind her, and smiled.

At the forest's edge, she paused. She heard the subtle murmur and rush of flowing water more clearly. It was coming from somewhere to her left, beyond the trees. She maneuvered

Zeke to an area where the brush and vegetation were less thick, jumped off his back, and, holding his reins, walked him into the woods. A good ways in, they came upon a crystal-clear creek that had cut a meandering path through the woodland.

The wolves rushed to the water's edge and began to drink.

Valeria held onto Zeke and watched. The tranquility of the moment was breathtaking, but like life itself, it didn't last. Somewhere in the dense forest behind her, she heard a loud rustling noise. Not long after, Jesse emerged with Cutter some thirty yards away or so upstream. He called out to her, waved, and made his way alongside the creek to where she was.

"Why did you leave me back there?" asked Jesse.

"Why do you think?" Valeria pretended to be adjusting Zeke's stirrups and didn't look at him.

"Okay. You've made your point." Jesse glared at her. "You don't like me. I get it. I've admitted I don't want anything to do with this crazy wolf nonsense of yours, but if something bad were to happen to you again way out here, everyone would blame me for your stupidity. Trust me, it's not safe to stray this far off the trails alone, not around here anyway. It's best we stick together, whether you like it or not."

"Stupidity?" Valeria balled up her fists and stared at Jesse. "I found this creek without your help, didn't I?" She took a step toward him.

"All right. Okay." Jesse backed away. "Wrong word. I'm sorry."

No more was said. They waited for the wolves to drink their fill before leading the horses on foot back through the woods, low brush, and maze of scattered rocks. Picking up the trail near where Valeria had left it, they rode off in search of the dead elk.

A half mile or so farther on, all six wolves, led by Roxie, suddenly raced ahead of the horses. At a bend in the trail, Jesse and Valeria lost sight of them. The uneven trail was much too narrow and littered with stones for Zeke and Cutter to chase after the pack.

"They must have picked up the scent," said Valeria, pleased but also worried the inexperienced pups might become lost in their rush to find the carcass.

Beyond the bend, past some fairly large boulders, the trail led to an open expanse of tall firs, grass, and wildflowers. The wolves were nowhere to be seen.

Jesse raised his hand, and they stopped.

"Where are they?" asked Valeria.

Jesse glanced around and pointed. "Look over there. What do you see?"

To the north, three ravens were perched atop a rock fifty to a hundred yards away. Several others were circling over the same area. Valeria had learned from her father that ravens often followed wolf packs so they could scavenge fresh kills. Unable to tear apart the fur of dead animals themselves, the ravens needed the wolves to rip through the thick hide of their prey with their teeth in order for them to get at the flesh.

"They must be on the other side of those rocks," said Valeria.

They dismounted and cautiously led their horses on foot over to the outcrop of rocks. The ravens scattered but quickly returned. Just on the other side, the wolves had already begun the gruesome but necessary process of eating the dead elk. Jesse and Valeria kept their distance and watched them gorge.

The young wolves wasted little time tearing apart the carcass. Although they growled and fought over choice pieces, most skirmishes were short-lived. There was more than enough meat to satisfy everyone, including the ravens, who nimbly avoided the wolves' objections as they jumped in and out of the fray. Valeria found a nearby rock to sit atop and rest while she looked on. And as usual, Jesse grew impatient and, without saying a word, wandered off to be by himself.

An hour later, Diesel and Tess were still pacing around the kill, ripping and biting off chunks, but at a much less frantic and unhurried pace, indicating they were nearly finished. The other four were lying near the carcass, resting after their meal.

By now, it was midafternoon. They'd soon need to return to the ranch. Valeria stood up to stretch her legs and attend to Zeke. There was a small cluster of trees nearby where she thought Jesse had gone to get out of the sun, but he wasn't there. Cutter was still tied off beside Zeke.

She looked around. "Jesse?" she called out.

No answer. There was no sign of him anywhere.

Thinking Jesse had to be somewhere close by, she called his name a second time. When again he didn't respond, Valeria became curious. She walked over to where she'd last seen him by the trees. Maybe he'd lain down to take a nap in the shade. She searched the area, but he was nowhere to be found. On the other side of the trees, she spotted a good-size outcrop of rocks a short distance away and guessed he might be someplace on the far side of them.

Valeria reached the outcrop and climbed over it, calling to Jesse several times, but again, nothing. He didn't seem to be anywhere. It was puzzling, but since his horse was still tied off with Zeke, he couldn't have wandered far. She decided to head back to the wolves and wait for him there. She turned around, picked her away past several rocks, and screamed.

"Didn't mean to startle you, miss," said one of two men standing in front of her. He had ahold of Valeria's arm, steadying her. She'd stumbled and almost hit her head on one of the rocks from the unexpected shock of accidentally bumping into someone in the middle of nowhere. He'd frightened her so bad; her heart was still pounding. "Take a deep breath," he said. "We heard something rustling around by the rocks. Thought it was an animal."

Valeria recognized the men immediately. It was the same two who'd nearly hit her with their truck back at the ranch, the ones she'd seen talking to Jesse. Both were dressed from head to toe in hunting camouflage and holding high-powered rifles with scopes. Each also had on a backpack like they'd been hiking.

"Jesse!" yelled Valeria. "Where are you?"

"Shh!" Still holding her arm, the first man put his finger to his lips. "We're not going to hurt you."

"What are you doing here?" Valeria stammered. With her free hand, she loosened his grip and yanked her arm away from him. "And *who* are you?"

"Enjoying the scenery," said the second man.

"It doesn't matter who we are," said the first. "But we know your name. You're Val, Officer Cortez's girl. Everyone in these parts knows you."

Valeria took a few steps back. "You two knew we'd be somewhere way out here and followed us. Didn't you?" She was careful not to say why she knew. "So, what are you really doing out here?"

The second man smiled. "Target shooting."

"Jesse!" she shouted.

"Yell for the boy if you want. It's okay, but there's no reason to be afraid. We're not here for you," said the first. "Besides, Jesse Hardin is a friend of ours." He glanced at his partner. "Isn't he?"

"Yeah, he is."

"To answer your question, we're professional trophy hunters who specialize in hard-to-find big game," said the first. His relaxed manner abruptly disappeared. He came much closer and glared at her.

"You mean illegal," said Valeria.

"Well, I'm sure your father wouldn't approve, but we

haven't actually accomplished what we set out to do…not yet anyway." He smiled. "We're talking no harm, no foul, right?"

"Plus, he has to catch us in the act," his partner chimed in. "And as you can see, it's a big wide world way out here in the backwoods. So, even if you tell dear ol' dad that you ran into us, there's not much he can do about it. He has a lot more on his plate to worry about than us."

"Where's Jesse?" asked Valeria.

"I'm sure he's around here somewhere," said the first. "But as you know, Miss Cortez, better than most, it's not uncommon for folks to become lost or hurt all alone in this incredible wilderness, and the authorities never find their bodies." He reached nonchalantly into his pants pocket, pulled out a magazine with bullets, and loaded his rifle. "But you've already learned that lesson the hard way. Am I right?"

He held up his rifle and pointed it at a tree in the distance. "You're damn lucky to have survived." He fired a shot that tore into the tree's trunk. Valeria flinched as the piercing crack of the rifle echoed in all directions. The two men exchanged glances. "Do us a favor, will you? When you find Jesse, tell him we said hello."

With that, the men turned and walked off. Valeria quickly climbed atop one of the rocks to watch and make sure they weren't coming back. She was able to follow their movement in and out of several stands of trees, but at the crest of a nearby hill, about a half mile away, she lost sight of them.

Valeria scrambled down, calling, "Jesse! Jesse!"

She decided to hurry back to where she'd left the wolves with the dead elk and wait for him there, but on her way, she stopped abruptly. Valeria thought she heard something peculiar nearby, an odd fleeting noise, possibly coming from somewhere in the dense brush a short distance away. Gone now, it had sounded like groaning.

Another few steps, and there it was again. Slowly and cautiously, she made her way toward it, traversing weathered rocks and a thicket littered with fallen trees, bleached by the sun and long dead. As she stepped over some downed branches, she heard a weak voice mumble, "Val?"

She found Jesse sprawled, face-up on the ground, his eyes half open. His lip was bleeding. Valeria rushed to his side. "What happened?" she asked.

"Let me think," he said, groggily.

She put her arms around Jesse's shoulders and helped lift him to a sitting position.

"Oh yeah… I got punched in the face with the butt end of a rifle." He opened and closed his mouth several times and massaged his jaw.

"Are you okay?" asked Valeria.

"It hurts like hell but doesn't feel broken."

With Valeria's assistance, Jesse got to his feet. At first, he wobbled a bit. "I feel lightheaded," he said, and leaned on her for support. After a few minutes, he began to look better and was able to steady himself.

"You sure you're all right?"

"Yeah. I think so."

In the next breath, Valeria gave Jesse a hard shove. He tripped backward over a fallen tree limb and fell head over heels, this time landing face-down on the ground. "Tell me what the hell's going on," she said angrily. "I just bumped into two hunters who said they were looking for you, but it looks like they lied to me. It's pretty obvious they already found you. What did you do to make them mad?"

Jesse dusted himself off and stood up. "I wouldn't do what they wanted." Grabbing Valeria by the wrist, he started to make his way out of the thicket, dragging her, kicking and screaming behind him. "We need to leave."

"Tell me! The truth, Jesse!" She broke his grip. "I'm not taking another step until you tell me what those men want with you."

He stopped but didn't turn around to look at her. "It's not me they want," said Jesse. He went over to an old dead tree trunk lying on its side and sat down. "It's the wolves."

Jesse reluctantly looked up, and she stared at him in disbelief.

"Explain!" she said.

Jesse was slow to speak. "This all started before I met you," he said. "I was part of a group of hunters who'd meet in online forums to exchange information on where and how to hunt big game, mostly legal, but we'd also share surveillance information on hard-to-find predators like mountain lions and wolves." He paused to rub his jaw again. "It was no big deal until you came along. We'd brag about our kills and share the various ways we tracked the animals or lured them to where we could safely shoot them without being caught." He went silent.

"Go on," said Valeria.

"Then I met you and stopped… I watched how you mother these pups, and it's like your love for them seeped into my brain." He looked away. "When word got out that a wolf pack was being brought to the ranch to be reintroduced into the wild, it attracted a lot of interest. Some of the more hard-core trophy hunters I'd met online–guys with too much time on their hands and a bucket list of animals they want to kill–started calling the house and sending me emails, trying to get information about them."

Valeria glared at him.

Jesse paused before continuing, "At first, I ignored everyone who tried to contact me, but then I received an offer that was hard to refuse. It was from one of the two guys you ran into. He and his buddy offered me an insane amount of money if I'd help steer them to some wolves. I figured any wolves would do, so I agreed to provide them with good intel on where to find and hunt the Togwolee pack."

"Jesse, so help me, God!" said Valeria. "I don't know if I can listen to any more of this because it's all I can do to keep from bashing you over the head."

Jesse stood up, picked his way out of the snarl of dead trees and thicket, and walked hurriedly in the direction of the dead elk and wolves. Falling in behind him, Valeria had a hard time keeping up.

"You can pound on me later, but right now, we need to get out of here," said Jesse.

As they rushed to get back to the wolves and horses, Valeria wouldn't stay quiet. "You haven't explained why they hit you."

Keeping his distance from her, Jesse stopped and turned around. "They claimed to be world-class shots with a rifle and experienced, said they knew how to track and hunt top predators, and all I had to do was give them a few landmarks and point them in the right direction. But for whatever reason, they can't find the Togwolee pack or any other wolf in the area on their own. I never should've accepted their offer. It was wrong and stupid, I know, and I'm incredibly sorry."

Jesse paused. "Somehow, these guys knew we were coming here. I'm not exactly sure how they found out, but they did. They were waiting for us so they could get me alone and renegotiate the deal I had with them. Mostly, they wanted to threaten me where nobody could see. They accused me of ripping them off. I told them it wasn't my fault they'd failed to track down the Togwolee pack and that I'd had a serious change of heart about the whole thing anyway. I asked them to meet me back at the ranch later so I could refund their money, every penny, but they refused my offer. That's when I realized they were up to something and—"

Valeria interrupted, "If they don't want the money, what

do they want?"

"The thing that enticed them to contact me in the first place. They want to hunt Roxie, Zeus, and the others. They're after your wolves."

Crying out, "You son of a bitch!" and with fists flying, Valeria rushed at Jesse and knocked him onto his backside. She landed on top of him, arms flailing, feet kicking, and they both rolled across the hard, stony ground several times. Pinning her with the weight of his body, he eventually was able to seize her hands and hold them down to keep her from hitting him.

"Stop!" said Jesse, out of breath from the struggle. "We don't have time for this." Valeria spat in his face, and he winced. "I told them if they ever came anywhere near these wolves, I'd turn them both in to your father and testify against them, said I'd make sure they did time in jail. That's when one of them cold-cocked me with the rifle."

Jesse got up and extended his hand to Valeria.

Without saying anything more to each other, they started walking. The wolves were anxiously waiting for them near the elk. Except for its skull and spine, it had been devoured. Zeke and Cutter were still tied off where Valeria and Jesse had left them.

Valeria called to the wolves, "Let's go!"

The pack didn't hesitate to come over and nuzzle her legs, and in return, she took a moment to shower each of them with affection.

Jesse and Valeria readied the horses and, with the wolves keeping pace behind them, headed back to the ranch as quickly as they could.

CHAPTER 19

At first light, Valeria began what had become her daily routine. She jumped out of bed, got dressed, and stepped outside to check on the wolves and Zeke before breakfast, but a bitter mid-autumn chill stopped her in her tracks. It was the coldest air she'd felt since the days she'd spent stranded in the mountains, snowed in with Philip. She rushed back into the house to retrieve a jacket, winter hat, and gloves.

Better dressed, Valeria was again on her way to the pen when she spotted a black SUV with government plates coming up the road. She recognized the vehicle immediately. It stopped in front of the ranch house, and three men got out: Dr. Irwin from the FDA; his uniformed army escort, Sergeant Norris; and a driver, another soldier who also wore military fatigues.

The three approached.

"Shouldn't you be in school?" asked Dr Irwin, his question dripping with sarcasm.

"Get away from me," said Valeria. "You have no business being here. There's still a restraining order."

Dr. Irwin smiled. "You intrigue me, Miss Cortez," he replied. "I'd think a young girl like you would much prefer hanging out with friends, not wasting your time babysitting a bunch of scruffy wolves."

Just then, Butch stepped out from behind one of the main tool and equipment storage buildings with Sam, his foreman.

"Can I help you, gentlemen?" asked Butch, wiping grease off his fingers with an oily rag.

"I'm Dr. Theodore Irwin…"

"I know who you are," interrupted Butch, ignoring the man's offer to shake hands.

Dr. Irwin smiled. "Well, I won't take up much of your time," he said. "We've come to conduct a visual inspection. I just need to verify that the wolf pack is still being cared for here on the ranch and that you've failed to reintroduce them into the wild."

The front door to the ranch house opened and out came Eleanor with Jesse by her side. The two made their way to Valeria and the group of men.

"This is private property," announced Eleanor, loudly. "I suggest you get right back in your car and leave immediately. You're not welcome here."

Dr. Irwin reached into his coat pocket and pulled out some official-looking papers. "I've already obtained permission from the judge who presided over this case," he replied, unfolding the papers. The bottom sheet looked to have a notary seal. "Time is running out, my friends. Per the judge's orders, you've got less than three days to clear the wolves off this ranch and return them to their natural habitat."

"And if we don't?" asked Butch.

"On behalf of the FDA, I've already prepared the necessary documents to gain legal custody of the wolves," answered Dr. Irwin. "That is…if they're still here on your ranch a few days from now."

"You bastard!" said Valeria.

"There's no need for name-calling," replied Dr. Irwin. "You didn't think we were going to just forget about all this and go away, did you?"

Eleanor responded, "Go ahead, Val, and take these gentlemen to the pen so they can inspect the wolves and file whatever report they've concocted as an excuse to come out here."

Turning to Dr. Irwin, Eleanor raised her ever-present cane and jabbed him in the chest with it. "You've got some nerve, mister. This incredibly smart, dedicated young lady has been working her tail off to see that these wolves are never subjected to your torture or whatever you call your experiments." With everyone looking on, she jabbed him again, even harder. "And this is the last time you'll ever march onto our land and make threats. You understand? Now you go have your little look-see, then turn on around and climb back into your car. I want you out of my sight."

Dr. Irwin glared at the elderly woman. "You've got three days. Remember that," he repeated. "When I come back, I'll have a court order in hand and the necessary people to remove these wolves from this property, by force if necessary."

Everyone except for Eleanor, who went back inside the house, followed Valeria to the old converted pigpen, where the wolves were all napping, half of them lying in their favorite spots inside the pen, and the rest curled up beside the fence. When they heard Valeria coming, their eyes opened, and all six heads perked up.

"The gate is open," observed Dr. Irwin.

"Yes, it is," said Butch. "And if I were you, I wouldn't venture too close. They don't take too kindly to anyone who's not a member of their pack." He went up to Yoko, who was lying out in the open near the fence, and extended the back of his hand. She looked up and nuzzled it.

Jesse walked over to Tess and did the same.

"Amazing," said Dr. Irwin. "I don't know how you accomplished that." He and Sergeant Norris took a few steps closer. "They're such impressive creatures."

"Be careful," said Sam. "You fellows ought to back off

some because you don't know what you're doing."

Dr. Irwin ignored him. Emulating Butch and Jesse, he carefully approached Diesel and offered the wolf his hand. He was met with a low, menacing growl. Diesel bared his teeth and sat up. Dr. Irwin yanked back his hand and retreated several steps. Roxie and Scout, who'd both been lying in the pen, also sat upright and growled.

"Tried to warn you," said Sam.

"Yes," replied Dr. Irwin. "You most certainly did."

Dr. Irwin then turned to Valeria. "We'll be back, Miss Cortez. In the meantime, I suggest you say your goodbyes to these wolves while you have the chance."

"I'll make sure you're never able to lay a hand on them," replied Valeria. "Trust me."

That's when everyone noticed Roxie and Scout getting to their feet. Together, the two quickly made their way out of the pen and into the open with heads lowered. Both wolves stepped slowly toward Dr. Irwin and growled.

"Uh-oh. You're in for it now," said Sam. "They must've been listening."

"What do we do?" asked Sergeant Norris. "Someone needs to back them off—"

Butch interrupted him. "Val's the only person around here with the magic touch." He chuckled. "She has the power to stop them from tearing you apart, but I doubt she'll step in and help. You shouldn't have threatened her. These wolves are very sensitive to how she's treated by people they don't know, and like you've been told already, you ain't a part of this pack."

"Don't make any sudden moves," said Sam. "My best advice is to just slowly walk away and don't make eye contact with them."

Dr. Irwin motioned to Sergeant Norris and the other soldier. "Let's go," he said.

The three turned and immediately headed toward their vehicle, taking turns to glance back over their shoulders. Halfway there, they were on a dead run. Roxie, Scout, and Diesel had given chase.

Sergeant Norris and the other soldier managed to make it to the car and jump inside just before Roxie and Diesel were able to descend upon them, but Scout caught Dr. Irwin's pant leg outside the passenger door and ripped at it with his teeth.

"Call him off!" shouted Dr. Irwin, frantically trying to get the determined wolf to loosen his grip.

Valeria pretended not to hear him.

Cursing and kicking wildly, Dr. Irwin knocked Scout back and shook himself free. He then leapt into the car and slammed the door shut.

The car sped off.

The three wolves ran after it but soon gave up. When they returned to the pen, Valeria showered them with a flurry of hugs and kisses.

Butch and Sam wandered off, discussing what to do about a broken piece of machinery, and Jesse quietly disappeared. Valeria went to the stalls to tend to Zeke and, afterward, came back to the pen to spend the rest of the morning alone with her babies. With the earlier turmoil over and their fate shelved for another day, all was peaceful, except for a good-natured tussle between the wolves involving Scout, who had a long scrap of fabric hanging from his mouth that he let his siblings sniff but not take.

The next day, Jesse and Valeria saddled their horses and headed to the Gros Ventre River. Another fresh elk carcass had been laid for the pack somewhere near the seventy-five-mile-long tributary east of Black Peak. Like before, only a smattering of landmarks were divulged beforehand to help sharpen the wolves' sensory skills.

The two had agreed not to tell anyone about their earlier close encounter with the rogue trophy hunters. Valeria was worried that if her father found out about the men, he'd put an abrupt end to the reintroduction project out of concern for her safety. And if she stopped now, it'd mean surrendering the young wolves to Dr. Irwin, and she was willing to do whatever it took to prevent the scientist from getting his hands on them.

As they passed through a narrow valley surrounded on either side by mountains, Jesse pointed to an area of rocks along a nearby ridge south of the trail. "I'm sure they're out here somewhere," he said. "Keep your eyes peeled for a glint of steel from the barrel of one of their rifles or any unusual movement. That spot would be a perfect place to spy on us."

"This wilderness is so huge; it's hard to believe they'd be able to know in advance where we're going," said Valeria. "I'm watching everywhere you tell me, though… I haven't noticed anything suspicious yet."

The wolves were trailing behind them but keeping up with the horses. Despite getting a later than usual start, they were making good time.

"I've been wondering how those hunters found us near that dead elk the last time," said Jesse. "I think I've figured it out. They're either following the ranch hands to where the venison is being left for the wolves or using telemetry to locate the pack. I asked our two guys, and they don't believe anyone saw them shoot the elk or move the carcass."

"Telemetry?" asked Valeria.

"It's the radio collars the wolves are wearing." Jesse glanced back at the pack. "Your dad did it to keep track of them, right?"

"Yes. Some of the pups were starting to get loose," answered Valeria. "He said the radio collars were a safeguard in case he needed to locate them quickly if they escaped the yard."

"I don't know for sure, but the sons of bitches might have hijacked the radio frequencies to these wolves," said Jesse. "The signal that each collar emits is proprietary. I mean, only the animal researchers are supposed to know the exact frequencies, but I've met several hunters online who've bragged about cheating the system. They've gotten ahold of the frequencies and used a special radio receiver and antenna to track and kill entire wolf packs using telemetry."

"That's terrible," said Valeria, more than just a little upset. "People like that should be made to serve time in prison for doing something so rotten."

They continued to ride in and out of a mostly rocky terrain, where the trail became much steeper in places and the footing more treacherous, and downslope through an area of dense woodland until they reached the banks of the Upper Gros Ventre. The two climbed off Cutter and Zeke to rest a bit before pressing on and led the horses to the water's edge for a drink. The wolves took advantage of the break and gathered for a sip as well. After drinking their fill, they lay near one another beside the river and waited.

After everyone had a chance to catch their breath, Jesse opened a leather saddlebag draped over Cutter's back and pulled out a large hunting knife. "In town, your dad was smart to put radio collars on them. It makes sense." He unsheathed it. "But if these wolves are going to survive out here on their own, the collars are a mistake."

"What are you doing?" asked Valeria.

Jesse walked over to Roxie, who was lying near the stream. "Come help me," said Jesse. "I'm getting rid of these collars."

Valeria approached Roxie, knelt, and stroked her head and muzzle while Jesse leaned over and ran the knife blade under the leather collar along the back of the wolf's neck. "Don't let her bite me." Grabbing the collar with one hand and slicing upward with the other, Jesse sawed at the thick, wide collar. It wasn't coming off easily. "I've got to bear down some. They used locking brackets and nuts to attach these collars, and this leather is heavy duty. I can barely cut through it."

With Valeria keeping Roxie calm, Jesse finally was able to slice off the collar and remove it from around the wolf's neck. He set it aside on a nearby rock and approached Yoko. Together, he and Valeria went from wolf to wolf and detached every collar.

"We should return these to my father," said Valeria, glancing at the pile of severed radio collars.

"I've got a better idea," Jesse responded. "Wait here." He walked away from her, disappearing off into a nearby brush thick with fir and blue spruce. When he returned, his arms were filled with dead branches. He dropped the pile on the ground, retrieved a coiled length of wilderness cord from his saddlebag, and began separating the cord into smaller strands.

"He's not going to be happy that we removed them," said Valeria.

"I'll explain it to him." Jesse looked over at Valeria. "I know you'll be mad when I tell you this, but before I met you, I'd thought of doing the same thing, using the radio frequencies to help me hunt collared wolves." He went back to dividing the cord into strands. "The hunting forums are full of information on how to track all kinds of animals. I know every trick other hunters use to lure and kill wolves."

Jesse cut the dead branches into shorter pieces about the length of his arm. Then, using the strands of cord, he quickly tied four or five pieces of wood together. He repeated the process until he had what looked like six miniature rafts.

"Most of these radio collars have a mortality mode." Jesse grabbed a collar and started tying it atop one of the makeshift rafts. "If the collar doesn't move for several days, it broadcasts a mortality signal that lets the researchers know the wolf has died and where to find the body."

Jesse finished lashing the collars, one to each raft. "What we want to do is dupe the hunters into thinking the wolves are alive, but somewhere else, a long way from here. We can use these collars to send them on a wild goose chase."

He picked up several of the crude rafts and took them to the river's edge. Valeria helped him bring over the rest. They both placed a raft on the water to see if it'd float. Each did.

"The river will carry the collars downstream, which will prevent the motion sensor from activating the mortality mode. On a radio receiver, it'll look like the wolves are roaming along its banks, using the stream to hunt for prey. If hunters are tuning into their frequencies, the signals will lead them to the wrong areas," said Jesse. "It should, at least, buy the pack some time to disappear off into the wild before anyone catches on."

Valeria and Jesse knelt by the river and set the collars adrift. The small rafts bobbed close to shore for a time but soon caught the shimmering current and quietly floated away. They vanished around a bend.

The wolves had no trouble picking up the scent of the dead elk. They led Valeria, Jesse, and the horses off trail through an adjacent valley and found it a mile east of the Gros Ventre. As usual, they were greeted by a small congregation of hungry ravens.

With the radio collars gone, Valeria felt less nervous about the trophy hunters possibly finding them. Jesse helped her clear away some stones from a small area on the ground and spread out a blanket. From inside a saddlebag, she retrieved two neatly wrapped foot-long hoagies on fresh home-baked bread, a pint of coleslaw, and a huge slice of cake that Giuseppe, the cowboy chef, had prepared for them.

"I don't think the old cowboys, a hundred years ago, ever

ate grub this good," slurred Jesse with his mouth half full. He took another bite of his hoagie.

"This is so delicious," said Valeria. Like the wolves, she devoured everything in front of her.

Not much more was said. Valeria and Jesse sat and watched the wolves and ravens go at the carcass. By now, the day was winding down. As soon as the pack showed signs of being finished, the two would need to hurry back to the ranch before it got dark. They'd lost track of time at the river.

An hour and a half later, they both stood up and started to load their things and ready the horses. The wolves appeared to be nearly done. As Jesse was helping Valeria fold the blanket, he looked at her and said, "Thank you."

"For what?" Valeria asked, a little taken aback. She paused for a moment from what she was doing, then resumed folding and handed the blanket to him.

Jesse secured the blanket inside his saddlebag. "I, um…I enjoy your company." He turned his back to her.

Valeria was next to Zeke, rechecking his bridle and cinch, making sure everything still fit comfortably and was secure. "I thought you hated me."

"No. I never… Well, I might have at first, but I didn't know you." Jesse looked up. "Then everything happened, and I'm not sure what else to say. You're okay…great, actually," he stammered. "I mean, I've explored these mountains hundreds of times, always alone, just me by myself riding off to wherever, and it's nice to have someone around to share it all with. I like being out here with you, just the two of us."

"I didn't know you felt that way," said Valeria. "But thank you." She hesitated, then added, "I've misjudged you too… Growing up on your family's cattle ranch next to the Tetons, how could that experience not help shape who you are and your attitude toward animals? I've learned a lot just by getting to know you. Everyone's nature is special, and nature isn't good or bad, is it? It just is. I'm me. You're you. And despite everything, you're here with me, helping." She smiled at him. "I'm glad we met, Jesse, and I couldn't do this without—"

Just then, Jesse spotted a grizzly bear cub coming out of the brush less than thirty yards away. "Hush!" he whispered, bringing his finger to his lips. "Don't make any sudden moves, Val."

Two more nearly identical-looking yearling cubs appeared behind the first, followed closely by their mother, a huge sow. They were headed in the general direction of the dead elk, now mostly bits of skin and bone.

"Oh, no. This is bad, really bad," said Jesse. "If the sow sees us, we're in serious trouble." He grabbed Cutter's reins. "Whatever you do, Val, don't look her in the eyes. Grizzlies perceive it as a threat, and she's apt to charge."

Valeria whispered, "What do we do?" She glanced at the wolves, who, still engrossed in their meal, didn't seem to notice the bears were nearby.

"Very slowly, slowly, climb onto your horse and get ready to ride away hard and fast."

Turning her back to the grizzlies, Valeria put her foot in a stirrup and quietly lifted herself onto Zeke's saddle. Jesse did the same, mounting Cutter without saying another word. But for some reason, Cutter whinnied. Jesse and Valeria both glanced over to see if the bear heard. It had.

The grizzly glared at them for a few brief seconds and roared. In the next breath, it came charging. With the bear nearly upon them, Zeke suddenly spun and reared up, tossing Valeria hard to the ground. Jesse shouted, "Val!" and jumped off Cutter. He rushed to get between the attacking sow and where she lay, waved his arms wildly, and shouted, "Get out of here! Go!"

But the bear didn't leave. It knocked Jesse down violently

and lashed at him with its claws. Furiously punching and kicking, Jesse fought to get the grizzly off him but was pinned. Valeria got up and screamed. She grabbed a rock and threw it at the bear's head, but it had no effect. The sow sunk its teeth deep into the boy's shoulder. Jesse groaned. Another jagged rock–this one struck the bear in the eye. For a moment, the grizzly hesitated and stepped away.

Valeria turned to run, but before she could take a step, the bear trapped her. She felt its breath on her neck and fell face-first, screaming. It was then she heard the wolves growling. The sow abruptly backed off and stood erect on its hind legs. The whole pack had encircled the huge female grizzly and, with teeth bared, were lunging at her feet, trying to bite her. The bear aggressively defended itself. Whirling around, it attempted to strike or bite any wolf that came near but quickly dropped to all fours and retreated, hurrying off in the direction of its cubs. The wolves gave chase but stopped when the bear disappeared into the brush with its young.

Jesse lay dazed and bleeding.

Valeria rushed to his side, sat him upright, and took off his shirt to assess his wounds. Jesse's chest and arms had been slashed, but the deepest and bloodiest damage was to his shoulder, where the bear had bitten him. Using his shirt, she applied pressure in an attempt to stop the bleeding. When it failed to stem the flow of blood, she quickly grabbed the hunting knife from his saddlebag and cut the picnic blanket into smaller pieces and strips. She packed the deepest wounds to his shoulder and chest with bits of cloth from the blanket, then tied a tourniquet just above an ugly gash to his upper arm.

"I had her right where I wanted…in a bear hug," joked Jesse, wincing. "How do I look?"

"You've looked better." Valeria kissed his forehead. "We need to get you home."

She helped lift him off the ground and onto his saddle.

CHAPTER 20

Glorious shades of orange tinged with deep violet hues filled the sky as the sun began its descent beyond the mountains. Jesse was lying on a gurney. Along with his father and grandmother, several of the ranch hands had gathered around him outside the ranch house. Off to one side, trying to give his family some space, Ray and Valeria looked on as well.

"Absolutely not!" said Ray under his breath. "You're not going back out there by yourself. I've lost you once, and I'm not losing you again.

"But Dad, what choice do I have?" whispered Valeria. "Dr. Irwin will be here in two days. There's no other way."

Eleanor knelt over her grandson, wiped away some sweat and dirt from his brow, and took hold of his hand. "Hang in there, boy," she said.

One of the two paramedics attending to him finished attaching an IV catheter to a vein in his arm. "We need to raise his blood pressure," he said. "It's too low." They finished strapping Jesse to the gurney and, together, loaded him into the back of the ambulance.

Butch gave Eleanor a quick kiss on the cheek and headed to his truck. "I'm going to follow them," he said. "If they decide to keep Jesse overnight, I'll stay with him at the medical center. I'll be by his side until they release him."

"He's lost quite a bit of blood," said Eleanor. "I'm sure

they'll want to test for infection and keep an eye on him for a spell. Just make sure they patch him up good. In the interim, Sam and I will take care of things around here while you're gone."

Valeria walked up to one of the paramedics. "He's going to be okay, right?" she asked.

"It's a good thing you stuffed those wounds like you did," he answered. "Or he would have bled out. How did you know to do that?"

"I'm not sure. I didn't exactly think it through."

"Well, you probably saved his life."

He climbed into the back of the ambulance and closed the doors. The other jumped behind the wheel, and with siren wailing and emergency lights flashing, they sped off.

Eleanor folded her hands as if praying silently and looked up at the darkening sky. She lingered for a few moments afterward. Then, without saying a word, she went into the house. Sam and the ranch hands dispersed.

Ray followed Valeria to the pigpen.

"Maybe the judge will give us more time," she said, kneeling next to Zeus. She stroked the wolf's neck.

"Going back to court and getting an extension is out of the question." Ray stood near the open gate. "Val, I realize you're not going to want to hear what I have to say, but maybe it's time to give up."

"What are you saying?"

"I mean, everyone needs to move on with their lives," said Ray, pointedly. "Listen to me. You've raised and cared for these wolves and done an amazing job. You love them and want what's best for them, but if they're not ready by now to set out on their own, there's nothing more you can do. The time has come for you to let go."

Valeria didn't respond.

"Promise me you'll stay here on the ranch with Mrs.

Hardin until I return. I don't want you wandering off somewhere by yourself and getting hurt." Ray walked over to his daughter, helped her up, and put his arms around her. "I miss having you near me, and in two days, it'll be time to come home."

Visibly upset, Valeria wouldn't look at him. Together, they made their way back to the ranch house. It was after dark now, and the stars, sprinkled across the sky overhead, were beginning to sparkle like rhinestones.

"I'm on duty and need to leave, but I'll be back tomorrow evening," said Ray. "We'll talk more about the wolves and Dr. Irwin then."

In the wee hours of the morning, long before anyone else was awake, Valeria climbed out of bed and got dressed. She put on her riding gear, heaviest jacket, and a wool cap, raided the refrigerator for lunch meat and the kitchen pantry for cookies and homemade bread, which she stuffed into several baggies, and snuck out the front door.

She went into the stalls, quietly brushed and tacked up Zeke, and walked him to the pigpen. The wolves, who somehow already had sensed Valeria's approach, were roused and waiting for her when she arrived. She took a moment to fuss on each of them individually before taking hold of Zeke's reins and getting up on his saddle.

"Let's go," Valeria whispered.

The wolves fell in behind Zeke and followed her.

After weeks of riding with Jesse, Valeria was now familiar with the various trails near the ranch that cut through the mountains and neighboring countryside. With only moonlight to illuminate her way, she led the wolves through a rolling woodland, surrounded on all sides by boulders and steep hillsides. She took her time, moving cautiously so as not to take a wrong step or make a wrong turn, listened carefully to the sounds around her, and glanced back every now and then to make sure everyone was keeping up and still together.

With every breath Valeria, Zeke, and the wolves exhaled in the cold night air, fleeting billows of colorless mist could be seen silhouetted against the vast darkness. They pressed on, down dimly lit paths that skirted enormous rockfaces and passed through dense forests, where the world turned pitch-black, and the eerie silence felt like a gaping void that might swallow them whole.

Two hours or so into the ride, Valeria stopped to rest beside a meandering creek near the edge of a valley, partially enclosed to the east and west by an expanse of rock-strewn cliffs. The sun had yet to come up, but the horizon beyond the mountains was just beginning to brighten ever so slowly. She jumped off Zeke and led him to the water for a sip. After he'd drunk his fill, she walked him to a fir tree near some soft grass and looped his reins over one of the branches.

Valeria found a small boulder to sit on next to the creek and watched as the surrounding night sky gently dissipated and the majestic light of a new day crept over the trees and cliffs in the distance. Before long, a brilliant morning, void of any clouds, revealed a lovely, unspoiled wilderness all around her.

"Well, my babies… This is goodbye," said Valeria.

The high-pitched bugle of a bull elk resounded nearby. Searching for the source of the distinctive call, Valeria looked across the valley and spotted a large elk herd, possibly one hundred or more, grazing and milling about roughly a quarter mile away.

Roxie was the first of the wolves to react to the herd's presence. She stood up, sniffed the air, and let out a low, almost inaudible growl. Soon, her siblings had joined her to take stock of the elk, standing nearly shoulder to shoulder a few yards from Valeria. And although they'd all been fed and cared for since birth, and none had ever stalked or killed anything on their own, by the intense expression on each wolf's face, she could see the pack's natural instincts were working out the logistics collectively in their minds.

This is what Valeria had hoped for when she set out that morning. To survive in the wild, the inexperienced wolves needed to learn how to be the feared predators they were and take down their own meal. But Valeria had run out of time to see things through the way she'd envisioned, and rather than give in and relinquish her babies to the likes of Dr. Irwin, she'd decided to lead the young pack into the mountains, one last time, with the idea of abandoning them in a place where they'd at least have a chance to live free and endure.

Valeria climbed down off the rock and went to where the wolves were gathered. With tears welling in her eyes, she knelt next to them, gently ran her hands over their coarse fur, and allowed their faces to nuzzle hers. Afterward, their body language changed almost immediately. With raised hackles on the necks of several, the pack became visibly restless, and Valeria understood by the steely way the wolves gazed at both her and the elk that they wanted her to lead a pursuit.

"I'm sorry," said Valeria, her voice quavering. "I want to stay and help you, but I can't. Some people are coming who want to take you away. If they find you, you'll just be one of their stupid experiments and never know what it's like to live free. You're almost grown now, and we can't go on like this together. I have to leave."

The wolves stared at her, seemingly transfixed.

"Go on! Be wolves!" she shouted, pointing at the herd. "You don't need me anymore. Do what you have to do!" Valeria fell to her knees, sobbing.

The wolves came to her en masse, rubbing their heads and bodies against her gently and nudging Valeria to get up.

After a minute or two, she composed herself and rose. Without saying another word, she turned and quietly walked off to where she'd left Zeke. Halfway there, she glanced back, and there they all were, a few yards away, their devotion unshaken, following her.

Valeria reached down and grabbed a good-sized stone near her feet. She spun around and flung it at them. "Get out of here!" she screamed. "Can't you see? I don't want you around no more!" She snapped up another stone and threw it. "I don't care what happens to you! I don't...love you."

The wolves didn't move. The troubled look on their faces said it all: they were confused.

With her eyes red from crying and her body trembling, Valeria reached for another stone. "Please! Leave me alone!" She hurled it over their heads.

Tess was the first to turn her back to Valeria. Then, one by one, Zeus, Yoko, Diesel, and Scout did the same. Together, they walked away. The last to leave was Roxie, who stared directly into Valeria's eyes and whined like a young pup before slowly turning and following the others.

Once Valeria was atop Zeke, she never looked back.

"I'm going to miss you so much," she whispered, unable to stop crying, though no one was there to hear.

The narrow trail leading back to the ranch appeared much more uneven and treacherous than it had earlier. A brisk autumn wind from the west had moved in, and seemingly without warning, the deep blue morning sky turned a sullen gray. Within minutes, the mountain air became frigid, and it began to snow. A bitter chill blew against Valeria's cheeks.

"Mom, if you're listening, please watch over my babies," she said, softly. Shivering, Valeria pulled up the collar of her jacket.

She tried hard not to think. It was better not to think, but feelings of guilt and regret over leaving the wolves to survive on their own were already tormenting her mind. Almost immediately, Valeria questioned her decision, though she was certain she'd made the right one. The young pack might not have been ready, but what choice did she have? She thought about riding back to where she'd left them with the elk, but there was no guarantee they were still there.

Valeria rode on, barely able to see the trail through the veil of snow.

Less than ten minutes into the ride, while rounding a bend, she signaled Zeke to stop. Blocking the trail were two large tree branches, lying crisscross to form what looked like an X. Rather than attempt a relatively long horse jump over them, Valeria decided it'd be safer to take a moment to move them out of the way. She hopped down, secured Zeke, and grabbed the top branch. Both were fairly heavy, and she wondered how they'd found their way onto the trail since there hadn't been any downed limbs on the path earlier, nor were there any overhanging trees close by.

It was then Valeria heard an odd noise, coming from behind some rocks and brush not far away. It sounded like a newborn wolf pup whimpering, which seemed impossible since it was autumn, and wolves typically give birth very late in the winter and early spring. But still, the unmistakable sound of a baby wolf in distress drew her closer. If there was a young animal either hurt or in trouble, she had to see for herself and try to help.

Not sure what she might stumble upon, Valeria cautiously made her way through the dense vegetation on foot until she reached a shadowy wooded area next to a cluster of big rocks. She peeked around the corner, and there, propped up against a pine, was the source of the disturbing sound, some kind of electronic device, about the size of a handheld radio, playing a recording of a newborn wolf pup whimpering for its mother over and over.

Valeria realized immediately it'd been put there by hunters, a heinous trick to lure unsuspecting wolves into a deadly trap. Furious, she seized the device and smashed it repeatedly against a rock until it exploded into pieces. That still wasn't enough to release all her anger and frustration. She let out a fierce scream that echoed far and wide across the mountains.

One or more hunters must have passed through the area sometime that morning, Valeria realized. It explained the two tree branches, which hadn't been on the trail earlier. Jesse had told her wolves routinely use trails created by humans when hunting for prey. So, the branches had to have been placed there to slow down a passing wolf and draw its attention to the baby in distress. And if the faked cries were a lure to attract wolves, the hunters more than likely had laid a trap close to the recorder. She quickly glanced around and then heard a low, menacing growl.

Valeria spun around, and there, in the shadows, less than ten feet from her, were two eyes and a face she knew all too well. It was the leader of the Togwolee pack, snarling, its teeth bared. Their eyes locked as it inched toward her. Not wanting to panic or show fear, she quietly tried to back away but tripped over a rock and fell. In desperation, she struggled to find a stone to throw but came up empty. The wolf lunged. Valeria closed her eyes and screamed.

Her screams echoed, and then, for a moment, all was silent. There was no pain. She was alive.

When she opened her eyes, the wolf was lying on its side, panting. It had leapt and come up short. One of its hind legs was caught in a snare halfway to the hock. Valeria sat up. The wolf thrashed about, but the more it fought to free itself, the tighter the snare–a simple wire noose anchored to a tree–became. The snare had cut deep into the wolf's leg, which was soaked in blood.

"Oh, God," said Valeria.

Keeping her distance, she took a second to catch her breath before getting to her feet. Valeria dusted herself off. The wolf, in turn, also stood up, growled angrily at her, and again bared its teeth, but this time, its vicious expression quickly softened to one of utter exhaustion and defeat. It lay back down and whined.

"Serves you right." Valeria's heart was still racing.

She abruptly turned her back on the wolf and began to storm away but stopped.

For more than a minute, Valeria didn't move as she stared off into space and thought about what had happened. She then did an about-face. "Please forgive me," she said, gazing at the wolf that repeatedly had tried to kill her but now was lying on its side, trapped and helpless, sure to be slain by hunters when they returned.

Valeria quietly stepped closer to where the desperate wolf lay, paused just beyond the reach of its fangs and claws, and knelt. "You're a mother, aren't you?" she said, softly. The wolf appeared weak and, for just a second, diverted its eyes. "You thought you heard a pup, maybe lost or hurt, that needed your help, didn't you?" She inched closer. "We were both tricked into thinking the same thing–that an innocent life needed to be saved. The trap worked because we both care. In the end, that makes us more alike than different."

Very slowly and cautiously, Valeria extended the back of her hand. The wounded wolf groaned, then raised its head ever so slightly and sniffed it but didn't attempt to bite or get up.

"Yes…yes. Just relax," said Valeria. She carefully brought her hand to the side of the wolf's neck and gently stroked its fur. The wolf remained still. "I'm going to help you."

The icy wind had abated a bit, but a steady dusting of featherlike snow continued to fall and blanket everything it touched. Little by little, the surrounding world was turning whiter and whiter.

On her hands and knees, Valeria crept to where the wolf's hind leg was caught in the snare. The bloody gash, where the wire loop had cut deep into the flesh, looked much worse close up than it had from afar. She took a moment to examine the wire, which appeared to be some kind of durable ultra-thin cable with a tiny locking mechanism attached. Easing the tension to the lock at the end of the loop seemed simple enough, but undoing the cable from around the leg also meant removing it from the wound, which surely would hurt.

"Easy now," Valeria whispered.

With both hands, she took hold of the snare's locking device at the end of the wire loop, and the wolf flinched. It raised its head, glanced over its shoulder at her, bared its teeth, and snarled before laying its head back down.

"Stay calm," she said. Valeria removed her hands from the wire in case she needed to back away quickly. "This is going to sting a little, and I don't want you to bite me."

The wolf shook its trapped leg several times and panted. Valeria checked to see if its eyes were open. They were. As gently as possible, she grabbed the cable, made sure there was some slack in the length anchored to the tree, and pinched open the small lock at the end of the loop. She then took a deep breath and, in one swift motion, loosened the wire, spread open the snare, and yanked it off the wolf's foot.

Valeria jumped up and quickly backed away. For a moment, the wolf didn't move, appearing dazed, before sluggishly getting to its feet. It sniffed and licked the bloody gash on its leg, then raised its head and stared at her. Just a few yards separated the two as they stood in silence, facing each other. The expression on the wolf's face was hard to read.

"You're welcome," said Valeria.

The wolf slowly approached her, favoring the wounded leg and limping. There were no outward signs of aggression, but

Valeria was prepared to run to a nearby tree and climb it at the first hint of trouble. She stood very still and let the wolf come closer. When it was within arm's reach, it stopped, looked her in the eye, and howled.

Almost immediately, Valeria heard a second howl beyond a steep ridge off in the distance, then a third.

She smiled and tenderly stroked the side of the wolf's face and neck with the back of her hand.

Seconds later, she heard the crack of a gunshot echoing across the mountains, followed by several more. They were a long way off but coming from the direction of the valley, where she'd left the six young wolves with the elk.

The Togwolee wolf turned and ran away.

"My babies!" cried Valeria.

CHAPTER 21

Six weeks before her mother died, Valeria went with her to a pawnshop near where they lived in East Los Angeles. She didn't want to go, but Rosa had insisted she come.

"It'll do you some good to get a little fresh air," said Rosa. "You lay around holed up in this apartment too much. Anyway, I'm not asking you–I'm telling you. Get your lazy butt up and walk with me."

"Ah, Mom!" It was a Saturday afternoon, and Valeria had been texting a friend while binge-watching one of her favorite TV sitcoms. She'd seen the same episode more than a dozen times, but whatever. The show was just getting to a particularly funny scene, and she didn't want to pause it. She had her orange soda and microwave popcorn and no intention of getting off the sofa.

Rosa stood by the front door with her sunglasses on and holding her handbag. "Come on. We both need the exercise, and I could use the company," she said. "I've barely seen you this week. I don't know why you keep avoiding me or what's happening, but we never spend any time together."

Valeria reluctantly turned off the television and put on her shoes.

On the way to the pawnshop, not much was said. Valeria continued to text her friend, groaning that her mother was making her hang out with her for no good reason and, in general, ruining her life.

Over the years, she'd accompanied her mother to this particular pawn dealer a number of times. Rosa had a penchant for flea markets, second-hand stores, and thrift shops. She liked to hunt for bargains in such places and was on a first-name basis with many of the store owners.

Located in an old building on a busy street corner, the Nuestra Tierra Pawn Shop had been around forever. Inside, it was clean and well organized, but it had a strange, musty odor that smelled vaguely like bleach. There were guitars and other musical instruments on one wall, a section dedicated to tools of all kinds, several glass cases with coins, jewelry, watches, and another with firearms, and much more.

Valeria didn't know why her mother had wanted to come and assumed it was simply to get out of the apartment for a while, browse the showroom for a few good deals, or maybe inquire about something she might have seen earlier in the shop's window display. But instead, Rosa walked straight to the front counter without once glancing about.

An older gray-haired man wearing glasses got up from behind a massive antique desk that was partly buried under a mound of receipts, other papers, and a hodgepodge of what could only be described as miscellaneous "things." He came over to the counter and, still distracted by whatever he'd been doing, took a quick look back at his messy desk. Valeria reckoned the guy must have been in the middle of recalculating the numbers on some recent sale or deal.

"May I help you?" he asked in a matter-of-fact tone that was both polite and a bit unfriendly.

Rosa reached into her handbag and plucked out two gold rings. She then laid them on the counter in front of the man.

Valeria was taken aback because she recognized both rings. They were the diamond engagement ring and wedding band that her father, Ray, had bought and given to her mother. After the breakup and divorce, they'd been put away for safekeeping in a jewelry box. That had been years ago when Valeria was still quite young. And though they hadn't been taken out and worn since the split, she never thought her mother would ever part with them. To Valeria, the rings were one of the few connections she had to her father.

"Are you wanting to pawn or sell them?" asked the man.

"Sell," answered Rosa, her voice cool and sure.

The man reached under the counter and brought out a jeweler's loupe, which he held up to his eye. Holding the engagement ring in front of the loupe's magnifying lens, he sighed and said, "Not bad. It's decent quality. The diamond is nearly colorless. On the GIA scale, it's an H, which is quite common but good." He studied the diamond some more. "The size is just a little over one carat. I do see a few minor flaws."

"What are you doing, Mom?" asked Valeria.

"Getting rid of a few things I don't need anymore," she replied. "You'll understand someday."

The man brought over a small digital scale to the counter and set it in front of them. He then placed the two rings on the scale. "Together, their total weight is right at ten grams," he announced. "Of course, they're both fourteen karat gold."

"Okay," said Rosa.

"Mom!" said Valeria. "Don't do this."

The man pulled out a calculator from his pocket and punched some numbers. "The worldwide spot price for gold fluctuates every day," he said. "And lately, the price has been down. I have to make a profit when I go to resell the rings. I'm sure you understand." He jotted a number on a piece of paper and slid it in front of Rosa. "This is the best I can do."

Rosa barely glanced at the offer. "All right," she said. "It's less than I thought, but I'll let you have them for that."

"Mom, please!" Valeria repeated. "Those rings are special.

They mean something."

"Not anymore," said Rosa.

The man wrote out a receipt in longhand, then opened a register and took out a stack of twenty, fifty, and one-hundred-dollar bills. He counted the bills in front of Rosa, put the money in a cashier's envelope, and handed it to her.

At least two or three times a week for the next month, Valeria would ride her bicycle, stop in front of the pawnshop, and stare at her mother's rings on display in the window alongside other jewelry. She wanted desperately to buy them back but didn't have any money. Boldly, she asked Abuela to lend her the money, but her grandmother refused to give it to her.

"It's sad, I know," said Abuela. "But what can I do? I'm not made of money."

Then, one day, Valeria pulled up in front of the pawnshop, and both rings were gone. She threw down her bike and rushed inside. The same older man from before was behind the counter, sitting at his cluttered antique desk, eating a sandwich. He glanced up at her but didn't bother to get out of his chair.

"May I help you, young lady?" he asked.

"The two rings in the window, what happened to them?" Valeria asked, frantically.

"I sold them."

As Valeria raced to the valley atop Zeke, flashes of the scene with her mother at the pawnshop swept through her mind repeatedly. She thought she'd buried the memory for good long ago, but here it was again, haunting her at the oddest moment. *Why?* she asked herself. *Why now?*

"They meant something to me, Mom," Valeria shouted it out loud, the snow flurries rushing past her face. "You shouldn't have done it. Those rings meant something to me. They meant something…to me!" Her eyes started to well up, but now wasn't the time for tears. She was able to fight them off.

"I didn't tell you how angry I was." She rode on while the long-suppressed thoughts and emotions poured out from somewhere deep inside her. "You were so wrong to do it, Mom. An old love like Dad's, even if it was dead and gone in your mind, there was no amount of money, no price high enough you could've ever put on it, because love, like a breath of air, lives on, no matter how fleeting it might have seemed. A love that once was will always be.

"What you did was cruel, Mom. You discarded the memory of my dad's love like it meant nothing at all, and you did it right in front of me. I was always a part of that love, Mom, and you forgot about me. And I hated…hated you for doing it!"

Several more shots rang out.

They jolted Valeria back to the here and now. Hoping and praying she wasn't too late, she shoved aside the unwanted but tenacious memory to focus on finding her wolves and making sure they were okay.

"Hurry, Zeke!"

Minutes later, with the valley coming into view, Valeria brought Zeke to a quick halt, tossed his reins over a nearby tree branch on a dead run, and, out of breath, sprinted into the clearing. The elk herd had scattered to the edges of the forest on the far end of the valley. Two elk could be seen lying on the ground; one was struggling to rise but was unable to. High on the cliffs to the east, atop a line of rocks, she saw the glint of metal. The barrels of two rifles were pointed at the valley below. She couldn't make out the faces of the hunters, but she didn't need to. She knew who they were.

At first, the wolves were nowhere to be seen, but then Valeria spotted something lying in the grass in the distance. It was one of the three females, Yoko.

Waving her arms wildly, Valeria shouted, "Stop! Stop!"

She rushed to where Yoko lay and fell to her knees. The wolf was in distress, conscious, and panting. It had been shot through the neck, its fur soaked in blood from the open wound.

"What have you done?" screamed Valeria, her hands covered in blood as she applied pressure to try to stop the bleeding. Yoko went to lift her head but couldn't and fell back.

A voice cried out, "Get out of the way!" She'd been right. It was one of the two trophy hunters who knew Jesse.

More shots were fired, a loud crack echoing off the surrounding cliffs and across the valley each time. Valeria quickly glanced around to see what they were shooting at. There, where the open expanse of the valley met an adjacent woodland, were the other five wolves peeking their heads out from behind a line of trees and rocks.

"Stay back!" she yelled, but the wolves didn't listen. The moment they made eye contact with Valeria, they came jogging out into the clearing toward her.

"Get the hell out of the way, girl!" shouted one of the men. A second later, another barrage of bullets came raining down. Diesel was hit and fell.

"No!" screamed Valeria. "No! Stop!"

The four remaining wolves rushed to where Valeria was tending to Yoko and encircled her. They were joined seconds later by Diesel, who somehow had managed to get to his feet and limp to where the others had gathered. His hip bleeding, he collapsed near Valeria and whined.

Valeria looked up. The two trophy hunters had their rifle barrels pointed right at them. She knew they were waiting for one of the remaining wolves to stray away from her and the pack so they could take a clean shot.

"Go on and get out of there!" yelled one of the hunters. "They're just wolves! They're no-good killers that don't belong here!"

"You're the real killers!" Valeria jumped up. "You're evil...evil...murderers! You just want to kill them so you can brag about it to your buddies!"

Just then, Roxie, who was staring up at the cliffs and men, carelessly strayed a few yards away from the others. Valeria saw one of the men rise and take aim. She screamed, "No!" and rushed to leap in front of Roxie.

She heard the crack of the rifle, felt a sudden searing pain, stumbled backward, and fell down. Her head struck a sharp stone. Valeria instinctively touched the wound where she'd been shot. Her fingers were covered in blood. The world around her was spinning, but she was able to sit up. She took a quick look at the damage. The bullet had grazed her upper arm.

There were several more deafening shots. Then, the shooting stopped.

Valeria rose and defiantly stared up at the hunters, but they weren't there. She heard some kind of loud commotion emanating from the same area of the cliffs. It sounded like a scuffle. The men were cursing and shouting. Then, all went quiet.

The snow continued to fall. Valeria hurried back to where Yoko and Diesel lay. Both wolves were lying on their sides, still conscious but barely, unable to move and bleeding. She tore at the sparse mountain grass all around them, wet and dusted with snow, and packed it into their wounds to stanch the flow of blood.

"Hang in there!" she said. "I'm not going to let either of you die."

Valeria ran her hands over each of the fallen wolves to calm them. The grass seemed to be working. At least the bleeding had slowed. She continued to apply pressure to the wounds but knew it wouldn't be enough. Somehow, she would need to transport them back to the ranch and contact Lauren. But how? There was no way to move the two wolves, and she dared not leave them to go get help with the hunters still nearby.

She began to cry. "I'm sorry. I didn't mean for any of this to happen. It was my job to protect you, and I couldn't do it." Valeria looked up at the falling snow. "I don't know what to do."

At the top of her lungs, she shouted, "Someone, please help me!" Her voice echoed across the valley and mountains.

It was then, on the far side of the valley, at the base of the cliffs, that Valeria spotted the two trophy hunters. They were approaching her on foot. Although she couldn't quite make out their faces, she knew it was them. But something wasn't right. They had their hands up. Someone else was behind them, holding the men at gunpoint with a rifle. At first, she couldn't see the other person's face, but as they drew closer…

"Philip!" she shouted. Valeria sprang to her feet and, with arms open, ran to greet him.

She rushed headlong through the two hunters, who appeared bewildered, and threw herself onto Philip, hugging him as tight as she could, not wanting to let go, and showering his face with kisses.

"Val!" said Philip. "My sweet, precious Val!" With the hunters looking on, he embraced her and kissed her warmly on the cheeks.

Seeing that Valeria's jacket and shirt sleeves were shredded and her arm was bleeding, he said, "Oh, God! You've been shot, Val." He examined the wound more closely. "We need to get you to a doctor. Do you feel all right?"

"I'm okay," she answered. "The bullet didn't go in." In truth, though, her arm was starting to hurt, like it'd been badly burned.

Philip was dressed in the same tattered clothes he'd worn when she first met him and had his old rifle with him again as well. It was as if nothing had changed.

"What happened?" Valeria finally let go of him. "The last thing Dad told me was a jury found you guilty, and the judge sentenced you to prison. But here you are!"

Philip quickly glanced at the two hunters, who were listening closely. "I'll tell you everything in time," he answered. "But first, we need to get you home as soon as possible so someone can tend to your arm."

"But how did you know I was here?" Valeria asked. "How did you find me? Was it through my mom?"

"It wasn't your mother." Philip smiled. "It was you, Val. When you scream and shout, your voice carries pretty far. I was hunting, not far away, and the second I heard someone yelling, I knew it was you. It could've only been you." He kissed the top of her head. "I came as fast as I could."

Philip spotted the two wolves lying on the ground, as well as the other four hovering near their fallen siblings. "Gypsy's pups! Oh, what a fine sight! You've done well, Val." He suddenly noticed the two on the ground weren't moving. With his rifle pointed at the hunters, he made his way to the wolves. "What's going on here?"

"These two jerks shot them." Valeria turned and looked at the hunters. "I've been trying to stop the bleeding. I'm not sure, but I think they're dying."

"Listen, they're just wolves," spouted one of the hunters, loudly. "And how were we supposed to know she was willing to take a bullet for them? That's not our fault."

Philip walked up to the hunter and punched him in the gut with the butt of his rifle. The man dropped to his knees, groaning and holding his stomach. "Put your hands behind your head," said Philip. He approached the second man. "Assume the same position next to your buddy. Now!" The second hunter quietly obeyed.

With both men on their knees, Philip handed his rifle to Valeria. "Here. Keep an eye on them," he said. "Don't let them get up."

Philip knelt beside Yoko and Diesel and inspected their wounds. "We need to get them back to Goshawk Pass Ranch as quickly as possible." He stood up. "I'm going to gather a few long branches and some bark strips for lashing to make a couple of travoises to lay the two wolves on so we can move them. Your horse can pull one, and the men will be able to drag the other."

He retrieved a hunting knife from his pants pocket, unsheathed it, and headed toward the nearby woodland. "I'll be back in a few minutes."

As soon as Philip disappeared into the woods, the hunter who'd been protesting the most spoke up, "Have you ever used a rifle before?" He lowered his hands and began to get to his feet.

Valeria had the rifle pointed at his chest. "Don't move!" she said.

Glaring at her, the man slowly dropped back down to his knees and put his hands behind his head.

"The answer to your question is no," she added.

The man had a smirk on his face. "Come on now, miss. You want me to believe you have what it takes to shoot us? A nice girl like you! If me and my partner here were to get up and simply leave you and your mangy pack of wolves in peace without a fuss, you'd have to let us go, right?"

With her finger firmly on the trigger, Valeria replied, "My friend's gun holds four bullets. There's one round in the chamber and three more in a magazine." She grinned. "All I have to do is pull back on this bolt and push it forward to reload it each time I shoot."

The two men exchanged nervous looks.

Valeria brought the rifle up higher and aimed it a little straighter. "Neither of you is leaving my sight, and I'd love to shoot you both. I guess the only way you'll know for sure whether or not I have what it takes is if you get up off your knees and try to make a run for it. Do you think I'm weak or bluffing? If you do, go ahead! Run fast! Give me a reason to pull this trigger."

No more was said.

Goshawk Pass Ranch was lit up with the flashing emergency lights of three Teton County sheriff patrol vehicles, the same ambulance that had come for Jesse just the day before, and Ray's game warden truck. Lauren had also driven to the ranch to see if she could save the two wounded wolves.

A deputy sheriff was cuffing one of the hunters. "Do you and your daughter intend to press charges?" he asked Ray. After securing the man's hands behind his back, the officer shoved him forcibly into the backseat of the patrol car next to his friend.

"We didn't break any laws!" the hunter protested.

"Definitely," answered Ray. "Keep them locked up until I get back to the station. I'll make sure they do some serious jail time for negligence, assault with a deadly weapon, and shooting endangered and federally protected wildlife on government land."

Eleanor stood on the other side of the patrol car, peering in at the two men in custody. "If you'd be so kind, Officer, could you roll down this window for a second?" she asked. "Before you haul these two gentlemen away, I'd like a quick word with them."

"Sure, ma'am." From his front seat, he pressed a button and lowered the back window halfway.

Eleanor brought her face close to the open window, scowled at the two men, and spat on them. She then took a step back and tapped the side of the patrol car with her cane. "I'm done," she told the officer. "Thank you."

"What the hey?" said the hunter, nearest the window. Both men's faces were dripping. "Are you going to let her get away with that?"

The deputy raised the window, smiled at Eleanor, and

drove off.

Meanwhile, Valeria was sitting on a gurney at the rear of the ambulance while one of the paramedics examined her arm. Standing next to her were Ray and Jesse.

"How does it look?" asked Ray.

"Your daughter's lucky. The bullet nicked her good, but the wound is too shallow to require any stitches." The paramedic was applying a thin layer of petroleum jelly to the gash. "She's probably going to have a permanent scar, though. I've cleaned the area." He tore open a waterproof pouch containing a field dressing and taped it in place. Valeria winced. "She needs to keep the wound dry. I'll leave you a few extra bandages so you can change them out."

A second deputy sheriff, standing beside his patrol car, called Ray's name. He had a hold on Philip's arm, and Philip's hands were cuffed behind his back. Ray walked over to see what he wanted.

"We're getting ready to head back to the station with this one," said the deputy. "I checked the system, and wouldn't you know it, there's been an APB out for this guy for several months. His name is Philip Wakska. According to dispatch, he's near the top of Wyoming's most wanted list. The warrant says he killed a man on Wind River and was recently sentenced to thirty years plus for second-degree murder."

A third deputy sheriff, who'd been surveying the scene, came over to where Ray and the second deputy were standing. "No one knows how Wakska did it," added the third deputy. "But somehow, he managed to escape custody while they were transporting him on a corrections bus from county lockup to the state prison. They have surveillance video of him being shackled and placed on the bus for transfer, but when it arrived at the prison, he was gone."

As if resigned to his fate, Philip stood stoically next to the patrol car and said nothing.

Valeria was listening to the conversation.

The deputy who had Philip cuffed opened the back door to his patrol car. "Take a good look around, Wakska," he said. "Where you're headed, they don't have countryside near this pretty. You're going to be spending the next thirty years of your life staring at the steel bars of a maximum-security prison cell and razor-sharp barbed wire." The officer laughed.

He started to guide the escaped convict into the backseat, but Ray stepped forward and stopped him.

"Here. Give him to me," said Ray, pulling out a pair of handcuffs from his pants pocket. "Other than my daughter, he's the only eyewitness to what went on out there today, and if we're going to prosecute the hunters and make the charges stick, I need some answers to a bunch of questions only he can provide."

The two deputies glanced at each other, a little puzzled. "I don't know, Ray," said the one holding Philip. "Bringing him in falls under our jurisdiction."

"I understand," said Ray. "But it's really all a matter of timing. If the hunters ever go before a judge or jury, anything Wakska says about their intentions or actions will be dismissed by their defense attorney as outright lies since he's a convicted felon. But if he can provide me with additional evidence right here and now at the arrest scene that corroborates my daughter's testimony, it'll carry greater weight in the courtroom. Anyway, I need to talk to Wakska some more before he's locked away for good."

Hesitant, the deputies again looked at each other.

"Don't worry. I'll bring him straight to the station when I'm done," said Ray. "You two can go on back. There's no need for either of you to stick around any longer. I'll be there shortly."

"All right," said the deputy who was holding Philip. "We'll leave him with you so you can ask your questions and do what you need to do." He spun Philip around, undid his handcuffs, and turned him over to Ray.

With his daughter, Eleanor, and others looking on, Ray re-cuffed Philip's hands behind his back and grabbed him firmly by the arm.

"I'm starting to get hungry," said the one deputy to the other. "Do you want to stop somewhere and get a bite to eat when we get back to town?"

"Yeah, for sure," answered the other. "I'm starving."

Waving a quick goodbye to Ray and the other people gathered around, the two deputies climbed into their respective patrol cars, turned off their emergency lights, and drove off.

The paramedic who'd been attending to Valeria stepped out from behind the ambulance with her beside him. "We're done, Ray," he said. "Your daughter's arm will be sore for the next few days, but the pain should subside. I've given her instructions on what to do and what not to do. It's important that she keeps the wound dry and clean so it doesn't get infected. Also, the first chance you get, you need to bring her to the medical center and have one of the doctors take a look at the damage."

"Will do," said Ray, still holding onto Philip. "I appreciate you guys coming out here as quickly as you did."

"Thank you," said Valeria.

"No problem," said the paramedic, closing the rear doors to the ambulance. "Try not to dash out in front of any more bullets in the future, and stay safe." His partner was already waiting for him behind the wheel.

As soon as the ambulance was out of sight, Ray undid Philip's cuffs.

"Aren't you going to get in trouble?" asked Philip, rubbing his wrists.

"You escaped…again," answered Ray with a wry smile. "And I don't have any idea how you did it."

The two followed Valeria and Eleanor to the old pigpen, where Lauren was on her knees, attending to Diesel with Jesse's help. The wolf was lying on its side, kicking sporadically. Yoko, eyes closed and motionless, was sprawled out in the pen as well. The others remained just outside the pen. Roxie was pacing back and forth, anxiously peering through the fence, while the rest of the siblings fidgeted. They were lying down together with heads up and ears alert.

Lauren looked up. "It's good you're here, Val. We can't seem to get Diesel to settle down," she said. "He took a bullet to the hip, and I need to remove it. I've given him a sedative, but he's still fighting me." Jesse was kneeling behind Diesel's neck, stroking the wolf's fur, trying to calm him.

Valeria knelt next to Jesse and brought her face close to Diesel's. "There, there," she said. "Just relax and let her help you." She nuzzled the wolf.

"Almost done," said Lauren. On the ground beside her, she had a large open veterinary satchel that was filled with medical tools and first-aid supplies. She was using an extractor to try to remove the lodged bullet.

A few moments later, Lauren exclaimed, "Got it!" She pulled out the bullet and held it up to the sunlight. "It didn't fragment. That's good." She finished sterilizing the wound, put the projectile in a baggie, and tossed it to Ray.

The full effects of the sedative must have finally kicked in because Diesel suddenly quieted and closed his eyes. While Lauren finished closing the gunshot wound with absorbable sutures, Valeria went over to Yoko and knelt. The wolf looked dead.

"Is she…?" asked Valeria, unable to say the word.

"No," answered Lauren. "I gave her a much stronger tranquilizer. She's out completely and will be for a few hours."

"Is she going to be all right?"

"I think so, but Yoko is very lucky." Lauren closed her satchel and stood up. "Incredibly, the bullet passed straight through the back of her neck without striking any bones or vital organs. She's lost a fair amount of blood, but if there's no nerve damage, she should recover quickly. I've closed both the entry and exit wounds. For now, it's best she just lies here and rests."

Valeria kissed Yoko on the head and got to her feet. She then went over to Lauren and gave her a quick hug. "I don't know what we'd do without you," she said.

"You're more than welcome, dear," said Lauren. "When the two wake up, they'll both be groggy for a while. It'll be important to give them some space until they're alert and acting more like their old selves again."

Jesse got up and followed Valeria and Lauren out of the pen. "Maybe now isn't the time to ask, but what were you thinking, Val?" he asked angrily. "I mean, riding off into the mountains like that by yourself? You could've been killed."

Valeria threw her arms around Jesse and kissed his cheek. "I did what was best for the wolves," she said, pulling away. "Dr. Irwin's coming tomorrow, and these are my babies. I love them and would rather die than let them become secret lab experiments for the government."

Just then, Butch and Sam joined the group gathered near the wolves and pigpen.

"Relax, Val," said Butch. "None of us are going to allow some bureaucrat masquerading as a scientist or anyone else to come take these wolves away. We're all behind you one hundred percent."

Eleanor interrupted. "Well, this certainly has been a long and interesting day, but it's nearly dinnertime. Given the good news that our dear Valeria has returned with her wolves, safe and sound, I've asked Giuseppe to prepare us something extra special this evening, and I insist everyone stay and eat."

"It's very kind of you to offer," said Philip. "But I need to head out now."

"I understand," Eleanor replied. "You have an open invitation to come, enjoy a good meal, and spend time with us whenever you want. Just know that. Okay?"

"I'll certainly take you up on your offer sometime." Philip turned to Valeria. "Will you walk with me to the gate and see me off? That is if you feel up to it."

Valeria nodded.

Ray said, "Wait here a second." He went to his truck, came back with Philip's rifle, and handed it to him. "This might come in handy when you do get hungry."

Philip took a moment to shake everyone's hand before leaving. After he expressed a few brief words of thanks, he and Valeria headed down the dirt road toward the main gate.

At first, neither said a word. The sky in all directions had cleared considerably. There were still more than a hundred head of cattle scattered across several fields, busy munching on fresh hay bales left for them when it had snowed earlier in the day. A few calves were nursing.

Valeria looked out across one of the fields. "How often do you think about your daughter?"

Philip was slow to respond. "Whenever I come across a fleeting moment, wonderful and sublime, like the morning sun's reflection in a mountain stream or a single wildflower emerging through the snowmelt in the spring, I think of Minsi." He paused. "There was a time when her death was so painful I tried hard not to think about her. I escaped into this wilderness, in part, to forget the past. Although the isolation and my love for the wolves helped ease the hurt a bit, it wasn't until I met you that I felt a kind of transcendent healing envelop my soul and could again embrace fully the shining light that my daughter was and is."

"I would've liked to have met her," said Valeria.

"You would have become good friends."

Valeria spotted two rabbits, one chasing the other along the fence line. They reminded her of the time Philip had fed her the jackrabbit stew after she was thrown off the pony and broke both her legs. Others said it was nothing short of a miracle that he'd found her at the bottom of the ravine in a near-blinding snowstorm and that she'd survived.

"Do you ever hear Minsi's voice whispering to you the way you heard my mother?" she asked.

"Sadly, no… But I do listen for her." Philip stopped and gazed out across one of the fields. "I can't explain it, but maybe my daughter's soul is at peace and has moved on to some other realm." He turned to look at Valeria. "What happens when our lives end and we cross over to the other side? I haven't a clue."

They continued on to the gate.

When they arrived, Philip unlatched it.

"What about my mother?" asked Valeria. "Do you think she's at peace?"

"I don't know." Philip opened the gate. "When you and I first met, and you were with me at the campsite, healing, I sensed your mother watching over you. And Gypsy and the other wolves also were in tune with her spiritual energy. It was exquisite." He paused for a moment. "After the avalanche, when you were gone from my life, her presence disappeared as well."

He looked Valeria in the eyes. "To be honest, I'd all but forgotten about your mother–that is, until today. A few minutes before your screams, I heard a soft voice whisper to me from above and recognized who it was immediately. It was her, your mother, but her voice was very, very faint."

Valeria's eyes lit up. "What did she say?"

"I'm sorry, but I couldn't quite make it out," he answered. "Her voice was like a passing breeze. She was there and not there. And at the time, I had no idea you were nearby." Again, he paused. "Your mother seemed to be repeating the same thing over and over, no more than a few words or phrases. Then something else flashed in my mind, for just a moment, a sign or symbol of some kind. I didn't understand it."

"What kind of symbol? What did it look like?"

With the heel of his boot, Philip drew a simple image on the dirt road: It was two perfect circles, both the same size, that overlapped. When he was done, he stood back so Valeria could see it.

"I don't know what it means," he said.

Valeria stared at the circles.

"Two rings, perhaps, intertwined?" he added.

CHAPTER 22

The morning air brushed against Valeria's cheeks. It felt chilly but refreshing. Sluggishly, she opened her eyes, unzipped the sleeping bag, and sat up. Sprawled atop the bag, across where her feet had been, was Tess. To her right, warmly pressed against her body, was Zeus, and on the left lay Roxie, with Scout next to her. Nearby, Yoko was awake and sitting up, as was Diesel. Neither looked to be in pain.

Valeria had insisted on spending one last night with the pups she'd help raise. Her father had discouraged her from sleeping outdoors, saying it was far too cold out and he didn't want her catching pneumonia. But shortly after Ray left for Jackson to file charges against the hunters, Eleanor brought Valeria an old sleeping bag and a heavy wool blanket.

"For God's sake, a little cold won't kill you, and it's just one night," Eleanor replied. "Forget what your dad said. I know how much blood, sweat, and tears you've poured into caring for these wolves. And after tomorrow, who knows if you'll ever see them again. I say, bundle up good and enjoy their company while you still can. You'll remember this fondly for the rest of your life."

Eleanor had been right. Valeria was already smiling as she recalled how reassuring it felt to lie down in the old pig pen and simply gaze up at the moon and stars nestled among her babies.

"Excuse us, Val."

She looked behind her. Big Duke and another ranch hand were standing just outside the pen's gate with two wheelbarrows, filled to overflowing with thick cuts of venison. Valeria slowly got to her feet and gathered up the sleeping bag and blanket.

"Since the wolves are leaving us today, Butch suggested it'd be nice if the pack had a proper send-off," said Big Duke. "A few of us went out and hunted this elk before daybreak, so it's as fresh and juicy as it gets." He opened the gate for Valeria and let her pass. "We're going to miss you and your furry pals when you're gone."

"Thank you," said Valeria. "I'll miss you too."

Before stepping into the pen, Big Duke set down his wheelbarrow and held out his arms. "Come on now!" he said. "Where's my hug?"

Smiling from ear to ear, Valeria dropped the sleeping bag and blanket and threw her arms around him.

The two embraced. "That's my girl!" replied Big Duke. The aging cowboy kissed her on the cheek before letting her go. "How in the world are we going to live without you, Hugger?"

After the men finished distributing the venison inside the pen, Valeria lingered nearby for a few minutes to see whether Yoko and Diesel had their appetites back. Fortunately, they did. She watched the two injured wolves carefully sniff the meat, then growl and tussle for choice pieces. Soon, they were guarding their scraps and eagerly devouring everything in sight right alongside their siblings.

Valeria headed for the ranch house to shower. On her way, she passed Jesse, who was making his way to the stable to help tack up the horses.

"Breakfast is ready," said Jesse. "I'll meet you out by the barn when you're done."

The warm smell of bacon, omelets, and jam on homemade buttermilk biscuits hit Valeria's nose the moment she came through the front door. She was going to miss Giuseppe's cooking.

"Just say the word, and I'll whip up whatever you want," said Giuseppe. "I've also prepared a large batch of your favorite fruit smoothie."

Valeria took a quick hot shower, then came back out to eat, gorging on most everything the cowboy chef served. Afterward, she went into the guest bedroom and finished packing her belongings.

Eleanor appeared in the doorway. "I wish you didn't have to leave," she said. "You have no idea how much I'm going to miss you." The elderly woman's eyes welled up as she stepped into the room. "Please come back to us," she added. "I never had a daughter, but if I did, I'd want her to be just like you–smart, thoughtful, kind, and brave. I love you, Val. Don't be a stranger."

Valeria threw her arms around Eleanor and held her tight. "I love you, too."

Just then, they heard Jesse shout, "He's here!" followed by the heavy rumble of multiple vehicles arriving on the property.

The two peered out a window to see for themselves who it was, but they already knew. Dr. Irwin's return had been a near certainty. Eleanor retrieved her cane, and with Valeria steadying her arm, the two rushed to confront him.

Dr. Irwin stepped out of a black SUV. He had a smile on his face. With him were Sergeant Norris and a driver, both dressed for combat. They'd brought along two animal transport vehicles, three all-terrain tactical Humvees, and a small army of a dozen uniformed men, all wearing camouflaged body armor and carrying a semi-automatic pistol, GPS locator, and other gear. Several of the soldiers also had Tasers, shaped like sidearms, in their hands.

Speaking directly to his men, Sergeant Norris said loudly for all to hear, "You'll find the six wolves over there." He pointed in the general direction of the pig pen.

One of the soldiers said, "Yes, sir!" He then picked up a canvas satchel off the ground and raised a closed fist in a sign of solidarity. "Come on, men! Work together, and let's get this over with."

The soldiers finished gathering their gear and hurried toward the pen like they were part of some secret special operations strike team.

Valeria was thirty yards or so ahead of them, running as fast as she could to get to the wolves first. Halfway there, Jesse joined her.

"What do we do?" he asked.

"I'm not sure," said Valeria, out of breath. "Try to hide the wolves from them, I think."

The wolves had finished their going-away meal and were lying about outside the pen with their eyes half closed, resting.

Shouting and waving her arms, Valeria tried to rouse them, but the pack barely stirred.

The soldiers came at a trot and overtook them before any more could be done. One of the men lifted Valeria off the ground and tossed her aside.

"Don't touch her!" yelled Jesse. He balled up his fists and took a swing at the soldier but missed.

Two other soldiers shoved Jesse to one side. "Stay back!" one of them shouted.

Several of the wolves rose, growled viciously, and bared their teeth, but the soldiers were efficient. In less than a minute, the contingent had secured the pack by binding each wolf's front and back legs together with heavy-duty zip ties and looping duct tape several times around their muzzles to close their jaws shut.

With Valeria and Jesse at their heels and chucking rocks at them, the soldiers quickly lifted the wolves by the zip ties around their feet, two men to each animal, and started carrying them back to the animal transport vehicles.

"You can't do this!" screamed Valeria. "It's not right! Put them down." She hit one of the soldiers in the arm with a rock and another in the back of the neck, but neither flinched.

On their way to the vehicles beyond the main barn, the soldiers were suddenly confronted by Eleanor and Butch.

"Stop!" Eleanor declared firmly. "The next one of you who takes another step will have to deal with me personally!" She raised her cane and pointed it at their heads.

The soldiers stopped dead in their tracks and glared at her. Unsure what to do next, one of the men radioed Sergeant Norris, who showed up within moments with Dr. Irwin by his side.

Dr. Irwin saw the bound wolves and said, "Good work, men!" He placed his hand on the head of the closest wolf to him. "They're remarkable creatures," he added before turning to face Eleanor. "As promised, Mrs. Hardin, I've brought along a signed federal court order giving me the legal authority to confiscate these wolves on behalf of the FDA. The girl and her father had their chance to set them free and failed." He nonchalantly pulled out a notarized document from a folder and handed it to her.

With Valeria and Jesse by her side, Eleanor held up the court order as if to read it, but instead, she ripped the document in half and tossed the pieces to the ground.

"You have no authority here," Eleanor replied. "And you won't be taking these wolves with you."

"Stand down, woman!" ordered Sergeant Norris. "My men have been instructed to seize these animals by any means necessary, and we're not returning to base empty-handed. We have our orders and intend to follow through."

Butch stepped forward, brought his face within inches of Sergeant Norris's, and shoved him. "Who do you think you're talking to?" he said, firmly. Before the sergeant could react, Butch shoved him hard again, knocking the sergeant back farther. "Let me put this in layman's terms you can understand: you're on our land, and you've got less than a minute to drop those wolves and leave quietly before we throw you out."

Sergeant Norris stood his ground. "We're not leaving without them," he repeated.

Butch whistled, and moments later, all the ranch hands, including Sam, dropped what they were doing and came running from near and far. With a nod from Butch, they encircled the soldiers, surrounding them.

"Let my wolves go!" yelled Valeria. "You have no right to come here and do this." She attempted to rush two of the soldiers, but Jesse grabbed her shoulders and held her back.

"Don't do it," Jesse whispered in her ear, trying to calm Valeria down. "These guys are no joke. You could get hurt."

Still carrying the wolves, several of the soldiers lowered their shoulders and attempted to force their way through the blockade of determined ranch hands but were immediately pushed back, which escalated the standoff into a full-fledged brawl. Men were shoved, punches thrown, and insults hurled, with both sides refusing to give in. When all was said and done, after a tense few minutes, the stalemate remained intact. The soldiers were still hemmed in by the ranch hands.

Frustrated, Dr. Irwin lashed out at the soldiers, "Don't let a bunch of good-for-nothing cowboys intimidate you!" He pointed a finger at Sergeant Norris. "You get your men to load these lousy wolves into the transport cages at once, and let's get the hell out of here."

Their arms growing tired, a number of the soldiers began to lay down the heavy wolves to rest. Valeria broke free of Jesse and rushed to Tess, who was the nearest wolf to her. Dropping to her knees, she held and tried to comfort the panic-stricken female, who was breathing heavily and kicking and struggling to break free of the zip ties.

One of the soldiers who'd been carrying Tess booted

Valeria hard in the shin and pushed her away.

Big Duke, who saw what happened, pushed past a couple of soldiers and came to Valeria's aid. He lifted her off the ground and helped her back to Jesse. Then, he turned to face the soldier who'd struck her.

"That was a big mistake," Big Duke said, angrily. "Weren't you ever taught to never hit a girl?" Without warning, he threw a punch, which knocked the soldier down hard onto his backside.

With that, tensions on both sides spiraled out of control, turning the impasse over the wolves into a free-for-all. Amid the seemingly endless cursing, faces were bruised and knuckles bloodied. The soldiers and ranch hands pummeled each other, wrestled, and rolled about on the ground.

Then, there was a loud boom.

The fighting stopped immediately, and everyone quickly looked around to see who'd pulled out a gun.

Ray had arrived. In his hands, he held a twelve-gauge shotgun, pointed at the sky. Beside him was Lauren, carrying her veterinary first aid bag. They'd pulled up without anyone noticing and were approaching the confrontation.

"Enough!" yelled Ray.

Pushing her way past several ranch hands and soldiers who were still grappling and shoving each other, Lauren saw what had been done to the wolves. "Oh, my God!" she cried. "What's going on here?" She dropped to her knees and opened her emergency kit to help Zeus, the closest wolf to her. She then pulled out a pair of medical scissors to cut off the tape wrapped around his muzzle.

"Stop her!" said Dr. Irwin.

The two soldiers who'd been carrying Zeus grabbed Lauren's arms and lifted her off the struggling wolf. They forcibly pushed back the veterinarian and kicked her bag away.

Valeria rushed to her father in near tears. Ray held her

close for a moment to calm her. "Don't worry," he said. "I'll take care of this, okay?" She nodded and moved aside.

Lauren found Valeria, and the two embraced.

With his shotgun at his side, Ray walked up to Dr. Irwin and stood in front of him. "You and your men have less than ten minutes to get back in your vehicles and leave," he said calmly.

"You must be confused, Officer Cortez," Dr. Irwin replied. "I have a notarized federal court order giving me, on behalf of the FDA and US Army, full custody of these wolves." He grinned. "And since you're an officer of the law around these parts, I expect you to uphold the oath you took and enforce our legal rights without bias. Tell these hooligans to allow us to pass."

"Nine minutes," said Ray.

Dr. Irwin glared at him. "You either let us leave with these wolves, or I'll make sure you're fired and never work as a game warden again."

Ray glanced at his daughter before responding. "In case you're confused or a little fuzzy about the details, Dr. Irwin, let me rephrase my command so you have a better understanding. If you don't heed my warning to leave peacefully, I'm prepared to toss you and every one of these soldiers in jail."

"On what charges?" asked Dr. Irwin.

"Trespassing and assaulting civilians."

"You can't be serious."

"I'll make sure you personally serve time in the county lockup for assault," said Ray. "And as this is your second go round with the local judge for attacking our law-abiding people without provocation, I'm pretty sure you'll be denied bail for being a repeat offender." He paused and smiled. "Look around you, Dr. Irwin. These folks are on my daughter's side and have helped support her efforts with the wolves. Every one of them is an eyewitness who'll testify against you under oath and corroborate my version of events."

Sergeant Norris stepped between the two men. "I've heard enough!" he blurted loudly. "You're interfering with an authorized mission of the US Army, Officer Cortez. You either stand aside and allow us to do our job or face the consequences."

Standing toe to toe, Ray looked the sergeant in the eyes and calmly handed Butch his shotgun. "What exactly are the consequences I'm facing, Sergeant Norris?" he asked.

Sergeant Norris glanced around at his men, who were all staring at him. Many looked beat up, their faces bruised and lips cut from trading punches with the ranch hands.

"Five minutes," said Ray. "Gather your men and go."

The sergeant turned his back to Ray for a moment as if to leave, then spun around fast and took a swing at him. Ray ducked the punch and countered with a hard blow to Norris's chin. The sergeant's legs buckled; his eyes rolled back in his head, and he dropped straight to the ground in a heap. With one blow, Ray had knocked Sergeant Norris unconscious.

Ray turned his attention to the soldiers. "You heard me!" he said. "Get back in your vehicles, all of you, and leave. Now!" He glanced down at the sergeant. "And take your fearless leader with you."

With some hesitation, several of the soldiers came over, picked up the sergeant, and carried him back to their vehicles. He was still out cold. The other men followed suit, leaving Dr. Irwin alone with Ray.

Lauren rushed to the aid of the young wolves. With Valeria helping to keep them calm, she gently and carefully snipped away the duct tape from around their muzzles, then sliced off the zip ties that bound their front and back legs. Once freed, each wolf rose but didn't flee. The expression on nearly every one of their faces was a mixture of both fierce indignation and bewilderment.

"This isn't over," said Dr. Irwin. "I'm still going to have a word with your superiors."

"You do that," answered Ray. "But first, you might want to mull this over in your mind: I'm ready to file a very damning and career-ending report on you as well, not just with whoever signs your paychecks but also with the world's largest animal rights groups and the local news media. They're always looking for a good story." He reached into his pants pocket and pulled out a pair of handcuffs. "And if you don't want to spend the next few weeks of your life behind bars, I suggest you get a move on and join your buddies before I have a change of heart and run you in."

Dr. Irwin didn't respond. Instead, he reached down to pick up the torn pieces of his federal court order.

Everyone heard a low growl. Still half-bent over, Dr. Irwin quickly glanced behind him. Staring back was Roxie, her teeth bared, eyes wild and intense, and the hackles raised on her neck.

"Oh, crap!" said Dr. Irwin. "Keep her away from me." He rose slowly, then stood very still.

Scout and Diesel joined Roxie. Their lips curled back, all three were snarling at Dr. Irwin.

"My best advice is don't look them in the eye," said Ray. "And don't make any sudden moves." He looked over at his daughter and smiled. "Above all, don't try to make a run for it."

The three wolves lowered their heads and crept toward Dr. Irwin. In a panic, he turned to run but fell flat on his face. With his mouth covered in dirt, he looked up, dazed and confused.

Ray and everyone else roared with laughter.

Eleanor had tripped him with her cane.

CHAPTER 23

At the edge of a rock-strewn cliff that overlooked an immense valley surrounded by steep mountains, Valeria squeezed back on her reins and brought Zeke to a halt.

"Good boy," she said.

She patted him and hopped off, then looped his reins over the branch of a nearby spruce. The panoramic view was breathtaking. Despite several recent snowstorms, autumn had yet to fully give way to winter. Against a brilliant blue sky sprinkled with white fluffy clouds, ribbons of bright orange, yellow, and red flowed down the cottonwood forests and aspen groves in the distance. A black bear with two yearling cubs could be seen moving along an outcrop of stark gray rocks on the other side of the valley. Closer below, an enormous bull moose was busy nibbling on willow leaves.

This was, indeed, an extraordinary land, and despite everything she'd endured, Valeria couldn't imagine ever moving back to Los Angeles. The rugged mountain range and untamed beauty all around her spoke in silence to the very core of her being.

Jesse, who'd been leading the way for a time on Cutter, arrived soon after. Following close behind him were the wolves, then Ray and Lauren, riding side by side. They were keeping an eye on Diesel, who was favoring his hip and struggling a bit to keep up with the others.

"Where did Philip say he'd be out here?" asked Ray.

"He didn't," answered Valeria. "He said he'd know when we were coming and would reach out to us in some way."

Lauren was off her horse and examining Yoko and Diesel's bullet wounds for any lingering soreness or signs of infection. "A needle in a haystack. That's what this feels like," she said. "You could hike in and out of this wilderness for years searching for someone and never find them."

"True," said Ray. "I saw Philip's wanted file back at the Sheriff's Office. The lawmen who are out looking for him were told the exact location of his hideout, the old mountaineer's shed. So, it's unlikely he'll return to it, at least not for a while, because that shed will be the first place they'll search."

"I say we rest here for a few minutes and figure out what to do next before wasting any more time looking for him," said Jesse. "It would have been nice to know where he disappeared to beforehand."

No sooner did the words come out of Jesse's mouth, when Valeria spotted something. "Look!" she blurted, pointing.

To the south was a twisting trail of white smoke rising from a narrow divide between two mountains.

"That's him," said Valeria.

"How do you know?" asked Jesse.

She shrugged. "I just do."

Ray retrieved a pair of high-powered binoculars from his saddlebag and held them up to his eyes. "It looks too concentrated in one spot to be a wildfire. And smoke from a small campfire typically doesn't rise that high. It smolders and remains closer to the source," he said. "The blaze is a good two to three miles away."

"We're already several miles off trail," said Lauren. "I don't see any way for us to get over to it."

"I don't see how either," said Ray. "There are no trails

in or out that I know of, and this sheer mountain terrain can be treacherous." He lowered his binoculars. "What do you think, Jesse? You're the expert when it comes to navigating these mountains."

Jesse was standing beside Valeria near the edge of the cliff. "I'm not sure there's any safe path to it," he said, before pausing to think. "A straight shot from here won't work, but there might be a way to reach the fire if we ride north off in the opposite direction about a mile, then cross back over. Still, it won't be easy. This area has a lot of dangerous cliffs, and in the places where it's way too steep, we'll need to lead the horses on foot."

Valeria turned to Lauren. "What about Diesel?" she asked. "He's limping pretty badly. Do you think he has the strength to make it that far?"

"I'm not sure he can," Lauren answered. "Given the fact his wound hasn't had a chance to heal properly, Diesel's doing much better than I expected. But this long trek is clearly aggravating his hip. He's in pain."

Not much more was said. Everyone stretched their legs, drank some water, and rested for a little while before getting back on the horses. They then headed north, following Jesse's lead, in search of a safe route down the cliffs and back toward the smoke.

Jesse had been right. The group soon encountered a massive outcrop of rocks along the cliff face, which proved to be both impenetrable and impossible to circumvent.

"What now?" asked Valeria.

"If we backtrack, there's a path–it's no more than a ledge, really–that runs along this cliff to a high wooded area on the other side," Jesse replied. "From there, we'd have access to the valley below, but the ledge is extremely narrow in places. I'm not sure the horses can make it, and there's a sheer drop beneath. It would save us time, but I wouldn't risk it."

"Show us the ledge," said Ray.

Jesse took everyone to a spot along the ridge where a cluster of boulders dangled precariously over the edge. The path was partly hidden by the boulders and dense vegetation. The horses were secured to nearby trees, and after snapping off a few sizable limbs that were blocking the way, Ray cautiously followed Jesse to the ledge on foot to see if it was wide enough for the horses and where it led. Valeria went with them, while Lauren stayed behind with the wolves.

The ledge's width varied, but it looked to be no more than three to four foot wide in most places. An uneven surface and loose stones made footing treacherous, and a sharp bend around the cliff face, some forty to fifty yards away, made it impossible to see where the path ended without exploring further. A sheer drop along the cliff face ran directly below the entire length of the ledge.

"How far down is that?" asked Valeria, carefully peering over the edge.

"A hundred fifty feet or more," Ray answered.

He went back to his horse and returned with a long coil of nylon rope, which he secured around Valeria's and Jesse's waists, then his own. "Let's not take any unnecessary chances," he said, "in case one of us slips." The threesome then slowly made their way down to the bend, with Ray taking the lead.

Halfway there, Valeria stumbled on a protruding stone but caught herself. Jesse, bringing up the rear, grabbed her shoulders to steady her.

Ray paused to make sure she was okay. "Careful!" he said.

The far side of the bend revealed another fifty yards of cliff face and ledge. It was just as Jesse had described. The precarious mountain path led to a sparse wooded area and what looked to be a more gently sloping ridge that extended to the valley below.

"What do you think?" asked Jesse.

"It's doable, but just barely," said Ray.

They returned to Lauren. Then, very slowly, one at a time, Ray and Jesse took turns walking each horse out onto the ledge and to the other side. Once across, the horses were tied off to a tree before going back for the next one. Then, with a rope again tied around their waists, both helped Lauren safely across, then Valeria. The wolves followed close behind her single file, with Diesel limping across last.

"No one's here," said Jesse.

They'd entered a narrow but very deep and rocky canyon-like area littered with huge boulders. Near the center of the canyon, atop a few flat rocks, was a good-sized bonfire, still burning brightly. Its billows of smoke were rising straight up into the atmosphere.

"Well, this fire didn't build itself," said Ray. "Let's secure the horses and take a look around."

The wolves lay down to rest. Above, the once-vibrant sky had begun to change as ominous pale gray clouds rolled in.

Lauren glanced up. "Sometime this afternoon, we're supposed to be getting a strong snowstorm," she said. "I don't think we want to be anywhere out here when it comes."

A northwest wind already had begun to gust.

"It's afternoon now," said Valeria.

While Lauren waited near the fire, Ray, Jesse, and Valeria fanned out across the remote canyon in search of Philip. Other than the bonfire, there was no shelter, no hunting gear, cookware, utensils, or survival tools lying around, nothing whatsoever to indicate that the Shoshone had ever been there.

"Philip!" shouted Valeria, repeatedly. "Philip!" Her voice echoed off the canyon walls.

"Philip!" hollered Ray and Jesse.

After thirty or forty minutes, Ray called out, "There's no trace of him." He met the others back at the bonfire. "It's possible someone else is responsible for building this blaze, but if it was Philip, it looks like he's moved on."

"How long do we wait to see if he returns?" asked Lauren.

"I'm not sure, but the skies don't look good. We ought to head back to the ranch fairly soon before the storm hits," answered Ray.

Just then, everyone heard a low, menacing growl. It had emanated from behind a mass of boulders some thirty to forty yards away. All six wolves sprang to their feet and gathered near Valeria. The hackles on several were raised, and both Roxie and Scout snarled in response.

Another growl, and then a large wolf appeared atop one of the boulders. It was joined by two others. They stood shoulder to shoulder, glaring at everyone.

Keeping his eyes fixed on the wolves, Jesse quietly walked over to Cutter and pulled a rifle from out of a leather scabbard.

Together, the three wolves on the boulder jumped down and, with heads lowered, began to slowly walk toward the group.

"Don't make any sudden moves, and let's see what they do," said Ray. "There's something not quite right. They're outnumbered and normally wouldn't be this aggressive."

Everyone stood still except Jesse, who raised his rifle and pointed it at the three wolves.

Valeria shouted, "No, wait!" She sprinted to where Jesse was standing and, with both hands, grabbed the rifle barrel. "They're not here to hurt us." She forced him to lower it.

"What makes you so sure they won't attack?" he asked.

"Their ears aren't raised. They're flattened against their heads," said Valeria. "Also, I happen to know these three wolves." She smiled and rushed to greet them. "Sparkle! Titan! Romeo!"

"No! Stop!" yelled Ray. "What are you doing?"

Valeria dropped to her knees in front of the three wolves, and after circling her several times, they let her put her arms around each of them.

"Oh, wow!" said Lauren. "That's incredible. How on earth did she do that?"

With her father, Lauren, and Jesse keeping their distance and looking on, Valeria continued to shower the new arrivals with affection, stroking their fur and letting them nuzzle her in return. "I never thought I'd see you again," she told them.

"How do you know these wolves?" asked Ray.

"They were with Philip the day he saved me. They lived with him at the mountaineer shed," said Valeria. "These two are Titan and Sparkle. They're brother and sister, Gypsy's older kids. And this guy here is Romeo. He was once a lone wolf who was allowed to join the pack." She gently stroked Romeo's neck. "This is all that's left of Gypsy's pack, just these three…"

She was suddenly interrupted. "Nine!" said a voice from somewhere behind the bonfire. "There are now nine, plus a few other honorary two-legged members."

Valeria instantly recognized the voice and jumped to her feet. "Philip!" she shrieked, joyously.

Philip stepped out from behind the fire. "Hello, everyone!" he said warmly. "I apologize for not being here to greet you when you arrived, but I had to make sure you weren't being followed."

He shook Ray's hand, acknowledged Lauren and Jesse with a nod and a smile, then slowly made his way to Valeria. He looked her in the eyes and said, "I'm so glad you returned to us, even if it's only for a short while." He kissed her forehead, and the two hugged.

"It's nice to see you, too," said Valeria.

"I wasn't able to control Sparkle, Titan, or Romeo when they sensed you were nearby. They left me in the dust to go find you." Philip laughed, then took a few steps back and added, "Do you recognize this place?"

"No," she answered.

Philip spread out both his arms and glanced up. "This is the ravine. This is where your mother led the wolves and where we found you in the snowstorm. You were lying unconscious right there, where you see the fire." He paused. "I come to this very spot sometimes to rest and think, to remember there are untold spirits in the heavens who watch over each of us, and if we take time to listen closely, they'll send an angel to clear a path and help guide our steps in our hour of need."

"Are you saying my mom's an angel?"

"I'm certain she is, but no, I was talking about you, Val," said Philip. "You're our angel. Gypsy had been shot and was dying, and you came, seemingly from out of nowhere, and helped save these wolves. By coming back for me when you did and rescuing the pups, you saved this pack. And the sad and ugly truth is, after Minsi disappeared, I kind of lost my way and came to these mountains, prepared to die a slow death out here in the wilderness all alone, with no one to bear witness… And you saved me. Somehow, you rekindled my faith in the things that truly matter in this world and gave me more reasons than I can count to live again."

Valeria threw her arms around Philip and kissed his face over and over. "And you came and rescued me," she replied. "You saved me."

As Valeria was letting go of him, she felt one of the wolves brush against the back of her legs. She turned and looked down. It was Zeus, and next to him was Yoko. A moment later, Tess approached and wedged her body between Philip and Valeria. She glared at Philip and snarled.

"Oh, I see how it is." Philip laughed. "Their bond to you is one of mother and child, unbreakable. You can see it in the pups' eyes." He reached down and gently stroked the back of Tess's neck. As soon as he did, she stopped snarling. "Right now, they're not sure what to make of me. It'll take time to earn their trust."

Meanwhile, Romeo had come over to Roxie and calmly pressed his nose against her nose and mouth. She let him do it. Soon after, Diesel and Scout circled and rubbed against their older siblings, Sparkle and Titan. All four took turns sniffing each other.

Still standing near the fire with Lauren, looking on, Ray asked, "Philip, is this where you're staying?"

"No," he replied. "I have a small campsite not far from here, but it's a rough setup and temporary. The sheriff's deputies are going to come looking for me, and when they do, I'll be constantly moving around from one hiding spot to another, one step ahead of them. Hopefully, they'll get tired of chasing after me and find better, more productive things to do."

"What about laying low somewhere else?" asked Lauren. "Maybe you'd be safer, say, if you moved to another state."

"Where would I go? There's no place on earth as beautiful as here," Philip replied. "This is my home, and these wolves are my family. I'm never going to leave."

A light snow began to fall.

"We really should start heading back to the ranch before the worst part of the storm comes," said Lauren.

"I agree," said Ray.

Jesse put away his rifle and grabbed Cutter's reins.

"This is happening too fast," said Valeria, trying hard not to tear up. "I'm not ready to let go of my babies." She knelt and began to cry.

Resting his hand on her shoulder, Philip whispered softly, "The pups are where they belong."

Sparkle, Titan, and Romeo instinctively backed away while the six pups, now nearly grown, drew near Valeria. They took turns putting their noses against her face and nuzzling her as she embraced each one. "I'm sorry, but I have to leave you here… You'll have Philip to help take care of you," she sobbed. "He knew your mother well. She was brave…very brave."

Valeria could barely breathe. "Tess, Yoko, Roxie, promise me you'll be good." She touched each wolf's face and tenderly stroked their necks. "Diesel, Scout…Zeus, you too…I love you. I love you all, and I'm going to miss you terribly. Please, please remember me."

"It's never goodbye," said Philip, "when someone's in your heart."

Jesse brought Zeke over to Valeria, handed her his reins, and mounted Cutter. Quietly, Ray and Lauren retrieved and got back on their horses.

With tears flowing down her cheeks, Valeria gave each of the wolves a last kiss. Then she stood, took a moment to settle Zeke, and climbed up onto his saddle.

Roxie and Scout both began to whine.

"Stay here," said Valeria. "You're not coming with me." Wiping away her tears, she fought hard to compose herself and stopped crying.

The four horses formed a line, with Jesse out front, ready to lead the way, and Ray bringing up the rear.

"Good luck, Philip," said Ray. "Hopefully, if things work out, we'll be able to visit you now and then. That is if we can find you."

"Thank you," said Philip.

The wind had picked up considerably, and the snow flurries were starting to become more intense.

Jesse interrupted them, "Let's go, everyone, before the storm gets any worse." With that, he tapped Cutter, and off they rode.

Valeria couldn't bring herself to look back. Behind her, she heard several of the wolves whimpering, but it soon receded, and by the time she reached the far end of the canyon, all she heard were the footsteps of the horses and the rustling of leaves in the trees.

The howling didn't start till later when she was well out of sight. It began with one lone voice, then another, and another in succession, until eventually, the howls became a chorus, unbound and wistful, and filled every inch of the wind-swept valleys, penetrated the deepest woodlands, echoed high off the surrounding mountain cliffs, and all but disappeared somewhere far above the sky.

CHAPTER 24

"Look out!" yelled Valeria.

Ray slammed on the brakes, and his truck began to slide out of control. "Hang on," he said.

They were on their way to the Silver Beaver to meet up with Lauren and have lunch when a mature bull elk stepped out from between two parked cars in downtown Jackson and into the path of Ray's truck. It had snowed overnight, and the streets were still wet.

At the last second, the tires gripped the pavement, and Ray was able to stop the truck mere inches from impact. Startled, the elk just stood there in the middle of the street, seemingly oblivious to the fact it had narrowly avoided being killed. It turned and sniffed the truck's grille before moseying on down the street. Ray and Valeria both looked at each other and let out a collective sigh of relief.

A few minutes later, they pulled up to the restaurant. Lauren was already there, standing outside, waiting. She waved at them and smiled.

"You're late," she said.

Ray gave her a kiss. "I had to go check on a pair of bighorn sheep fighting over breeding rights. The two were head-butting each other senseless smack dab in the middle of the main highway into town. They had traffic backed up for several miles in both directions."

"You should've seen them beating each other up," said Valeria. "It was awesome."

"Tourists always want to take pictures of things like that. I had to make sure everyone remained in their cars and didn't get too close to the action," said Ray.

"How did it end?" asked Lauren. "Who won?"

"They were still banging heads when we left," answered Ray. "One bighorn chased the other into a meadow, and I got the line of cars to eventually move on. After that, we came straight here."

Lauren reached out and grabbed a heart-shaped pendant dangling from a necklace that Valeria had on. "What's this?" she asked. The handcrafted silver pendant displayed two wolves within the heart, facing each other and touching noses. "Is it new?"

"It's a gift from Jesse." Valeria blushed. "He had Celeste and Quinn Pollock design and make it for me."

"Oh my!" said Lauren with a wry grin.

Ray rolled his eyes. "Who's hungry?"

They went inside and, at Valeria's request, found a table near George the buffalo. Two older cowboys, who looked like they'd been working outdoors for days and hadn't changed their clothes or shaved, were just getting up to leave. They nodded to Ray and then tipped their hats. "It's good to see you, Val, and you too, Doc," said one, and "Have a nice day, ladies," added the other.

Valeria had never seen either man before and had no idea who they were. "You too," she said. "And thank you." She flashed them an appreciative smile.

Hazel came out of the kitchen with three glasses on a tray and a pitcher of ice water. She was dressed from head to toe like an early seventeenth-century pilgrim, complete with a coif on her head, petticoat, and long apron. "Hello," she said, cheerfully.

Hazel set down the glasses and poured.

"What's with the get-up?" asked Ray.

"It's to remind everyone that Thanksgiving Day will be here next week," Hazel answered. "It's my favorite holiday. Has been since I was little. Some folks are all about Christmas, and others prefer Halloween, but I like Thanksgiving. There's something about having a special day set aside to give thanks for all our blessings that I find appealing."

Hazel brought over some menus, took their orders, and disappeared into the kitchen.

"Blessings," said Lauren. "You know, she has me thinking. We really don't ever stop and give thanks often enough for all we have in our lives. We get so busy with things and forget that tomorrow is never promised to us."

"You're right," said Ray. "We could do better." He took a sip of water.

"I agree," said Valeria.

A short while later, Hazel returned with their orders. "Be careful," she said, setting everything down. "Some of these plates are very hot."

"It all smells wonderful," said Lauren.

Hazel turned to leave, then stopped and said, "You know, Val, I had a young family with four kids drop by this morning for breakfast, and the parents asked me where they could see the wolves." She paused. "I told them they'd come too late but that the wolves were still in the area somewhere, nearby in the mountains, and if they were lucky, they might hear them howling." Before heading off to tend to another table, she added, "I miss the pups."

"Me too," said Valeria. "I think about them every day."

Just then, a half dozen people got up from their tables and rushed to the window. "Hey, look!" said one of them.

The bull elk Ray and Valeria had nearly run into earlier was wandering aimlessly down the center of the street right outside the restaurant. There were two cowboy-hat-wearing police officers on horseback near him, monitoring the elk's movements and directing traffic out of his way.

Ray glanced up. "It looks like the local mounted patrol has things under control."

Lauren added, "It's always something around here." She turned her attention to Valeria. "Have you given any thought to what you're going to do now that you don't have the wolves in your life, Val?" she asked. "I mean, when you're off from school. You're going to have a lot more spare time on your hands."

"I'll be old enough to get my learner's permit to drive next year," said Valeria. "I'm thinking about looking for a part-time job on weekends and after school to earn some money toward a car."

"This is the first I've heard you mention anything about wanting to drive or a car," said Ray.

Lauren smiled. "Get with the program, Ray. I was the same way at her age, strong-willed and ambitious. I couldn't wait to grow up." She gave Valeria a wink, then added, "You know, Kimberly and I could use some help down at the veterinary center. If you're interested, Val, you could come to work for me after school and on weekends. Mostly, you'd be assisting us with the animals, which I'm sure you'd enjoy, and I'd be grateful for the extra hands."

Valeria's face brightened. "I'd love to work with you," she replied. "When can I start?"

"Next week, if you're ready. You can stop by after school on Monday."

"What do you think, Dad?" asked Valeria.

"I don't have a problem with it," answered Ray. "As long as you don't neglect your schoolwork. With all that's happened, you've fallen a bit behind and are still in the process of catching up." He smiled. "But working at the veterinary center sounds like a great opportunity, especially since you like caring for animals."

A few minutes later, Lauren glanced at her watch and abruptly got up from the table. "Yikes. I'm late," she said. "I need to hurry back to the center. I have appointments scheduled this afternoon." She leaned over and gave both Ray and Valeria quick pecks on the cheek. "I'd love to stay longer, but don't want to leave my patients waiting." She smiled and headed for the door.

Hazel came over and immediately began to remove Lauren's dirty plates and setting. "The poor dear is always on the run. Is there anything else I can get the two of you? Maybe some dessert?" she asked.

Ray glanced at his daughter, who shook her head. "No, thank you," he answered. "I think we're good."

For a time, little was said. Valeria and Ray sat there and quietly finished their meal. The room had settled down considerably and felt hushed. On the wall across from the table, George the buffalo silently stared back at them. Valeria liked to imagine his gentle gaze was speaking to everyone, but she alone understood him. She could read his eyes and interpret his thoughts.

I have much to say, but few are willing to listen to a head hanging on a wall. George sighed. *Can you hear me?*

"I'm listening," muttered Val, under her breath.

"What?" said Ray.

It's now or never, whispered George the buffalo. *Wherever you go, Val, remember, there's far more sky than walls, and it's always now or never.*

"Dad," said Valeria in a faint voice. "Why didn't you reach out to me more often?"

Ray hesitated. "I meant to do better," he replied, averting his eyes when he looked up. "...but didn't."

"For years, I wondered where you were and what you

were doing." Valeria wiped away a few tears from her face. "But you hardly ever contacted me, just now and then, as if there was no thought behind it, no rhyme or reason, and it hurt…a lot. Eventually, I gave up on you because I had no other choice. It was too painful to think about you, not knowing whether you cared or not."

Ray sat there for a few moments, gazing off into space with a puzzled expression as if trying to recall something he thought he'd discarded from his mind long, long ago. Then he looked at his daughter and said, "I never wanted to live apart from you. But life…it's a one-shot deal, and I wasn't happy living in one place day after day. I wanted to see the world, at least some of it, while I was still young and brave enough to take some chances and explore, and your mother… She never wanted to come along for the ride and wasn't going to let me take you with me."

"Mom loved you," said Valeria. "She tried to hide it from me, but I could see she never stopped loving you. It was hard… really hard to live around someone whose heart has been broken. And it didn't help any that you weren't around for me to talk to."

Ray reached out and took her hands in his. "Please forgive me," he said. "Over time, I convinced myself you were better off without me and that if I came bouncing in and out of your life at odd moments and interfered too often, it would just make things worse for you and me both." He looked her in the eyes. "It's one of the few things in my life I've come to regret, Val. I made a mistake, and I'm extremely sorry I wasn't there for you. I should have made more of an effort. I love you."

Whatever else Valeria wanted to say seemed to dissipate. "I love you too, Dad," she said.

They both managed to smile.

"This reminds me," said Ray. "I have something I've been wanting to give you."

"What is it?" she asked. "A present?"

"Possibly." Ray reached into his pants pocket and pulled out his wallet. "Close your eyes for a second."

Valeria shut her eyes and, a moment later, felt her father place something small in the palm of her hand. He then took her fingers and gently had her make a fist around it.

"Okay," said Ray. "You can open your eyes now."

Valeria slowly opened her hand and looked. "Oh, my God!" she said. "But how?" In her palm were the two gold rings her mother had sold to the pawnbroker. She held Rosa's engagement ring and wedding band up to the light.

"When your mother sold them, Abuela wrote and told me how upset you were," said Ray. "So, I called the owner of the pawnshop, bought back the two rings, and had him ship them to me. I was going to wait until you were older to give them to you, but..."

Valeria leaned over and showered her father with kisses. "Thank you, Dad," she said. "I'm so happy! Thank you."

Hazel came out of the kitchen and greeted a few people who'd entered the restaurant. She showed them to a table, while nearby, several others got up to leave. At another, an older couple was laughing.

Admiring the rings on one of her fingers, Valeria looked over and winked at George the buffalo. She whispered to him, "Thank you."

There's far more sky than walls, repeated George with a sigh. *...always more sky.*

Russell Sebring is a novelist and poet who grew up in the south. He graduated with a photography degree from the Art Institute of Fort Lauderdale before going on to work as a journalist, independent copywriter, professional photographer, and web designer. Russell lives within a few miles of Hogwarts Castle at Universal's Islands of Adventure and Cinderella Castle at Walt Disney World in Florida.

www.ingramcontent.com/pod-product-compliance
Lightning Source LLC
Chambersburg PA
CBHW050737180626
46814CB00002B/793
* 9 7 9 8 8 9 1 2 6 1 5 8 7 *